RIVER OF BODIES

A gripping mystery about a terrible crime

NICOLA CLIFFORD

THE BOOK FOLKS

Published by The Book Folks

London, 2023

This book is a work of fiction. Names, characters, businesses, organizations, places and events are either the product of the author's imagination or are used fictitiously. Any resemblance to actual persons, living or dead, events or locales is entirely coincidental. The spelling is British English.

ISBN 978-1-80462-054-0

www.thebookfolks.com

To Brother Andrew
who has always provided the music.

Chapter one

Shortly after midnight, the River Wye began to rise steadily and quickly. Following three days of heavy rain in the hills surrounding Builth Wells, a wide expanse of muddy water rushed beneath bridges lit by a weak moon. The surge continued and a tall, languid wave spilled out of the river, crested the banks, swamped the footpath and claimed half of the town's main car park in a few seconds.

Still the river rose. Large tree trunks sailed along the watercourse, some becoming trapped upon the grey stone stanchions of the eighteenth-century Wye Bridge, creating turbulent waves beneath the six graceful spans. The flood grew and widened until it encompassed Llanelwedd. It gushed over petrol station forecourts, inside the builders' merchants, and inundated a large car showroom. Dirty water slipped silently beneath the doors, through vents and airbricks, and flowed between the new, highly polished vehicles.

Two staff members, denied their Sunday morning lie-in, arrived shortly after seven to assess the gravity of the situation. The manager stepped out of his low-slung, saloon car into six inches of freezing water. His younger employee – who had borrowed his father's Land Rover and thought to bring wellies – grinned broadly as the pair paddled inside the showroom. Being at a lower level than the car park, the water swirling around the cars was almost two feet deep and immediately breached the wellies of the younger man. The manager laughed, but within minutes of unlocking the glass and stainless-steel main entrance doors, he was on the phone to the police.

* * *

DCI Ben James and DS Jack Trent stood side by side, eyes cast low as they stared at the body of a woman, floating face down next to a flash sports car. One pale arm, a tattooed butterfly above her elbow, was draped over a front tyre as though she was clinging on, or trying to haul herself upright. A mass of long, dark hair was suspended in the water and wafted around her head like filaments of seaweed. She was dressed in a full-length gown, tightly fitted, made of a shimmery fabric. The dress was a striking aqua-blue with silver sparkles in a shell-shaped design, and when Jack first saw the body, he thought he'd found a mermaid. He pointed at the woman's feet.

'Only one shoe, guv,' he said. 'I'll have a scout about for the other. Is the team on its way?'

'Yeah, Carrie Salmon too. I'd like her to see this before the body is moved.'

Jack nodded and waded slowly and carefully through the water to check out the rest of the barn-sized building. Ben turned to the manager and the young salesman.

'Gentlemen,' he said, 'did either of you touch anything?'

'No,' the manager said. 'I saw her as soon as we walked in. I could tell she was dead just by looking at her, so I went to the office and rang you straight away.'

The lad in wellies shook his head. 'I didn't go anywhere near her either.'

Jack returned with a spike-heeled, gold sandal dangling from a ballpoint pen.

'Found it jammed in a metal grate in the floor,' he said. 'Heel snapped off. Could be the reason she ended up face down in river water.'

Ben nodded. 'Maybe, but what was she doing in here in the first place?'

He ducked his head through the open driver's window, peered into the sports car and suddenly jerked backwards, scraping his ear painfully on the edge of the door. He clamped a hand to the side of his head.

'What's up, guv?' Jack asked.

Ben didn't speak and took a few steps backward. Jack took his place at the side window and gasped audibly.

'I wasn't dreaming then?' Ben asked.

'No, guv. Guy in a dinner suit slumped on the back seat, with what looks to be a bullet hole in the centre of his forehead.'

'OK. I'll move the staff outside. You chase up the team and protect the scene.'

'Will do,' Jack said and slipped the broken sandal into a plastic evidence bag.

Ben ushered the men out to the car park. The group stood on a small island of saturated grass at the edge of the tarmac and Ben took out his notebook.

'Names and addresses please,' he said.

The manager spoke first. 'Tomos Jones. Got a place in Erwood, other side of the old station.'

Ben scribbled down the details and glanced at the younger man.

'I'm Caleb Griffiths and live on my folks' farm in Garth.'

'Thanks,' Ben said. 'Right then. Tell me what you saw this morning.'

Caleb chuckled nervously. 'Lots of water and a dead woman floating in the showroom.'

Ben frowned at the lad who stopped smiling.

The manager nodded. 'That was about it really. I unlocked the main doors, and we spotted her more or less as soon as we walked inside.'

'So the doors were locked?' Ben asked.

'Yes, they were. The alarm was set but failed to sound. I'm guessing the water took out the electricity.'

'Any idea how the woman got inside?'

Tomos Jones shrugged. 'No damage to any of the doors I could see.'

* * *

A large 4x4 crawled into the car park and Ben moved higher up the grassy bank as the resultant wake rushed towards him. The vehicle parked next to the others and Carrie Salmon stepped out. She nodded at Ben, removed a pair of fishermen's waders from the boot, pulled them on and splashed across the car park towards the stricken showroom.

Ben thanked the staff again, told them not to go anywhere, and followed the pathologist inside as a gang of uniforms got busy rolling out yards of blue-and-white tape. Carrie paddled past an ambulance parked close to the main entrance. Jack Trent, a cluster of plastic evidence bags in his hands, spotted Carrie and waded towards her. All three took a minute to survey the scene.

Carrie spoke first. 'Two bodies you said?'

Ben nodded. 'Young woman face down in the water. Thirty-something male on the back seat of the sports car with what appears to be a bullet wound between his eyes. Haven't touched either.'

'Let's take a look then.'

Carrie took photographs of the fallen woman, then she moved closer and beckoned for a pair of paramedics to bring a wheeled stretcher to the front of the car. Under her watchful gaze, they gently lifted the body from the water and placed it face down on a thin mattress. With gloved hands, Carrie carefully parted the victim's hair and searched for wounds, checked pale skin on wrists, ankles, upper arms and neck.

'OK,' she said. 'Let's turn her. Take it slowly. Ready? Then lift… and turn. Perfect. Thanks, guys.'

She stepped closer, examined the body, manipulated joints, peered closely at the hands and fingernails, and shone a torch into dead eyes.

'Well?' Ben asked.

'Nothing obvious. Bearing in mind where we found her, death by drowning would be top of my list, but can't be certain until I've completed the autopsy.'

Carrie moved back from the stretcher and the paramedics wheeled it out to the waiting vehicle. Carrie stretched her back, hands on hips.

'So, where's the other one?' she asked.

'Back seat of the car,' Ben said. 'As I said, looks like a bullet wound, not much obvious blood.'

Carrie nodded. 'Through and through maybe. How much of the skull is blown out will depend on the type of ammo used.'

'How can you talk so matter-of-factly about these things?' Ben asked.

Carrie chuckled. 'Because I'm used to it and what I say is, well, factual.'

She sloshed closer to the car and bent in through the open window, took photographs of the body in situ, then shone a torch towards the back seat.

'Definitely a bullet to the head, there are powder burns stippling the skin. The killer got up close.'

She gently moved the victim's head away from the upholstery and pointed her torch into the shadows. The light seemed to change from white to red as it illuminated a medium-sized patch of blood and brains plastered on the headrest. Ben took a couple of steps back, not keen on seeing much more. He'd never been good with excessively bloody crime scenes.

'Can't see any defensive wounds,' Carrie said. 'No sign of a struggle.'

She raised her head and waved the ambulance crew forward to pick up another client.

'I'll get to town and crack on. I'll call as soon as I have anything to impart,' Carrie said.

She watched the crew extricate the body of the man in a dinner suit. They placed him on a second stretcher, his wide-open, empty eyes, staring at nothing. Carrie took another quick look before the stretcher was rolled out of the showroom. Jack followed and was shocked to see Caleb hop out of the back of the ambulance, a mobile in his hand.

'Oi!' Jack yelled. 'What the hell are you up to, boy?'

'I wanted to see if it was her,' Caleb said.

'Who?' Ben asked.

'Kitty. Our receptionist.' He rubbed his face. 'I liked Kitty, she was a laugh.'

'Is it her?' Ben asked.

Caleb sniffed. 'Yes. Kitty Phillips.'

'Do you mind taking a look at the guy on the stretcher?' Jack asked.

Caleb shrugged. 'I guess not.'

Jack led him towards the second body, then he lifted the sheet covering the man's face and Caleb gazed down.

'Fuck,' he muttered. 'Is that a bullet hole?'

'Maybe,' Jack said non-committedly. 'So, do you know him?'

'No. He doesn't work here, and I haven't seen him before.'

Jack beckoned the manager over. 'How about you, sir? Do you recognise this man?'

'No, sorry, I don't.'

Movement on the far side of the car park caught Jack's eye. He nudged Ben and nodded towards one of the narrow grass islands.

'Press is here, guv,' he said.

Ben peered across the shallow lake and spotted Stacey Logan, reporter for *The Mid Wales Times*. She waved and pointed a camera at him as he walked towards her.

'No point in asking why you're here,' Ben said. 'When did you arrive?'

'As soon as the tape started rolling out.'

'That was quick. Llanagethin is a good thirty minutes away, more with the bridge closed.' He smiled. 'Have you been peering into your crystal ball again, *cariad*?'

She returned his smile. 'Didn't need to. A mate of mine from town rang first thing and said the flood was worse than usual. Photogenic was how he described it, so I popped out for a look.'

'Took some good pictures then?'

'Of course.'

'Where's your car?'

'Parked in the high street. I sweet-talked a couple of coppers who let me walk across the bridge.'

'Hmm, I'll have to have a word. I'm not sure the bridge is safe with water so high above the tops of the spans.'

Stacey changed the subject. 'I saw two bodies removed from the showroom. Gonna tell me what happened?'

Ben sighed. 'You know I can't.'

'I'll find out as soon as I chat to the staff.'

'Yes, you're good at your job, but like I said…'

Stacey stretched up and brushed a quick kiss on Ben's cheek while his officers were all looking the other way.

'Supper at seven any good for you?'

'Perfect,' he said and returned her kiss.

He walked back towards the crime scene as a patrol car pulled out of the car park. Jack had obviously arranged for Tomos and Caleb to be taken to the local nick for statement gathering. He was still in the showroom, and when he saw Ben enter he splashed closer, more plastic evidence bags in one hand.

'Some of this is probably crap from the river,' he said, 'but there was ID on Kitty Phillips, and I collected the contents of the second victim's pockets.'

'Name?'

'Jonathon Haddon. Thirty-two-years-old, lives in Hay-on-Wye according to the driving licence. Credit cards, cash and a photo of a woman in his wallet, together with a plastic key card for a room at the Caer Beris hotel opposite the golf course.'

'Got an address for Kitty?'

'Yeah, she lived with her husband in a cottage halfway between Garth and Llanwrtyd just off the main road. Caleb gave me directions.'

'OK, let's go and talk to the husband first before word gets out. Ring the station and have Kevin Biggs confiscate Caleb's phone. We don't want to run the risk of inappropriate photos appearing on the net. I'll have a word with Ollie Langdon and Tegan Hedges. They can protect the scene and keep an eye on SOCO.'

Jack nodded. 'I'll go and get the car started.' He gazed at the bridge and the water pounding the old stonework. 'Do you think the bridge will hold?'

Ben grinned. 'Course it will. Just easier to close it. Keeps the rubberneckers away. Make sure you contact the nick and get hold of that mobile.'

* * *

Stacey waited until the ambulance had driven away then trudged carefully around the edge of the flood, collecting vox pops from locals and keeping her ears open for any useful gossip. After half an hour she had enough to put a story together. A description of the young salesman convinced her locals were talking about Caleb Griffiths. She knew his parents, and thought she'd pop into the farm on the way home. Consequently, she was disappointed to hear he and the manager had been driven away in a police car, presumably to the local nick.

She captured a few last photos of the scene, then she crossed the bridge again and decided to grab a quick fry-up at her favourite cafe, before heading for the station and settling down to wait for Caleb to leave. She'd talk to him then.

Chapter two

At the end of a long, rutted track dividing fields of sheep, Jack pulled up outside a small white cottage with a low porch and grey slates on the roof. He discovered a metal bell pull to the right of the door and gave it a tug. A dull discordant jangle sounded on the other side.

Ben gazed around the property and cast an eye over a large, pretty garden and attached paddock where a solitary hill pony grazed on late spring grass. A flight of swallows swooped low over the meadow, snatching insects from just a few inches above the pasture.

Jack rang the bell again and this time, after a short wait, a casually dressed man wearing slippers, maybe in his early thirties, opened the door.

'Yes? Can I help you? If you're Jehovah's Witnesses you can just leave. I've told you before.'

The officers displayed their warrant cards and the man blinked.

'Mind if we come in, sir?' Jack asked.

'Why? What do you want?'

'Just a quick chat.'

The man shrugged, opened the door wider and asked, 'Cuppa?'

'We're fine thanks,' Ben said.

'Please, take a seat.'

The detectives perched on a squishy sofa and Ben continued, 'We understand you are Leo Phillips, husband of Kitty.'

'That's right.' Leo frowned. 'Has something happened to her? Is that why you are here?'

'Do you know where she was yesterday evening?' Jack asked.

Leo smiled. 'One of her weekends with the girls. You know the sort of thing, fancy hotel in Cardiff, spa, posh restaurant.' He laughed. 'She calls it her "seasonal spoiling".'

'When is she due home?'

'Early evening. They usually choose a place that does a decent Sunday roast and head for home after desert and coffee.' Leo crossed his legs. 'Is Kitty in some sort of trouble? Is that why you are here?'

Ben took a deep breath. 'I'm very sorry to have to tell you that we found the body of a woman in Builth Wells this morning and have reason to believe it might be your wife.' He held out a driving licence protected by a plastic bag. 'We found this in the victim's evening bag.'

Leo began to swing his head from side to side, breathing heavily, almost groaning. 'Can't be Kitty,' he muttered. 'She's in Cardiff Bay. I told you.'

'I have a photo of the victim I'd like you to look at,' Ben said quietly.

The head swinging stopped. Leo reluctantly held out a hand and took the offered smartphone. The man's eyes widened before he clamped his free hand over his face, shoulders quivering as he sobbed silently.

After a while he looked up and asked, 'What was she doing in Builth? Where did you find her?'

'Inside a flooded car showroom in Llanelwedd.'

'The showroom?' Leo scrubbed his face. 'Why was she in there?'

'We were hoping you could tell us?' Jack said.

'I don't know. She only works there four days a week and never at weekends. Likes to spend time in the garden and ride her pony. Weekends are sacrosanct.' He took a huge breath, closed his eyes and asked, 'Do you know how she died?'

'We're not certain,' Ben said, 'but Kitty may have drowned. She was found lying in the water between the cars. We think she fell – one of her shoes was broken.'

Leo hauled himself to his feet, crossed to the kitchen area, removed some brandy from an overhead cupboard and gulped directly from the bottle. Without turning around, he asked, 'Was she alone?'

Jack cleared his throat. 'There was a man in his thirties, sitting on the back seat of one of the cars.'

'Did he say who he was and what he was doing with my wife?' Leo asked, voice full of anger.

'No, sir,' Ben said. 'He didn't say anything. He was also deceased.'

* * *

Stacey spotted Caleb as he left the police station, got out of her car and waved. He returned the wave and clumped closer, rubber boots slapping his calves.

'Stacey. What are you doing here?'

She smiled. 'Heard you'd been brought to the station and thought you might appreciate a lift home.' She saw his eyebrows raise. 'I've been covering the flood.'

Caleb shook his head. 'I'm OK, thanks. I drove Dad's Land Rover to the showroom so I ought to get it back to him.'

'The bridge is still closed, but I'll drive you there if you want. We can probably cross the river at Erwood.'

'That's a long way.' He shrugged. 'Go on then, a lift home would be good. Me and Dad can get the truck later when the river's gone down.'

'Sure. Hop in.' Stacey turned the car around and pulled onto the main road. 'I was a bit worried when I saw the ambulance.. Your mum told me a while back you were working there and when someone said a police car took you away, I was more worried. Are you OK?'

'Yeah, fine I guess.' Caleb took a deep breath. 'Boss called me first thing, said the showroom was flooded and he'd meet me there. Move the cars or something, but…'

'But what?'

The young man scrubbed at his face and took a deep breath. 'There were two dead people inside. Kitty Phillips, drowned I reckon, floating in the water, and a bloke.'

Stacey felt her heart speed up and concentrated on the road.

'Kitty Phillips your receptionist?'

Caleb nodded.

'Had the bloke drowned too?'

Caleb shook his head and swallowed hard. 'No, he was sitting in one of the cars. He'd been shot in the head, Stacey. I saw the bullet hole. Cops asked if I could identity him and uncovered his face. Grim.'

'Bloody hell,' she said, indicated and pulled into the side of the road, needing a moment to order her thoughts. 'Did the police say anything?'

'Not much.'

'So tell me what happened.'

Caleb wiped his eyes with his fingers and related the story, while, unknown to him, Stacey recorded what he said on her mobile.

'I've never seen Kitty dressed up like that,' he said. 'Her dress was beautiful, like she is… uh… was.' He covered his eyes again. 'Poor Kitty. I can't believe she's dead.' He swiped tears from his cheeks.

'Let's get you home,' Stacey said. 'Looks like you could do with a strong cup of tea.'

She started the car, checked her mirrors and pulled out.

'Drop me by the chapel,' Caleb said, 'opposite the school. I'll walk from there. What with all the rain there are some seriously deep potholes in our track. Not sure your old car would make it.'

'Nonsense. I can't let you walk home.'

'I'd like it better. Bit of time on my own before I have to tell Mum and Dad all the gruesome details.'

'If you're sure.'

'I am, and do me a favour, don't put my name in the paper. I'm not sure I should have told you all that.'

'I'll report the story but I promise I won't use your name.' She pulled up next to the chapel. 'Are you sure you don't want a lift down the drive?'

'No really, but thanks.' Caleb opened the door and stepped out.

'Keep in touch,' Stacey called.

Caleb raised an arm and began the mile-long hike to the farmhouse, dodging the worst of the crater-like potholes. Stacey watched until he rounded the bend, then pulled back onto the road and turned left towards the Epynt and her cottage on the edge of Llanagethin.

Large raindrops began to splatter against the windscreen as she pulled into the drive. She grabbed her kitbag and managed to open the front door before the storm clouds broke. She draped her damp coat on the newel post, dumped her bag in the office and headed for the kitchen. The coffee she'd drunk with the fry-up had been a long time ago, so she filled an old-fashioned pot and plonked it on top of the Aga.

While waiting for her brew, she uploaded photos from her camera to the laptop and worked through them slowly, deleting the rubbish and cherry-picking from the rest. She paused at a landscape shot of the turbulent, muddy river and a low, early morning sun. The pink-tinged light made the picture seem apocalyptic. By a gradual process of elimination, she whittled down the clutch of images to four: a body being wheeled inside the ambulance, groups of police officers wading around in the temporary lake, a candid shot of the staff, and lastly the eerie landscape. She sipped from her mug, then picked up the phone and dialled the number of her editor, Sam Jenkins. It rang once.

'Jenkins,' Sam growled down the line.

'Morning, boss. You sound happy.'

'Well I'm not! Shouldn't be here at all by rights. My house was flooded during the night.'

'God, I'm really sorry. Why *are* you at work? One of the subs could have covered for a couple of days.'

'No they couldn't. I wanted a paper to come back to.'

'I don't think you should have left your wife to deal with it on her own.'

Sam almost chuckled. 'Her sister – a difficult woman – arrived two days ago for a mini break, so she isn't on her own. They've already employed a couple of lads for the heavy work and I–' he paused '–was deemed surplus to requirements. So, what do you want?'

'You know I can cope with you being grumpy, but you're getting quite rude in your old age.'

Sam sighed heavily. 'Just tell me why you called.'

'Two bodies discovered in flooded car showroom in Builth.'

'Is that a headline?'

'Yep, tomorrow's front page. I went to town just after dawn to document the flood and stumbled on the story by chance. I know one of the people who found the bodies and gave him a lift home. He told me enough for a decent article.'

'Did they drown?' Sam asked.

'One did. Seems the other was shot.'

'Shot you say? That's certainly front-page news.'

'Give me an hour and I'll send everything over. I'm in all evening, so if you want changes, zip it back and I'll give it a tweak.'

Stacey hung up, worked through her notes, wrote a decent draft and pinged it through to Sam. She got up from the table, stretched and began preparing supper – chicken frittata with fresh salad leaves from the greenhouse. The rain had stopped and the evening sun had slipped below the goose-grey clouds, hovering in the gap between the sky and the Epynt Mountain. She paused and took a moment to take in the view, before the click of the side gate made her jump.

'Hello?' she called, peering into the gathering dusk.

'Just me, Pumpkin,' Ben said and walked closer.

'Perfect timing,' she said and stretched up to kiss him. 'I was just about to start cooking supper.'

'Sounds good to me,' he said. 'Need a hand?'

Stacey smiled. 'Thanks, but you'll get in the way.'

Ben dropped onto the carver. 'Been a bit full on today. Only managed a very substandard bacon roll from a van in a lay-by.'

'Frittata and salad meet with your approval?'

'Perfect. Any chance of a few fried potatoes? I'm pretty hungry.'

'No problem. Coffee or shall we open some wine?'

'Wine,' Ben said and headed to the larder, returning with a bottle of white which he put in the freezer to cool. 'Been home long?' he asked.

'Long enough to write tomorrow's front page.' She leaned across the table, woke up her laptop and turned the screen to face him. 'Take a look.'

While Ben read through the article, Stacey beat eggs and grated a bowl of cheese.

Ben chuckled. 'You really are good. Where did you get all this from?'

'I gave Caleb Griffiths a lift home and he told me everything.' She poured beaten egg into a hot frying pan containing chunks of chicken, leftover vegetables and sliced peppers, and sprinkled the cheese. 'Do you know who the male victim is?'

Ben nodded. 'Strictly off the record, his name is Jonathon Haddon. He'd been staying at the Caer Beris. Some sort of conference for independent financial advisers.' He snorted. 'They probably swanned around all night, drinking champagne and congratulating each other on how much money they've made.'

'Perhaps he lost a client a lot of money and the loser sought revenge?'

'Maybe.'

'So what was he doing in the showroom with the receptionist?'

'Not a clue. We spoke to Kitty's husband this morning. He's in bits. Thought his wife was on a mini break in Cardiff and now thinks she was having an affair. Not an easy visit.' He sighed. 'At least we solved the mystery of how they got inside the place. Kitty had a key.' He tapped the screen. 'This shot of the flood is brilliant. Looks almost biblical. Maybe we should start building an ark.'

Stacey laughed. 'No need. It's why I live on a mountain.' She carried the meal to the table and began dishing out. 'I know Haddon was shot and assume Kitty drowned. Any more info on that?'

'Off to talk to Carrie tomorrow. As you know, the autopsy suite is not my favourite place.' He picked up his cutlery. 'Anyway, enough of that. I'm hungry and this looks wonderful. Thank you, *cariad*.'

Chapter three

Ben left Noddfa before eight the next morning, and after Stacey had tidied the kitchen, she packed her kitbag, went out to the car, and headed through the lanes towards the main road.

Yesterday's storm clouds had floated away to bother England and the unbroken sunshine was already warm. Stacey opened the car window and enjoyed the clean, dust-free air, heavy with birdsong and the scent of blackthorn blossom. Fields of sheep and their lambs edged the lanes. A mile or so from the main road, a group of three roe deer suddenly burst out of a forestry plantation, galloped across the tarmac and immediately disappeared into undergrowth on the opposite side. She drove on cautiously, past a high verge completely covered in bluebells, and joined the A483. A little over ten minutes later, she pulled into the car park of the country hotel on the edge of Builth.

She turned off the engine, dragged her kitbag from the passenger seat and locked the car. She took a minute to gaze at the impressive black and white timbered building, smiled as she remembered Ben giving her a "be mine" ring several years ago over lunch there, and the wedding of her friends, Heidi and Erica, at the end of the previous year.

Stacey slung her bag over her shoulder and strolled into reception. A smartly dressed young woman looked up from behind the desk and smiled.

'Good morning,' she said. 'Can I help you?'

'Thought I'd treat myself to a coffee in the conservatory,' Stacey said. 'Not too early, am I?'

'Not at all. Please go and find a table. I'll arrange for someone to come and take your order.'

'Thanks.'

Stacey walked through the dining room, nodded at a pair of late breakfasters and settled herself at one of the tables next to the windows. The eighteenth-century manor house had been constructed on a rise and Stacey looked out over the long expanse of grass leading to the river, a tributary of the Wye. She was pleased to see the water had dropped, leaving a swathe of flattened, muddy vegetation in its wake. She glanced up as a teenaged lad in white shirt and black trousers, a pad and pen in his hand, approached her table.

'Morning,' he said. 'Lovely day.'

'Much better than all the rain,' Stacey said. 'I was beginning to wonder if it would ever stop.'

He chuckled. 'It's the rain that makes Wales so green. Now, what can I get you?'

'A large pot of strong coffee and a couple of Welsh cakes would be perfect.'

'I'll see to it.' He placed a folded copy of *The Mid Wales Times* on the table. 'Check out the photos,' he said. 'Awesome picture of the flood in town.'

He bustled away in the direction of the kitchens and Stacey smiled as she opened the paper. The waiter was right, the picture was awesome. She didn't have time to read through the article before he reappeared, a silver tray in his hands. He unloaded a large coffee pot, sugar, cream, a small dish of butter and a plate of sugar-coated griddle cakes, bursting with sultanas.

'Thanks,' Stacey said and refolded the newspaper. 'Just what I need. I'd planned to call in yesterday but there were police cars parked out the front. I wondered if the hotel had been flooded.'

'No, it missed us thankfully, we're too high up to be affected by the river.' He leaned closer and whispered conspiratorially. 'One of our guests was found dead in town.'

'Wow.' Stacey reopened the paper. 'Says here a man was found dead in the car showroom in Llanelwedd. Was he your guest?'

The waiter nodded and took a quick glance around the conservatory.

'We held a conference this weekend with a ball on Saturday night. Jonathon Haddon was staying here.'

'How awful. Did he drown?'

The young man shook his head. 'I don't think so. The paper said he'd been shot.'

'Yes, I read that, but why would someone shoot him?'

'I don't know. I served him dinner before the ball and he seemed like an OK guy. Left a decent tip.'

'What was the conference for?'

'My boss said the people who attended were financial advisers.' He smiled. 'I'm not sure what they do. Never met one before – not having any money.'

Stacey chuckled. 'You and me both.'

The waiter straightened. 'Can I bring you anything else?'

'No thank you, this is perfect.'

He wandered back towards the kitchen. Stacey buttered a Welsh cake and took a large bite. Thinking about what the young man had said, she noodled on her phone, searching the internet for financial advisers, individuals and companies, and googled the name of the victim.

* * *

Carrie Salmon looked up from her work and smiled as Ben and Jack entered the autopsy suite.

'Morning, Chief Inspector,' she said. 'You don't look like your usual sparkly self. Rough night?'

Jack grinned.

'Having to be here first thing on a Monday morning is not the way I'd choose to start my week,' Ben said. 'This really isn't my favourite place.'

'I know and I'll do my best not to show you anything too gruesome, apart from the gentleman who was shot. Let's get that over first shall we?'

Carrie walked closer to a gurney at the end of the room and lowered the sheet covering the victim's face to just below the base of his neck, concealing the 'Y' incision.

'Cause of death confirmed as gunshot wound to the head. As we discovered at the scene, the bullet exited the back of the skull and lodged itself in the headrest. I've sent it to FSS ballistics, but it's in poor shape and not hugely useful.'

'Any chance of identifying the weapon used?' Jack asked.

'Not really unless we find a spent shell case.' She pointed at the wound on Jonathon's forehead and the livid powder burn marks surrounding it. 'Looks like a .38 to me. A smaller bullet would probably still have been inside the skull, after whizzing around and shredding the brain.'

'That's a nice thought,' Ben muttered. 'So a bigger bullet then?'

Carrie nodded. 'I reckon. Mass plus velocity equals penetration. Thus, greater mass and velocity–'

'Yeah, I get it.'

'We need the casing to be completely sure.' Carrie glanced up from the corpse. 'Seen enough, gentlemen?'

'More than enough,' Ben said. 'Let's move on. What can you tell us about Kitty Phillips? Anything useful?'

'Certainly interesting. First case like it that I've seen in a murder investigation.'

'I thought she'd drowned,' Jack said.

'Yes, technically she did, but there's not a drop of water in her lungs – I checked, obviously.'

Ben paled and swallowed. 'So how did she die?'

'Something often referred to as "dry drowning". Not an official term but it describes what happened perfectly.'

'I think I've heard of that,' Jack said. 'Some sort of protective mechanism employed by the body when someone falls into water. Closes the throat and keeps water out of the lungs.'

Carrie nodded. 'That's about it. I'm impressed, Sergeant. The victim suffers a spasm of the vocal cords – a laryngeal spasm. The airways shut down and without oxygen, the victim suffocates. There are some theories that shock plays a part. For example a dousing in cold water can bring on the spasm.'

'Any marks on her at all?' Ben asked.

'Nothing to raise concern and no defence injuries.' Carrie removed the sheet from the lower half of the body and pointed at a red mark on Kitty's upper foot. 'This could have been sustained when her shoe broke.' She pointed again. 'Two bruised knees from the resultant tumble, and a damaged wrist, possibly from trying to save herself a dunking.'

'Any theories?' Ben asked.

Carrie chuckled. 'Not my job!'

'But you're bound to have formed an opinion. All I'm asking is for you to share your thoughts.'

Carrie sighed. 'OK, so how about this? I don't think the woman witnessed the shooting because I believe she wasn't present when it occurred. Whoever shot Haddon probably thought he was alone. If the killer knew someone else was in the showroom, I think they'd have probably shot her too.'

'Makes sense,' Ben said.

'Where would she have been?' Jack asked.

Carrie raised her hands in frustration. 'I don't know, Sergeant. Powdering her nose maybe? She returned to the main showroom to find the place flooded – we know how fast the river rises – and her date with a bullet between the eyes. She stumbled, hit the water face first, suffered a laryngeal spasm and dry-drowned.' She paused. 'Just a theory.'

'Anything else we should be aware of?' Ben asked.

'Nothing of consequence. Small amounts of alcohol present in the blood of each victim. Full stomachs with what looks to have been a good quality meal.'

Jack raised his eyebrows. 'Good quality?' he queried.

'Found a quantity of semi-digested caviar in both of them.'

'To sum up then,' Ben said, 'murder by shooting plus an accidental death?'

'Up to you,' Carrie said, 'but I'm fairly sure Kitty Phillips wouldn't have died if her friend hadn't been shot. I'd like to think if the case ever gets to court the CPS will go for murder and aggravated manslaughter.'

'Any trace evidence on the bodies?'

'I couldn't find any, but I've collected blood and DNA swabs. FSS will let me know as soon as they have something. The car was taken to the pound for SOCO to look at.' She smiled. 'Cuppa before you leave?'

'No thanks, no time,' Ben said. 'Overdue at the station. We'll be in touch.'

'I'll look forward to it.'

The detectives left the autopsy suite and walked back to the car. Ben took deep breaths.

'Glad that's out of the way,' he said. 'You'd think it would get easier, but the older I get the more difficult it seems to become.'

Jack unlocked the car and they got in. 'You'll feel better with some fresh air inside you, guv.'

* * *

An hour later the officers walked into the squad room on the top floor of the police station. Ben was pleased to see the place busy as his officers worked the new case. Jack fetched drinks while Ben assembled his team around the large, central table. He stood in front of the incident board where photos of the victims, in life and death, had already been pinned up.

'Morning, everyone,' Ben said as he removed his jacket and draped it on the back of his chair. 'We've just been speaking with Carrie Salmon who has conducted autopsies on Kitty Phillips and Jonathon Haddon. We don't have much more to go on I'm afraid. Haddon died after being shot in the head. A .38 was probably the weapon but we can't confirm that without the shell case.' He took a sip of coffee. 'The second victim dry-drowned. Her throat closed when water hit her vocal cords and she suffocated. There is nothing to suggest the shooter killed her.' He sat and looked expectantly at his team. 'Anyone got anything to tell me?'

'I've collected CCTV footage from the hotel,' Ollie Langdon said. 'Doesn't really show us much we don't know but it does record the victims leaving the place just after 1am, Sunday morning. They got in a taxi. I'm still trying to trace the driver. No registration number on the clip and the car looks to be an owner-operator.'

'Couldn't reception give you the name of the company?' Jack asked.

'No, Sarge. They didn't order it.'

Ben nodded. 'OK, keep on with it. We need to talk to that driver.'

'Yes, sir.'

Tegan Hedges got to her feet and passed some printed pages to her boss.

'What's this?' Ben asked.

'Early research on Jonathon Haddon and his company.'

'So he is an IFA?'

Tegan nodded. 'He founded a company with two friends a few years after leaving university. Theo Watson and Dominic Willis.'

'Have you spoken to them yet?'

'Trying to, sir. Watson is on holiday, according to his secretary who is trying to contact him. Willis has promised to call before close of business today. He's apparently in the middle of some huge meeting he can't leave.'

Ben sighed. 'Did you inform the secretary that Haddon has been killed?'

'No, sir. Thought it was better coming from you. I'm still trying to trace the victim's family.'

'What's the hold up?'

'Basically, lack of information. We have his mobile, but it was saturated. Maybe he dropped it. The backroom boys are working on the thing and should be able to give us a list of contacts as soon as they've dried it out.'

'OK. First off we need details of Haddon's clients. Find out if he lost someone money – someone who couldn't afford to lose it. Maybe he was diverting profits to himself. Money is a strong motivator.'

'Maybe,' Tegan said, 'Kitty's husband did for him. Revenge is also a motive.'

'I agree,' Ben said. 'We need another conversation with Leo Phillips, sooner rather than later.' He got to his feet. 'On with it then. We'll meet up here again before anyone clocks off.'

Chapter four

Stacey was lost in cyberspace, laptop open on the kitchen table as she researched Jonathon Haddon's past and his company. She'd discovered he had two partners and was about to start digging when there was a rap on the back door. It swung open and a petite woman in her twenties, with nearly white hair, walked in.

'Heidi,' Stacey said. 'How are you?'

'Fine. Any coffee going?'

'Help yourself.'

Heidi set up the machine and plonked herself at the table. 'What are you working on?' she asked.

'I'm looking into the guy found dead yesterday morning. Turns out he was an independent financial adviser. Runs his own company.'

'Maybe he lost the wrong person a barrowload of money and they caught up with him. A shot to the head sounds like organised crime, or a punishment killing.'

'You're right, it does.' Stacey shut the laptop and got up to pour the coffee. 'What have you and Erica been up to? Enjoying married life?'

'I like being with her – when I see her – but pretty much all she does is work. She often double-shifts as the police are so short-staffed. She said she'd back off a bit after the wedding, but that hasn't happened. I'm beginning to feel like a bloody housewife.'

Stacey laughed. 'Well you don't look like one. More like a sulky teenager.'

'That's nice,' Heidi grumbled. 'I came here to be cheered up.'

'Sorry.' Stacey returned to the table.

'So what have you discovered about this guy?' Heidi asked.

'His name is Jonathon Haddon, lives in Hay-on-Wye. Company name, Haddon, Watson and Willis. That's about it so far. I spoke to one of the waiters at the hotel. He served Haddon the night of the financial advisers' bun fight and said he seemed like a nice guy, but it would be good to talk to someone who really knew him.' She sighed. 'I also need to dig around in the murky world of finance but know practically nothing about it. I wondered if you fancied giving me a hand.'

'Why would you think I'd know anything about it?'

Stacey smiled. 'Cos you haven't worked since you resigned from the police and never seem to be broke.'

'I've worked!' Heidi muttered. She ripped a sheet of paper from a notepad and began tearing and folding.

'Doing what?'

Heidi shrugged. 'This and that.'

Stacey waved a hand. 'Whatever, I just know that you know about investments. You know about pretty much everything else.'

'True.' Heidi fiddled with the paper, rolled it between nimble fingers, appeared to turn it inside out and placed an origami turtle next to the pepper grinder. 'Go on then,' she said. 'I'll buy it.'

Stacey opened a packet of chocolate biscuits and passed them to her friend.

'I want to talk to Jonathon Haddon's partners, Watson and Willis, but not as a journalist, as an investor.'

'Someone left you a lump of cash?'

'Unfortunately not, but I want to try and work out whether anything dodgy is going on.'

Heidi snorted. 'You won't find that out just by visiting their offices.'

'Probably not, but I could get a feel for the company maybe. They might offer me a too-good-to-be-true-and-highly-suspect product.'

Heidi grinned and topped up the mugs. 'And you'd know one of those if you saw one, would you?'

'Possibly not.'

'So you want me to teach you how to act like an investor – what to say, that sort of thing?'

'Yes, that's about right.'

Heidi snorted again. 'I'm not being funny, Stace, but you haven't the brain for it.'

'Are you saying I'm stupid?'

'Of course not, but words are your thing, not numbers.'

'You have a point. What do you suggest?'

'I'll play the investor.'

Stacey smiled.

'I know,' Heidi continued, 'I look fourteen years old and a little like a space cadet. I'm not going to change my look, but I do have contacts.'

'In the financial industry?'

'A few, but I also have a wealthy father with many wealthy friends. I'll ask one of them to give me an introduction. Money and the old-school-tie brigade go hand in hand. Should be a doddle.' She grinned. 'Make an appointment for sometime this week and tell them I'll be bringing my PA.'

'Who's that?'

'You of course. That way you'll get to meet the partners too and can legitimately take minutes of the meeting.'

Stacey grinned. 'You're brilliant, you know.'

'Yes,' Heidi said, 'I do know. Now let's take a walk down by the river. We'll finalize our scheme after we've stretched our legs.'

* * *

Leo Phillips' face fell when he opened the door of his cottage and recognised the detectives. Without a word, he waved them inside and closed the door.

'How are you, Mr Phillips?' Ben asked.

The man frowned. 'How the bloody hell do you think I am?'

'Sir, I understand this is difficult for you, but we'd like a chat. We have some questions to ask.'

'I knew you'd get around to it sooner or later,' Phillips said and flopped onto an easy chair next to the fireplace.

'Get around to what, sir?' Jack asked.

'Accusing me of killing Kitty.' Phillips glanced up. 'That is why you are here?'

'We're here,' Ben said, 'to investigate your wife's death. To do that, we need to question anyone connected to her – yourself included. We aren't here to accuse you of anything.'

'OK if I make a cuppa?' Jack asked. 'I think we could do with one.'

'Yeah,' Phillips said, 'help yourself.'

Ben sat on the sofa and took out his notebook. 'So, tell me,' he said, 'how are you, sir?'

Phillips sighed and scrubbed at his short hair. 'I don't really know, if I'm honest. After you left yesterday, I rang Kitty's parents. A dreadful call to have to make and of course they wanted to know the circumstances, and I couldn't… just couldn't…'

'What, sir?'

'Tell them she was with another man.' Phillips wrapped his arms around his midriff and groaned. 'Not like I can get my head around any of it myself.'

Jack placed three mugs of tea on a low table and sat on the sofa next to his boss. Phillips grabbed one of the mugs, slurped loudly, then wiped his lips with the back of his hand.

'Tell me about Kitty,' Ben said. 'How did you meet? What was she like? Just talk to me.'

Phillips took a huge, shuddering breath and began to speak.

'Kitty was beautiful, always had been, deep green eyes and the brightest smile I have ever seen.' He gulped more tea. 'We met at a music festival, Cropredy in Oxfordshire. She was nineteen, I was twenty-five.' He smiled at the memory. 'She'd managed to lock herself in a portaloo. I heard her yelling, forced the door open and she flew out and kissed me.' He closed his eyes.

'Love at first sight then?' Ben prompted.

'Yeah, guess it was. A month later we moved in together, married three years ago, same time as I inherited some money. We found this place for sale and have lived here ever since.'

'You enjoyed a happy marriage?' Jack asked.

Without hesitation Phillips answered, 'Yes.' Then he added, 'Well I thought it was. Not so sure now.'

'We know Kitty worked in Builth,' Ben said. 'What do you do?'

'I'm a boring accountant, but it pays well enough and I can work from home.'

Ben scrawled in his notebook. 'Self-employed?' he asked.

Phillips nodded.

Jack slipped a photograph from his inside pocket. 'This is a picture of the man found with your wife,' he said. 'Do you recognise him, sir?'

Phillips took the photograph and stared at it for a brief moment. He shook his head. 'No, I don't. Does he have a name?'

'Jonathon Haddon.'

'Never heard of him.' Phillips handed the picture back.

'Where were you on Saturday night?' Ben asked.

'Here, working. Didn't leave the house.'

'Can anyone confirm that?'

'Check my phone records. I made some late calls and sent a few emails too.'

'Did you speak to your wife?'

'No, she doesn't usually ring when she's on a weekend away. She sent a couple of texts.' He swallowed hard. 'She told me what she had for dinner. Oh God, I can't believe I won't see her again. My beautiful girl, taken from me.' He glanced up at the officers, eyes brimming. 'Make bloody sure you find out what happened, that you catch the person responsible, and then lock them up for the rest of their life.'

* * *

As Jack negotiated the long track leading back to the road Ben asked, 'So, what do you think? Did Phillips shoot Haddon? A jealous killing?'

Jack snorted. 'Couldn't honestly say, guv. No doubt the grief is genuine, but I can't decide if it's stoked by guilt. He doesn't seem the type, but ordinary people sometimes do extraordinary things.'

'Did you get Kitty's parents' contact details?'

'Yes, guv.'

'Better put a visit to them on the to-do list.'

Ben's mobile rang. He removed it from his pocket, peered at the screen and answered the call.

'Hi, *cariad*,' he said. 'Everything OK?'

'Good thanks,' Stacey said. 'Just wondering if you're coming for supper tonight.'

'Why? Got a better offer?'

She chuckled. 'Not tonight I haven't. Heidi's here so I need to know how much food to cook.'

'Supper would be great, thanks. I need to pop back to the station so I'll be over about six thirty.'

'Perfect, see you then.'

Chapter five

Ben pushed through the main door of the police station just before eight the next morning. The desk sergeant caught his eye and Ben walked towards him. The sergeant leaned closer and spoke quietly.

'The bloke behind you is the taxi driver you were looking for. He saw the appeal in the press.'

'Has he said anything?'

'Not much but I reckon he's definitely your guy. He described the victims including Ms Phillips' dress.'

'OK. Give me five to chat with Jack. Put the cabbie in the back office and give him a cuppa.'

'Yes, sir.'

Ben passed through reception and ran upstairs to the squad room. Tegan looked up from her screen as he entered.

'Morning, sir,' she said.

'Morning. Where is everyone? Where's Jack?'

Tegan shrugged. 'No sign of DS Trent. Ollie's down at the vehicle pound. SOCO rang half an hour ago.'

'Do you know why?'

'No, sir, they just asked for one of the team to pop down.'

'What about the others?'

'Elsa Duffin and Kevin Biggs have gone to Llandeilo to talk to Kitty's friends.'

'Right then, come downstairs with me. The cabbie who collected the victims from the Caer Beris is here and wants to talk to us.'

'That's a bit of luck.'

'Isn't it. Let's get down there before he changes his mind.'

Tegan slipped into her jacket and followed Ben down to the slightly scruffy office behind reception. A middle-aged man with a decent-sized beer belly got to his feet and smiled nervously, unsure whether or not to offer a hand.

'Please, take your seat,' Ben said. 'Good of you to come in, Mr…?'

'Goodman,' the man said. 'Charlie.'

Ben introduced himself and Tegan and said, 'You told the desk sergeant that you picked up two customers from the Caer Beris early Sunday morning. That you believe they may have been the couple discovered at the car showroom in Llanelwedd. Is that correct?'

'Yes, it is. I read about their deaths in the paper and knew it was them. The timing was right and the article said the woman had been wearing a blue ball gown.'

'How did they contact you?'

'By phone. Mr Haddon called me at nine o'clock that evening and booked a taxi to pick him up at one in the morning.'

'Did he provide a destination?'

'No, he joked about me not making my fortune as it was a short trip but said he'd tip well, so I agreed.'

'Tell us what happened.'

'I left home at 12.45am. It had just started to rain again, foul night. I parked as close to the entrance of the hotel as I could and just after one, the door opened and a bloke stepped out. A woman in a blue, sparkly dress, a dinner jacket over her head, dashed out and got in the car with the bloke and I set off.'

'To the car showroom?' Ben asked.

'No. He asked me to drive to the golf club. It was closed of course, but he posted a thick envelope through the letterbox, then we went to the showroom.'

'Do you know what was in the envelope?' Tegan asked.

The cabbie grinned. 'Unfortunately not, love. Left my X-ray specs at home.'

'Did you see anything written on the envelope?'

'No, sorry.'

'So you drove through town and over the bridge?' Ben asked.

'That's right. Man, you should have seen the river, heard the roar of it as we crossed over.'

'Had the Wye burst its banks?'

'No, but I knew it wouldn't be long. I warned the couple what was coming, but they insisted I let them out in the car park.'

'Did they tell you why they wanted to go there?'

'No, they just handed over a hefty tip and left the car.'

'Did they talk about anything on the journey? How did they seem?'

'OK I guess. They didn't seem overly pleased about having to go out and I thought they said something about meeting someone.'

'Hear a name?'

'No, sorry, that's it. I dropped them where they asked and drove back home to the wife. Last job of a very long day.'

Ben nodded. 'Thanks again for coming in. Constable Hedges will take a written statement then you can get on with your day.'

'No problem,' Charlie said. 'Glad I could be useful.'

Ben left the room and walked back upstairs to the incident room. Jack was standing next to the coffee machine.

'Fancy a cuppa, guv?' he asked.

'Yeah, a quick one. We need to get over to Bwlch and talk to Kitty's parents.'

'Are they expecting us?'

'I told them we'd be there mid-morning. On the return journey, we need to drop into the golf club at Builth. I've just been speaking with the cabbie who drove the victims to the showroom. He told me Jonathon Haddon delivered an envelope to the clubhouse shortly before he was shot.'

* * *

Jack turned off the A40 just before Bwlch and drove towards Llangorse Lake. A few miles further on, he pulled up outside a large, detached house, two cars parked on the drive.

'Nice place, guv,' he said as he got out of the car. 'Lovely views.'

'Dad used to bring me fishing here when I was a kid,' Ben said, 'and he had the time. Can't remember catching much but I loved floating about in the boat.'

Jack led the way to the front door and rang the bell. A few moments later, a man in his mid-fifties, dressed in what looked like gardening clothes, opened the door. His hair was tousled, as though he had just got out of bed, and his face tired and sagging; a deep frown creased his high forehead.

'Are you the police?' he asked and receiving a nod from the officers, he held out his hand. 'Raymond Gardiner.'

Ben shook his hand and introduced them, then they followed the man inside to a large kitchen where a woman sat at the table, nursing a mug of tea. She glanced up, skin deathly pale, eyes red and swollen, full of tears.

'My wife, Geraldine,' Raymond said. 'Please, take a seat and I'll make some tea.'

The detectives sat at the table as Raymond filled the kettle and put it on to boil. He perched on a stool next to the worktop.

'Have you any news for us, gentlemen?' he asked. 'Do you know the circumstances of our daughter's death?'

Ben cleared his throat then he explained as delicately as he could what had been discovered during autopsy, and how Kitty's death may have been accidental.

'Do you have any idea why she might have gone to her place of work in the middle of the night?' Ben asked.

'No, we haven't,' Raymond said and poured boiling water into a brown teapot which he carried to the table. 'Like her husband, we believed she was spending the weekend with her girlfriends in Cardiff.'

Geraldine spoke for the first time, slowly and quietly.

'We always knew she'd get herself into serious trouble,' she said, 'but never imagined she would end up dead.'

'Why do you say that?' Ben asked.

'She got in too deep. We told her over and over that it wouldn't end well, but she was addicted and wouldn't stop. I blame Rowan, her brother. This is all his fault. He shouldn't have involved her.'

'Involved her with what exactly?' Ben asked.

Geraldine sniffed and dabbed her eyes. 'Saving souls, she called it.'

'You mean they were preaching? Trying to convert people?'

Geraldine shook her head. 'No, trying to help migrants who cross the Channel in overcrowded boats. She couldn't bear the suffering.'

'How did she save them?' Jack asked.

Geraldine didn't answer for several seconds while her husband gazed out of the window at the lake.

Eventually, Geraldine took a deep breath and said, 'Kitty and her brother smuggled people out of the camps in France and into the UK.'

The officers weren't expecting the answer and for a couple of minutes, no one spoke, until Ben asked, 'Does Rowan live with you?'

'No,' Raymond said. 'He hasn't lived here for three years.'

'Do you have an address for him?'

'I wish we did, but no. Haven't any idea where he is. He bought a van, put a bed and the bare essentials in the back, and drove away.'

'Do you hear from him at all?' Jack asked.

'He rings every now and again,' Geraldine said, 'but he doesn't visit.'

'Does he know about his sister's death?'

Geraldine swallowed a sob. 'We haven't spoken. Don't even have a phone number for him.'

'You said you blamed him for getting your daughter involved. How did that happen?'

Raymond sighed. 'After he completed his degree, he travelled to the so-called Jungle in Calais with a friend from university. When he came home, he was a different lad. We hardly recognised him.'

'He was ill,' Geraldine said, 'couldn't stop crying and wouldn't eat. I took him to the doctor who diagnosed something called "compassion saturation".'

'Load of nonsense,' Raymond grumbled. 'Bad things happen in this world and it's best not to get involved if you can't do anything to change them.'

'So he told Kitty about his experiences?' Ben asked.

'Yes, he did. Kitty spent a lot of time with him, helped him get back on his feet. She joined a charity to raise money for asylum seekers in the camps, but that wasn't enough for her. She began driving to Calais regularly with her brother. They took supplies to France and brought illegal immigrants back with them.'

'Sounds as though you don't approve, sir.'

'Of course I don't approve! They were breaking the law. Little better than people smugglers, the pair of them.'

'Did they charge for their services?' Jack asked.

'I don't believe so, but what they were doing was illegal.' Raymond snorted. 'We're a small island, bursting at the seams, not enough housing or services for our own people, so why bring those people here? What are we supposed to do with them?'

'Britain has a history of offering a safe haven to refugees,' Ben said. 'There were many schemes before, during, and after the Second World War.'

'But we're not at war, Inspector. Economic migrants, that's what they are. Refugees?' He snorted again. 'Of *course* they are. I see them on the news, strapping young men. They all have mobile phones, trainers on their feet. Those escaping the Nazis had nothing. Nothing at all!'

'One last thing,' Jack said, holding out a photograph. 'Do you know this man?'

'Yes, I do,' Raymond snapped. 'Jonathon Haddon. He was the one who took my son to those dreadful camps.'

* * *

Stacey leaned back in her chair and dialled Heidi's number, jiggling impatiently until her friend answered.

'Speak first. You're paying.'

Stacey chuckled. 'That line's getting old now.'

'Habit. Funny though, I was about to call you.'

'What for?'

'You first.'

'I've made an appointment at Haddon, Watson and Willis. Tomorrow morning I'm afraid, ten thirty. Sorry for the short notice.'

'No worries. Erica is on early shift this week and still hasn't learnt how to creep out of bed without waking me up. Must get a bigger place with a spare room. Anyway, where are the offices?'

'Just off the A485 on the edge of Carmarthen.'

'I'll meet you at yours then. Nine o'clock. That should give us plenty of time. Make sure you dress like an important person's PA.'

'What does one of those look like?'

'Smart suit, nothing flashy, semi-invisible.'

Stacey laughed. 'I'll check my wardrobe. So, why were you going to ring me?'

'I've been digging about online into the pasts of the main players.'

'Find anything?'

'Just the usual sort of crap everyone has, except…'

'Except what?'

'Leo Phillips has a criminal record. Picked it up four years ago for drunken brawling. He was fined and handed a six-month suspended sentence. Nothing before or after.'

'Is that relevant do you think?'

'Probably not, but if he thought he was defending Kitty, or smashing some guy's face in for ogling her… maybe.'

'Can we find out the circumstances?'

Heidi snorted. 'Given time "we" can find out anything.'

'Did you look into Kitty's background?'

'Of course and that was interesting. Her elder brother was fined for smuggling a refugee into the UK in the back of his van.'

'Wow. When did he do that?'

'A couple of years ago, but my gut tells me that wasn't the first or last time he'd done it.'

'Why do you say that?'

'He's all over the web raising money and supporting charities set up to help asylum seekers.'

'Does any of that have anything to do with the two dead people?'

'At first glance, I can't see it does, but as ever I'll keep an open mind. More data required.'

'How about Haddon, Watson and Willis? Find anything on them?'

'I didn't look. I want to talk to the partners first and not run the risk of influencing my instincts. Meantime, I'll send you some links to Rowan Gardiner's activities.'

'OK, thanks. I'll have a look and see you tomorrow.'

Chapter six

The team gathered early in the incident room for a progress report. Jack had brought in pastries from the local bakery and while they were consumed, Ben updated his staff.

'You'll probably know this already,' he said. 'SOCO found the shell case from a .38 in the sports car Haddon was sitting in when he was shot. FSS are checking their records to determine whether the gun has been used in a crime prior to this, but that will take some time. DNA was also recovered, from four different individuals. We need to collect samples from the staff at the showroom and see what we're left with, but nothing already on file matches.'

'It's good SOCO found the brass though,' Ollie said. 'We haven't got many clues to work with. The flood contaminated the scene and more than likely washed away any evidence.'

'We have to work with what we've got,' Ben said.

'How did it go with Kitty's parents?' Tegan asked.

Ben told them what he and Jack had discovered at the Gardiners', and what Kitty and her brother appeared to have been involved in.

'Bloody hell,' Kevin said. 'Kitty isn't someone I'd put down as being a people smuggler.' He sniggered. 'Can you honestly see that girl wandering up and down a French beach and herding people into plastic boats?'

'No,' Ben said, 'and we haven't heard anything that suggests she was engaged in that sort of operation. Her mother told us Kitty and her brother made regular trips to Calais delivering food, clothes and aid for those at the camps, but didn't always return with an empty car.'

'People smuggling just the same.'

'There's no evidence they were charging for their services,' Jack said. 'Her mother said they were "saving souls", and seemed more sympathetic than the father. He's afraid the British Isles will sink if we let in any more illegal immigrants.'

'I'm with him on that,' Kevin said. 'We shouldn't get involved. Our own people need homes.'

'Why can't people put themselves in other's shoes?' Tegan asked. 'I can't imagine how desperate you have to be to get into one of those blow-up boats and try to cross the world's busiest shipping lane.'

Ben nodded. 'OK, we have two priorities,' he said. 'Firstly, we need to track down Rowan Gardiner, thirty-one years old and of no fixed abode. Left home three years ago and his parents have very limited contact with him. His mother reports occasional phone calls, never any visits, and she doesn't have a phone number for him.'

'Should we check with homeless charities?' Ollie asked.

'I don't think that will be necessary. Seems Rowan bought a van, kitted it out so he could live in it, and left. A couple of years ago he was fined for bringing an asylum seeker into the UK. We have an address on record for that offence and it looks as though his bank account, HMRC records and driving licence are registered at the same place. Big house outside Abergavenny.' Ben glanced up at his team. 'Ollie and Tegan, follow this up today and take a statement from anyone living at the property.'

'Yes, sir,' Tegan said.

'On the way back from the Gardiners',' Ben continued, 'Jack and I called in to Builth golf club. The cabbie told us Haddon delivered an envelope there a little while before he died. No one working in the place admitted seeing the envelope, but I believe the driver was telling the truth and we need to find it. That's your job, Kevin.'

'I'm on it.'

'Jack and I have an appointment at Haddon's firm this morning, but if you need either of us, get in touch. How did you and Elsa get on talking to Kitty's friends in Llandeilo?'

'Not great,' he said. 'Seems Kitty Phillips stopped attending girlie weekends away a couple of years ago. No one admitted to a falling out but contact with Kitty declined. None of the women we spoke to could remember the last time she met up with them.' Kevin grinned. 'Obviously a story she spun her old man. Maybe she *was* having an affair with Haddon.'

'Maybe she was, but like everything else, we need proof.'

'Bet her husband knew about it,' Kevin said. 'I can see him in my mind's eye, wading through the flood, in the dark, loaded revolver in his hand…'

'Sergeant Biggs!' Ben snapped. 'You know better. Now let's get on with it.'

'What would you like me to do, sir?' Elsa asked.

Ben smiled. 'Person the phones and start checking Rowan's bank account records, find out if he uses a card and where. Speak to the mobile phone providers, the DWP – you know the drill.'

'Yes, sir,' she said and turned back to her screen.

* * *

Stacey strode up to the main entrance of Haddon, Watson and Willis, straight-armed the heavy glass door and held it open for Heidi to enter. As usual, her petite friend wore black; jeans, T-shirt, open leather jacket and Doc Marten boots, a striking contrast to her pale skin and white hair. Heidi marched up to the desk and Stacey noticed the young receptionist's eyes widen slightly as he spotted her.

'Yes?' he said. 'Can I help?'

'Ms Holtz,' Heidi snapped. 'I have a ten thirty appointment.' She glanced at a chunky watch on her wrist. 'If I'm still here at ten thirty-two, I shall leave. Time is money after all.'

'Yes, of course, madam. Please take a seat and I'll inform Mr Willis you have arrived.'

Heidi didn't reply, she spun on her heel and caught Stacey's eye, who tried hard not to giggle. Heidi's appearance, out of sync with her upper-class vowels and manner, had clearly put the receptionist on the back foot. The waiting room was chic, lots of glass and brushed stainless steel. A low table, covered with tastefully positioned piles of the obligatory magazines, also supported what could only be described as a statement plant – a long green stem with a weird-looking, red flower on the tip. Stacey was about to check if it was real, when a door next to the desk opened and a smartly dressed man in his mid-thirties, with an overly unrealistic smile packed with too many, too large, white teeth walked through it. His right hand was already outstretched.

'Ms Holtz. Good morning. Dominic Willis, pleased to meet you.'

Heidi nodded. 'And you. I've read good things about your firm.'

Willis grinned again. 'That's what we like to hear.' He turned to Stacey. 'And you are?'

'My PA,' Heidi said dismissively. 'Now the pleasantries are over, let's get to it. I have other appointments.'

'Of course, we're all busy. My diary is pretty packed, but we have an hour.'

'Should be sufficient. Lead the way.'

Willis set off along a carpeted corridor, pushed open the door to his office and waved his visitors inside.

'After you, ladies. I'll arrange some coffee.'

'No thanks,' Heidi said. 'We've already established how busy we are.'

'Of course.' Willis sat behind his desk and steepled his fingers. 'We should begin by assessing the health of your current portfolio and how much you are looking to invest.'

Heidi slipped a memory stick from her jacket pocket and slid it across the table.

'Everything is on there,' she said, 'and I have another half mill available to top it up – if you can point me in the right direction of an appropriate investment.'

Stacey peered at Willis from beneath her fringe and thought she spotted a tightening of his mouth, but the dazzling, fake smile reappeared almost instantly. She tuned out of the resultant discussion regarding bonds, stocks, high-yield savings accounts and a brief mention of bitcoin. She knew Heidi was listening – and understanding – so she concentrated on Willis' body language and how he had chosen to furnish his personal space.

She allowed her eyes to drift towards the glory wall behind his chair and noticed a framed degree certificate, diplomas, memberships of various financial bodies and heaps of awards. On the desk were half a dozen glass paperweights, sparkling in a patch of sunshine shafting through the large office windows. No family photos anywhere. Willis wore an expensive watch on his right wrist and Stacey scribbled, "left-handed" on her pad.

Heidi got to her feet and walked to the window with Willis who pointed at something. She looked at the view for a moment and then suddenly turned.

'Well,' she said, glancing out of the window a second time, 'my contact details are on the stick. We're done here. I need to be elsewhere. We can see ourselves out.'

Stacey scrabbled to her feet and followed her friend from the office.

'What's up?' she hissed halfway along the corridor.

'Ben and Jack just pulled up in the car park. We've gotta get out of here.'

Heidi entered reception, marched towards a fire door, pushed it open and discovered a staircase.

'This way,' she said. 'With a bit of luck we'll come out at the rear of the building and we can melt away.' She grinned at Stacey. 'This is quite good fun, isn't it? Makes the blood pump a little faster.'

* * *

Later that day, Stacey had just taken a huge bite of takeaway pizza, one of her favourite treats, when Ben said, 'I didn't know you were planning to go to Carmarthen today.'

Stacey chewed slowly, grey cells zipping about inside her skull as she worked out how to reply.

Ben continued, 'I spotted Heidi's truck parked outside the offices of Haddon, Watson and Willis.'

Stacey swallowed, picked up her glass of wine and sipped.

'I'm a bit miffed, to be honest,' Ben said. 'I gave you Jonathon Haddon's name off the record.'

'I know you did,' Stacey said, 'but I went for morning coffee at the Caer Beris and the waiter told me all about the guest who turned up dead.'

'You could have warned me you were planning something.'

'You would have got grumpy and told me not to go.'

'Of course I would and can you blame me? A man was found dead in Builth, just a few miles down the road, in what looks like an execution, and we haven't caught the killer yet.'

'I didn't go alone. Heidi was with me.'

Ben nodded. 'As I said, I saw her truck, but what would you have done if Willis pulled a gun on you?'

'Hardly likely, and how do you know we spoke to Willis?'

Ben sighed. 'Because I'm a detective and Watson is on leave.' He rested a hand on Stacey's cheek. 'I worry because I love you.'

'I know,' Stacey said, 'and I love you too, but you really don't need to worry about me.'

'It's part of the deal.'

'What deal?'

'Love and worry go together. I can only stop worrying if I stop loving.'

Stacey kissed his palm. 'We don't want that do we?'

'No, we don't. Promise me you'll take a couple of steps back from this – at least until we have a better idea what "this" is?'

'You can't ask me not to do my job. I've never given you hassle over yours.'

'No, you haven't and I'm grateful, but it's different for me. I'm police. I have back-up.' He held up a hand. 'Heidi Holtz is not back-up.'

'I'm not so sure.'

Ben laughed. 'Just promise me you'll be careful. Things tend to get dangerous when money is involved.'

'You think the murder is related to some sort of financial shenanigans? That Haddon lost someone a lot of money?'

'It's possible, but we are following other avenues.'

'Something to do with Rowan Gardiner's criminal record?'

'How the hell?' Ben sighed. 'Your back-up, of course. Listen, Pumpkin, I'm not trying to clip your wings, but you really can't print anything about that, and I mean *really*.'

'Have you spoken to him?'

'No, not yet.'

'Why not?'

'He doesn't have an address, lives in a van and his parents don't have a contact number. We've been looking but no luck so far.'

'Heidi's good at finding.'

'There's no stopping you, is there? Just be warned, this case could be much larger than it looks. If Heidi pokes around and she's caught breaking the law – or you come to that – I won't be able to help either of you. Be careful, *cariad*, be safe.'

The landline rang and glad of the distraction, Stacey snatched up the handset.

'Hello?'

'It's me,' Heidi said. 'You busy tomorrow?'

'Not especially.'

'Good, I'll be over at ten. There's a woman we need to talk to.'

'Oh?' Stacey asked, but the line had already disconnected.

Ben raised his eyebrows and Stacey shrugged.

'Heidi,' she said, 'she's popping in tomorrow.'

'Make sure you pass on what I've said. You both need to be careful.'

Chapter seven

The next morning, Heidi pulled up outside Noddfa and tooted the horn. Stacey ran down the path and climbed into the passenger seat and Heidi headed for Carmarthen. While she threaded through the lanes to the main road, Stacey told her how Ben had caught them out the day before.

'Ooh, was he angry?' Heidi asked.

'Not really,' Stacey said. 'More disappointed – which is actually much worse. He warned us to be careful if we're going to keep digging, and not to break the law.' Stacey sighed then asked, 'Now you've had time to think about yesterday's meeting, what was your impression of Willis? Is he up to something?'

'Shifty character, like most money men. I wonder if it's because they know they don't really do anything that useful. Charge hefty fees and commission for advice – which isn't always the best – and help the rich save tax.'

'I thought that was accountants. The tax thing.'

'IFAs talk about it when they're advising people what to do with their money. Helps them sell investment products.'

'Like you said, numbers aren't my thing.'

'Don't worry, I'm looking at him. I'm searching for a way in.'

Heidi slowed and turned right at the Llandeilo roundabout.

'So tell me,' Stacey said, 'who is the woman we're going to see.'

'She's called Sorrell. I looked at Rowan Gardiner's social media accounts and that's where I found her. She lives not far from Aberglasney and definitely worked in the camps with him.'

'Maybe she knows where he is.'

'Maybe. I haven't been able to find him yet. The address he uses for bank accounts, driving licence etc. is not where he lives.'

'Who does live there?'

'A very elderly, upper middle class, and utterly delightful woman called Felicity Savage. She lives alone in a big place Abergavenny way.'

'Have you spoken to her?'

Heidi nodded. 'Fantastic conversation. Back in the day she was one of the women who camped on Greenham Common protesting about the Yanks stationing nukes there.'

'Why does she let Rowan use her address?'

Heidi chuckled. 'Because, although she's over ninety, she still has the heart of an activist. At least twenty individuals have been granted permission to use her place as a postal address.' Heidi chuckled again. 'Hell of a woman that one.'

'Wow. I'd like to meet her. Feels like you stumbled on an underground network.'

'There's a lot of them about,' Heidi muttered.

A few miles down the road, Heidi turned left at Broad Oak and slowed in the lanes. The mid-May verges were lush, banks of cow parsley swayed in the breeze, the last blush of bluebells at their feet, and pure white stars of stitchwort scrambled through the long grass. Stacey wound down the window and breathed in the sharpness of spring. A few minutes later, Heidi took another left onto a dirt track.

'Does this Sorrell woman know we're about to descend on her, or what I do for a living?' Stacey asked.

Heidi shook her head. 'I haven't spoken to her.'

'So, what do you suggest?'

Heidi pulled up next to a five-bar gate, turned off the engine and cracked her knuckles. 'Have to see how it pans out.'

* * *

Tegan looked up from her computer screen as Ben entered the incident room.

'Morning, sir,' she said. 'The DNA results are back.'

'That was quick for once. Anything useful?'

'Certainly curious. Come and take a look, they're on my screen.'

Ben draped his jacket on the back of a chair and moved closer to Tegan's workstation.

'Show me what you've found,' he said.

'As you know, four unidentified samples were collected at the scene and from the bodies. We took swabs from the showroom staff and discovered' – she took a deep breath – 'DNA belonging to Caleb Griffiths in the mouth of Kitty Phillips.'

'In her mouth?' Ben asked.

'Yes, sir,'

'FSS offer any explanation?'

'No but they confirmed the sample wasn't from semen.'

Ben rubbed a hand across his short hair. 'That's something I suppose. OK, I'll have Kevin and Ollie pick him up. Is Jack around?'

'He nipped out to buy coffee beans for the machine.'

'If you see him before I do, tell him not to go anywhere. I want him here when we speak to Caleb.'

* * *

An hour passed before Ollie ushered Caleb Griffiths inside the interview room and encouraged him to take a seat at the table facing Ben and Jack. The lad looked nervous, younger than his years, and his eyes flicked busily around the room as Jack started the recording machine and logged the date, time and those in the room. Ollie Langdon leant against the wall next to the door.

The machine buzzed loudly and when it fell silent, Caleb asked, 'Do you think someone could tell me what's going on? Cos, to be honest, I'm a bit freaked by this. Well, a lot freaked to be fair.' He rubbed his face. 'When I saw you lot pull up in the yard, I thought you were there to ask me about the mess in the showroom, not arrest me.' He glanced at the officers in turn. 'Well?' he asked.

'We need to ask you some questions,' Ben said, 'under caution.'

'What does that even mean?'

'You were cautioned when you were arrested and it means what it says. Anything you say can be used as evidence if you go to trial.'

'Trial!' Caleb squeaked. 'You're not serious. What for? Do you think I had something to do with Kitty and that bloke's deaths? That's mad. Fucking mental. I had nothing to do with it.'

'Have you finished?' Jack asked quietly.

Caleb nodded, shut his mouth, then thought better of it and asked, 'Do I need a solicitor?'

Jack shrugged. 'It's up to you. One of your own or the duty solicitor?'

Caleb stared at the table and said, 'I don't know.'

Ben glanced at Ollie. 'Constable, can you find out if Mr Nyle is still on site and if he is, brief him and send him in?'

'Yes, sir.'

'DC Langdon leaving the room,' Jack said.

The stuffy, overly warm space and the silence didn't do anything for Caleb. He began to sweat, pulled at the neck of his hooded top and one knee bounced rapidly. After a short wait, the door reopened and a small wiry man, with wild, wire-wool-like hair, scruffy shoes and carrying an ancient, battered leather briefcase entered. He nodded at the detectives, shook his client's hand and sat.

'Mr Dick Nyle has entered the room,' Jack intoned for the tape.

'Would you like a moment to confer with your client?' Ben asked.

'Let's see how we get on,' the solicitor said. 'Caleb, if I touch your arm at any point, say "no comment". Got that?'

Caleb nodded.

Nyle smiled at Ben. 'We're ready.'

'Caleb, where were you Saturday night and into Sunday morning?' Ben asked.

'At the farm with Mum and Dad.'

'Can they confirm you were there?'

'Definitely. That night there was a difficult calving – twins. Dad and I were out dealing with it most of the night. We got back to the house around five. Mum cooked us breakfast and I'd planned to go to bed after we'd eaten.' He frowned. 'I'd just finished when Mr Jones from the showroom rang, so I had a quick shower, borrowed the Land Rover and drove to Builth.'

Nyle scribbled on a legal pad with a cheap ball-point and nodded slightly as though agreeing with what had been said.

'Where were you before the calving?' Jack asked.

'Uh… I ate supper, then I watched something on telly and went to bed at ten. Dad woke me just after one in the morning.'

Jack removed an evidence bag from a cardboard file. It contained a mobile phone. He placed it on the table and slid it under Caleb's nose.

'That's my phone,' Caleb said. 'When am I gonna get it back?'

'Not yet. It's evidence.'

Jack slipped the phone from the bag, switched it on, swiped the screen and held it in front of Caleb's face. Caleb gulped as he saw a photo of Kitty's face, eyes closed in death, long, wet hair plastered to her pale skin. Jack swiped the image and it was replaced by another, Kitty's face and torso.

'You agree this phone is yours?' Jack asked.

Caleb nodded.

'Speak up for the tape.'

'Yes, it's mine. I said so didn't I?'

'Did you take these pictures?'

Nyle reached out a hand and placed it on his client's arm.

Caleb blinked and said, 'No comment.'

'OK,' Jack said. 'Let's talk about something else.' He removed a sheet of paper from the file and pushed it across the desk. 'These are DNA results from the crime scene and the victims. Swabs are routinely taken from various parts of the body, and these show your DNA inside Kitty's mouth. Care to comment now?'

Nyle grasped Caleb's arm tightly. 'I wish to request a short break,' he said. 'I would like a few moments to consult with my client.' He smiled at Jack. 'Some tea wouldn't go amiss.'

Ben nodded. Jack terminated the interview and all three officers left the room.

Chapter eight

At the end of a footpath leading from the five-bar gate, was a mid-sized detached house, partially obscured by what looked to be an apple orchard, its trees covered with blossom. A large garden was surrounded by a wooden picket fence, and in a tidy yard next to the house a flock of russet-coloured chickens pecked at the dirt, squabbling amongst themselves.

'Wow, what a great place,' Stacey said.

'I could live here,' Heidi said, 'as long as there's internet, which I doubt.'

She opened the gate, skirted the industrious hens and rapped loudly on a polished brass knocker. After a few moments, the door was opened by a slim woman, early thirties maybe, wearing loose-fitting, purple trousers, a pink vest top, colourful tattoos on show, and green boots on her feet. Her hair was dreadlocked and piled on top of her head, held in place by a scrap of multicoloured material.

'Hello,' she said. 'Are you lost?'

Heidi smiled. 'I don't think so, we're looking for Sorrell.'

The woman blinked. 'Can you tell me why you want to speak to her?'

'We're trying to contact Rowan Gardiner and saw on social media that you've carried out charity work together,' Heidi said, bending the truth and smiling again. 'I know you're Sorrell, I recognise you from your posts, so any chance of a quick chat? My name's Heidi and my friend is Stacey. I can assure you we're both housetrained.'

Sorrell chuckled. 'OK then. I can spare you some time. Go on round to the back of the house and I'll bring lemonade. Don't let Rufus out.'

'Rufus?' Stacey asked.

'Skinny mongrel. He barks a lot but doesn't bite. I won't be long.'

Heidi set off along a narrow path and walked around the end of the building, past the orchard, through a small gate and into a large vegetable garden. A black, hairy dog, with two white socks, shot out of a wooden kennel barking madly.

'Oi!' Heidi yelled. 'Shut up!'

The dog stared at her, then plonked its bottom on the earth, mouth closed. Sorrell emerged from the house with a tray holding a jug of lemonade and three glasses. She placed the tray on a wooden table and the women sat.

Sorrell giggled. 'Poor Rufus. You've shocked him rigid. Do you have a dog?'

Heidi shook her head. 'Pa had a couple when I was young but I've never felt the need to own one myself.'

Sorrell filled the glasses. 'So,' she said, 'tell me how you know Rowan.'

Stacey felt her cheeks flush. She didn't enjoy lying, had never been very good at it, and knew she couldn't keep the falsehood going.

'Actually,' she said, 'we don't, but we need to find him.'

Sorrell frowned. 'Who are you then and why are you looking for my friend?'

'I'm a journalist, working on a story relating to the deaths of a man and a woman in Builth Wells the weekend of the flood.' She took a gulp of air. 'The woman who died is Kitty Phillips, Rowan's younger sister.'

Sorrell's hand flew to her mouth. 'Kitty's dead? How?'

Heidi told Sorrell about the flood and the bodies found in the showroom. She passed over a photograph of Jonathon Haddon she'd gleaned from the net. 'Do you know this man?' she asked.

Sorrell stared at the picture and began to cry. 'Jonathon.' She sniffled. 'Rowan's best mate.' She scrubbed at her eyes. 'Is he dead too? Is he the man found with Kitty?'

Stacey nodded. 'I'm very sorry,' she said. 'That's why we want to find Rowan.'

'Is he in danger?'

'To be honest,' Stacey said, shaking her head, 'we don't know, but it's why we need to talk to him. Can you tell us how you met each other?'

'I don't know,' Sorrell said. 'I'm not sure I want to talk to you, given you're a reporter.'

'I won't write about anything you tell me, I promise. Not a chance your name will appear in print, we're just concerned for Rowan. His parents don't have a contact number for him. He might not even know his sister has died.'

'How do I know I can trust you? The press hasn't been kind to the likes of us in the past.'

'Us?' Stacey asked.

'Charity workers trying to help the desperate stuck in the camps in France.'

'Tell us about the camps, how you help.'

'I'm really not sure–'

Stacey placed a gentle hand on Sorrell's forearm. 'I won't betray your confidence, you have my word, but something bad is going on and we want to stop it. We want to find out who killed your friends, so please talk to us.'

Sorrell gulped from her glass and set off a coughing fit. Stacey patted her back.

'Tell us how you met them, all we want to do is help.'

Sorrell glared at her visitors. 'You better not let me down,' she said. 'If you do, you could put others at risk.'

'We won't do that,' Heidi said.

'OK, then. I'll tell you. I met Kitty and Rowan in Calais. They drove regularly from the UK bringing supplies. Clothes, food, sleeping bags, medical supplies, stuff like that.'

'Where does it all come from?' Stacey asked.

'Donations mainly. We have people throughout the country collecting vanloads of gear that volunteers drive across the Channel.' She smiled. 'For example, there's a guy in Cardiff, best blagger in the business. Taps anyone with money – individuals and companies.' She chuckled.

'Can you give us the guy's name?'

'We call him Bilbo.'

Heidi laughed. 'As in Bilbo Blaggins?'

'Yes, exactly.' Sorrell topped up her glass for a second time.

'Tell me what it's like in the camps,' Stacey said.

Sorrell took a deep breath. 'It's like hell on earth. We build basic plywood shelters with a solar panel on the roof to charge a phone and run a single light bulb. A few days later the French police tear them down, forcing people back into leaky tents, floating in a sea of mud. Worse than anything I've ever seen at Glastonbury.'

'Sounds utterly dreadful,' Heidi said.

'There isn't a word to adequately describe the conditions. Little kids with no shoes wading through it, slicing feet open on broken glass and rusty metal, human waste mixed with the mud. Adults queuing in the rain for food at the free kitchens.' She covered her face with her hands.

The side gate clicked, Rufus barked and a small boy with dark curly hair, deep brown eyes and light brown skin, scampered across the yard and hurled himself at Sorrell. She wrapped her arms around his small body and hugged him tightly.

'Rebin, my beautiful boy. Where have you been?'

'By the pond watching the kingfisher catching his breakfast. He caught four or seven fish.'

'It's nearly time for us to have some food, so go inside and wash your hands,' Sorrell said.

'Yes, Mummy,' the boy said and dashed in through the back door.

'Sorrell,' Heidi said, 'I hope you don't mind me asking, but did you bring Rebin into the UK?'

'No, I brought his father.' She got to her feet. 'You should stay for lunch and I should stop drinking, it's too early to hit the bottle. You may as well hear the rest of the story. Come into the kitchen and I'll tell you.'

* * *

The recording device whirred quietly in the cramped space. Ben and Jack, having re-entered the interview room, sat opposite Caleb and his legal adviser. Dick Nyle spoke first.

'Having had the opportunity to consult with my client, we have decided he will read from a prepared statement.'

'OK,' Jack said, leaning back in his seat and folding his arms. 'Let's hear it.'

Caleb cleared his throat and began by confirming his name, address and date of birth. A single sheet of paper quivered in his fingers.

'I admit I took two photographs of Kitty Phillips, after she died, lying on a stretcher in the back of an ambulance.' Caleb took a deep breath. 'I also admit to kissing her.'

The detectives glanced quickly at each other but said nothing.

Caleb read on. 'Kitty was my friend. She was kind to me when I started working at the showroom. She was funny and beautiful, and I probably had a crush.' He swiped at his eyes. 'It broke my heart when I saw her on the stretcher. I took the photos so I could remember how lovely she was and kissed her so' – he faltered – 'so she would know someone cared.'

Caleb allowed the paper he was reading from to drop to the table and covered his face, sucking gulps of air through his fingers, shoulders shaking with grief. Eventually he uncovered his face and stared into Ben's eyes.

'I didn't kill Kitty,' he said. 'Really I didn't.' He snorted and a spray of snot and saliva landed on the table. 'I couldn't kill anything,' he said. 'I'm the only vegetarian farmer I know.'

He put his arms on the table and his head on his arms.

Dick Nyle cleared his throat. 'Well, gentlemen,' he said, 'that's all we've got.'

Ben leaned close to Jack, whispered in his ear and Jack nodded.

'OK, then,' Ben said. 'We won't make any charges now and we'll release your client on police bail, under investigation.' He looked at Caleb. 'Go home, boy,' he said. 'I can see this business has upset you, but we may need to talk to you again' – he smiled – 'so don't leave the country, OK?'

'No, I won't. Thank you.'

Ben got to his feet. 'The desk sergeant will issue your bail.'

'I'll walk him through the process,' Dick Nyle said, 'and give him a lift home.'

'Thanks,' Ben said and followed Jack from the room.

'Bloody hell,' Jack said. 'That was hard to listen to. I'll admit I was touched.'

'You think Caleb was telling the truth?'

'Yeah, I reckon. That love-from-afar syndrome can be really tough.'

'Speaking from experience, Sergeant?'

'Don't go there, guv. Right then, having solved the DNA puzzle, what's next?'

Chapter nine

Ben hadn't been back at his desk, updating the details of the investigation, for long when Ollie and Tegan walked in.

Ben looked up from his work and asked, 'How did it go in Abergavenny?'

'Not great, sir,' Ollie said.

'No one in?'

'No, the owner was home. Miss Felicity Savage, in her nineties and not a huge fan of the police.'

'Did she tell you why?'

'Oh, yes, chapter and verse. Protested at Greenham Common in the eighties, marched with the miners, active member of Greenpeace – it's quite a list. Seems her encounters with the boys in blue haven't always been positive.' Ollie chuckled. 'I have to say that even though she's a stroppy old boot, I actually quite liked her. She's certainly got the right name.'

'What did she tell you about Rowan Gardiner?'

'We asked if she had given him permission to use her address and if she knew where he was at present.'

Tegan grinned. 'She told us in no uncertain terms that even if she has allowed anyone to use her address it was her business and no one else's.'

'No further forward then.' Ben glanced at Elsa, working at the far end of the room, eyes fixed on her computer screen. 'Constable Duffin,' he called. 'How are you progressing with Rowan's banking records? Any flashes of enlightenment?'

'Not really, sir. He uses ATMs and makes purchases with his card at locations all over the place. He has used the same machines more than once, but months apart. I can't see a pattern at all.'

'Define, "all over the place".'

'Scotland, Wales, Yorkshire, Kent, France.' She shrugged. 'Stick a pin in a map and Rowan has probably been there.'

'Any withdrawals in Abergavenny?' Jack asked.

'I haven't found any, but there have been a couple in Builth, one in Carmarthen and two in Cardiff over the last year or so.'

'That's interesting, withdrawals or purchases in Builth?'

'ATM withdrawals, one last August, another at the start of this year. January 26th to be precise.'

'What are you thinking, Sergeant?' Ben asked.

'We've proven that Rowan is often in the area,' Jack said, 'yet his mother said she never sees him.'

'Perhaps she doesn't. It could be that the conviction a while back made his position at home untenable. His father didn't strike me as the understanding type.'

'Or,' Jack said, 'he was visiting Kitty. We should have another chat with her husband.'

Ben rubbed his eyes and looked back at Elsa. 'Did you find time to look into Haddon's firm? Get a list of his clients?'

'Trying to, sir. Theo Watson rang first thing this morning. He's back from his break and has refused to hand over anything until we have the proper paperwork. That's slowed things down, but not by much. He'll have to hand it over tomorrow.'

'OK, good. Anything else?'

'Background on the firm and the partners. Nothing earth-shattering so far.'

'Keep on it.'

The door opened, Kevin Biggs walked in and headed for the coffee machine in the corner.

'No envelope?' Jack asked.

'Nope.' Kevin filled a mug. 'Staff at the golf club denied ever having seen one.'

'CCTV on the premises?'

'Yep, but old styley and the tape had run out sometime during the day on Saturday.' He flopped on a chair. 'What a bloody waste of time that was.'

Ben glanced at the clock above the incident board.

'We should knock off,' he said. 'Everyone, get some rest and we'll start fresh in the morning. Seven o'clock start. Anyone who turns up with a good idea gets a Mars bar.'

* * *

Sorrell and Rebin walked their guests back to the truck and waved as they pulled away.

Stacey took a huge breath. 'Gosh,' she said, 'that was all a bit intense. I knew about the camps but until now have never spoken to anyone who has actually been to them.'

Heidi nodded. 'Such a mess, such misery. More like the dark ages than the twenty-first century.'

'What was Sorrell's husband's name again?'

'Bilal. It means victorious or a winner. The name of her son, Rebin, means pathfinder.'

'That's appropriate. Where do you think his father is?'

'Somewhere safe, hopefully, if Immigration is after him.'

'Why would they make him leave the country though? He has an English wife and a child born in the UK. He has the right to a family life.'

'The current government, much like many before them, don't appear to want people coming in.'

'I don't think that's fair. We took in refugees during the war.'

Heidi chuckled darkly. 'You need to read more. Many were labelled as undesirable aliens, namely heaps of German Jews running for their lives, who ended up being sent to Australia. The UK does not have a great record.'

'You're right, I don't read enough. Do you think Bilal is safe?'

'Probably. Sorrell seems more angry than distressed. Rebin spoke about his father a few times, so I reckon they are still in touch.' She chuckled. 'For all we know, he's living in the attic.'

Stacey glanced at her watch. 'I hadn't realised it was so late,' she said. 'Be good if we could get back to Noddfa before Ben. I don't want the third degree again.'

'Do my best,' Heidi said and put her foot down. 'Got any curry in your freezer? Lunch seems like a long time ago.'

'Aren't you going home to Erica?'

'She sent a text earlier, got involved in something and is working a double. I'm in no rush to leave.'

'Yes, I've got curry and you're welcome to stay for supper, just…'

'What?'

'Best not tell Ben about today; where we've been. I don't want to be responsible for Bilal being deported, or a load of coppers turning up on Sorrell's doorstep.'

'Not a problem. Where shall we say we've been?'

'I'll think of something.'

Just over thirty minutes later, Heidi pulled up in the lane behind Ben's car.

'Bugger,' Stacey said. 'He's early.'

She slipped out of the passenger seat and walked around the end of the cottage towards the back door, Heidi on her heels. Ben was sitting in the sun on the wooden bench, a can of lager in his hand, shirtsleeves rolled up. He smiled when he saw his partner.

'Hi, you,' he said and got to his feet. 'Heidi too, good to see you. What have you been up to?'

'Checking out the possibility of a new bed,' Stacey said, 'at that warehouse place on the A40.'

Ben plonked a kiss on her cheek. 'Didn't know we needed one.'

Heidi interrupted, sensing Stacey was about to get in too deep. 'Any coffee going?'

Ben nodded. 'Yeah, I've loaded up the machine, just needs switching on. Do we have anything for supper or shall I make a takeaway run?'

'Freezer curry,' Stacey said, 'won't take long.'

'Need a hand?'

'No thanks, stay in the sun and chat to Heidi. We'll eat outside. Amazing weather after all the rain.'

Stacey went into the kitchen, switched on the coffee maker and raided the freezer and larder. By the time a pan of rice was simmering on the Aga, the coffee was ready and she carried the pot outside. As Heidi filled the mugs, Stacey returned to the kitchen for crockery and cutlery, and placed nightlights in jars on the wooden table. Twenty minutes later, she carried three bowls of curry out to the patio.

'Smells great,' Heidi said. 'I'm starving. Got any ice cream?'

Stacey laughed. 'As a side dish, or on top of the korma?' She sat and the meal began. 'What have I missed?' she asked between mouthfuls.

'I shared the details of our trip to Haddon, Watson and Willis,' Heidi said.

Stacey blinked. 'You did?'

Heidi shrugged. 'No reason not to as Ben already knew we'd been there.'

Ben smiled at his partner. 'Don't worry, I've said my piece but what Heidi found out about Haddon is useful.'

'Is it?' Stacey asked, not sure Heidi had said anything about Haddon. 'Which bit?'

'For starters that all of Haddon's clients appear to be charitable organisations. No private companies or individuals.'

Ben put another forkful of food into his mouth and chewed.

'What does that mean? Anything?'

'It proves Haddon isn't your bog-standard IFA, for one thing,' Heidi said. 'Also, a large percentage of the charities have been set up to help asylum seekers.'

'What it means,' Ben said, 'apart from anything else, is that Haddon was still heavily involved in the same business as Kitty and her brother Rowan. Didn't stop when he formed the company.' He sighed. 'We really need to find that lad.'

Chapter ten

Stacey got out of bed a couple of hours after Ben had left for the station. She used the bathroom, got dressed and tapped on the door of the spare room.

'I'm putting coffee on,' she called.

She went to the kitchen, filled the machine, flicked on the switch then opened the back door, stood on the step and gazed at the garden. The sun shone from a cloudless sky and a gang of sparrows had gathered on the edge of the birdbath, waiting in line for a splash. Droplets of water, flung into the air by their fluttering, caught the light and sparkled like airborne gemstones. Stacey smiled and turned back to the room as the kitchen door opened and Heidi appeared.

'Sleep well?' Stacey asked.

'Yeah. Thanks for letting me stay over. Should have kept away from the wine bottle.' She helped herself to coffee and perched on the wooden carver. 'Have you got anything planned for today?'

'Not really, other than write up what we learned yesterday. How about you?'

'Nothing pressing. Wondered if we'd take a trip to Cardiff, see if we can track down the Bilbo bloke Sorrell told us about.'

'I'd be up for that.' Stacey put a couple of slices of bread in the toaster and a honey pot on the table. 'Any idea how we might find him?'

'I've compiled a list of places we might try, free kitchens, food banks and a free shop.'

'What's a free shop?'

'Basically a charity shop full of second-hand goods, but if you're an asylum seeker with limited funds, you don't have to pay for the things you choose.'

'That's a great idea. Anywhere else?'

'I found mention on social media of a night club that occasionally hosts charity nights. Bet you a quid Bilbo Blaggins has something to do with that.'

'Sounds good. Give me half an hour and we'll get off. I'll drive.'

* * *

Ben sat in the waiting room of Haddon's firm while Jack ambled around peering at the brightly coloured, modern artworks hanging from the walls. The male receptionist kept an eye on the detectives. Five minutes passed before a door next to the desk opened and a large man with a healthy tan and dressed in a dark suit emerged. Ben got to his feet.

'Theo Watson?' he asked.

'Yes, that's me. Come to my office where we can talk. Can I get you anything to drink?'

'No thanks,' Ben said. 'We're fine.'

Watson held open the door, directed his guests along a short hallway and ushered them inside his office.

'Please, gentleman, take a seat.'

The officers sat. Ben unbuttoned his jacket. Jack did the same and removed a notebook and pen from his inside pocket.

'As you know, we're here to collect your client list,' Ben said, 'but before that I'd be grateful if you could talk to us about Jonathon Haddon, his position in the firm and what his work entailed.'

Watson sighed heavily. 'He wasn't helping the business, that's for sure. It felt like he was trying to run it into the ground.'

'Why would he do that?'

Watson snorted loudly. 'Why did Jonathon do anything?'

'Care to illuminate us?' Jack asked.

'Not entirely sure I can, and I'm not being purposely obstructive. The best way I can describe it is he took his eye off the ball.'

'Tell us how.'

'Jonathon came from good stock as the saying goes. Fantastic education, best schools, place at Oxford, majored in mathematics, and didn't have a student loan to pay off at the end of it. Brilliant man, Jonathon.' Watson sighed. 'I'll be honest, the company wouldn't exist without him.'

'You referred to him apparently running things into the ground. Is the company not doing well?'

'It's certainly not failing – yet.' Watson flapped a hand. 'We've still got our company cars, but Jonathon needed to get a grip.'

'So what was he doing – or not doing – that worried you?' Jack asked.

'All this pissing about working on charity accounts. No money to be made there.'

Ben recalled what Heidi had told him the night before and pricked up his ears.

'Pissing about?' Jack queried.

'Too much *pro bono* and selective billing.'

'What's selective billing?'

'National charities, with CEOs earning six figure salaries, would pay more than… well… others.'

'Is that ethical?' Ben asked.

Watson smiled. 'The partners set their own rates. It is our company.' He sighed. 'Thing is, the hefty fees he charged, he gave away. Redistribution he called it.'

Ben nodded. 'I can't see anything illegal with that.'

'Nothing illegal about it,' Watson snapped, 'but it wasn't doing my bank balance any good.'

'What did Dominic Willis have to say?'

'Reckoned Jonathon had gone mad. Lost the plot.'

'We've been unable to trace any of Jonathon's family,' Jack said. 'Can you help us with that?'

'He hasn't got any,' Watson said. 'His parents died while he was at uni.'

Jack reached into his pocket and pulled out an evidence bag containing a small photograph. He offered the bag to Watson.

'Could you take a look at this?' Jack asked. 'We found it in Jonathon's wallet. Do you know who this woman is?'

Watson peered at the picture and groaned. 'Yezda. Last name escapes me. Her and Jonathon met up at Oxford and quickly became inseparable. She supported him when he lost his folks.'

'Do you know where she is now?'

Watson rubbed his face. 'I honestly don't.'

'You said they were inseparable. What happened?'

'No idea. I don't think Jonathon knew for certain. Yezda was Kurdish. Arrived in the UK as an unaccompanied child. Another brilliant individual. Somehow she found her way to Oxford, then one day just vanished.' He sighed. 'Jonathon was devastated. If I remember correctly, he found a note. She'd written something about saving her family. Shortly after she went missing he started travelling to France with his mate, Rowan Gardiner.'

'One last question,' Ben said. 'Who do you think had such a huge issue with Jonathon that they killed him?'

'Actually, one more,' Jack said. 'Where were you the night he was shot?'

* * *

Heidi and Stacey had spent all morning trudging around Cardiff in search of Bilbo Blaggins, the charity worker Sorrell had mentioned. At one o'clock, Heidi called a halt and demanded food before she did any more walking.

They wandered along Tudor Lane. The street displayed a certain randomness, shops full of creative oddities and strange curios. On one side of the street was a large, former coach house, now home to an eclectic range of businesses and craft workers. Next to a cycle repair shop was a small cafe. Heidi pushed open the door, they walked inside the warm, coffee-scented room and took a seat at a table in the window.

'This is nice,' Stacey said, removing her jacket. 'I've never been to this part of the city before.'

'Nor me,' Heidi said.

A young woman with braided hair, beads woven into the ends, approached the table and smiled.

'Hi,' she said. 'Are you ladies ready to order?'

Stacey returned the smile. 'Two strong black coffees and two all-day breakfasts would be great.'

'No problem. I'll bring the drinks over. The food will be a few minutes.'

She headed back to the counter and Heidi scrutinised the menu.

'It's all vegetarian,' she grumbled. 'Breakfast without bacon doesn't do anything for me.'

'Won't hurt you for once.'

The coffee arrived and Stacey sipped. 'Why do you think we haven't tracked down Bilbo?' she asked.

'I'm not entirely sure,' Heidi said. 'A few of those we spoke to knew him, but not where he lives.' She snorted. 'No chance of finding an address without his real name.'

'From what we've been told, he sounds like a saint. Fed the hungry all through the pandemic, kept the free shop stocked with essentials, and made sure the pop-up kitchens had enough food to cook.'

'He's certainly a busy boy.'

The waitress returned with laden plates which she placed on the table together with cutlery wrapped in paper napkins.

'Enjoy,' she said.

'Thank you, this looks fab,' Stacey said.

'I don't suppose you know a man people call Bilbo do you?' Heidi asked.

The waitress grinned. 'Yeah, I know him. He comes in after closing time most days to collect food we haven't sold and redistributes it. Can't bear throwing away good food.'

'Do you have an address for him?' Stacey asked.

'No, only that he lives in Cardiff.'

'Does he come in every day?'

'Pretty much.'

'What time do you close?'

'Usually around six. Now, can I get you anything else?'

'No, this is perfect, thanks.'

Heidi poked about with her fork, speared a button mushroom and a chunk of fried potato.

'What should we do?' Stacey asked. 'Hang about in here and hope Bilbo turns up?

Heidi shook her head. 'No, there's a few more places we can check. We'll come back if we don't find him.' She cut a small slice of veggie sausage, sniffed it suspiciously and put it in her mouth. 'Actually,' she said, 'this isn't bad.'

* * *

Jack drove away from the offices outside Carmarthen, turned onto the A40 and headed back towards Powys.

'You know,' Ben said, 'I'm beginning to warm to Jonathon Haddon. Seems he did a lot of good things.'

'Makes me wonder why he teamed up with Watson and Willis,' Jack said.

'What do you think about what Watson told us? Was he spinning a story?'

'Don't reckon so, guv. I'd like to find out more about this Yezda woman.'

'Yeah me too.' Ben ran a hand across his short hair and glanced at his watch. 'Let's call in at Leo Phillips' place. It'd be daft not to as we're passing the end of his drive. I want to ask him about his brawling conviction a few years ago and find out if Rowan visited his sister in January.'

'Good plan,' Jack said as he joined a section of dual carriageway and overtook a slow-moving wagon full of lambs on their way to market.

A little under an hour later, he indicated and turned onto the track leading to the cottage Kitty had shared with her husband. The detectives left the car and discovered the front door standing open. Ben rapped his knuckles on a small pane of dimpled glass set at eye-level.

'Hello? Mr Phillips? Police.'

There was no answer, so he knocked and called again before stepping inside the living room. The place was a disorganised mess. Empty bottles and glasses littered the coffee table, more on the worktops in the kitchen area, together with mounds of dirty plates, mugs and saucepans.

'Mr Phillips,' Ben yelled. 'Where are you?'

Jack climbed the stairs, checked the bathroom and bedrooms and reappeared on the landing.

'Not here, guv.'

Together they walked back into the sunshine and Ben headed towards the rear of the building. He reached the corner and saw Leo Phillips suddenly emerge from a wood store. He ran towards the officers, fists raised.

'Get off my land,' he roared and as soon as he was in range, took a swing at Ben.

Unable to avoid the unexpected assault, Leo's fist connected with Ben's nose before Jack waded in. He grabbed Leo's arms, spun the man around to face him and shoved. Leo stumbled, got his feet tangled and hit the stony ground hard. Fuelled by alcohol, he scrambled to his feet, charged at Jack and swung another fist. Jack dodged the blow, snatched it from the air and twisted the arm between Leo's shoulder blades. With a free hand, Jack snapped on handcuffs.

'How dare you,' Leo screamed, slurring badly. 'How bloody dare you break into my home?'

Jack ignored him, recited the caution and made the arrest – for assaulting a police officer – official. He dragged the angry man to the front of the cottage and locked him in the back of the car. The prisoner secure, Jack turned to look at his boss.

'What's the damage, guv?' he asked, offering a handkerchief from his pocket to staunch the flow of blood.

Ben snatched it from his sergeant's hand and clamped the material over his nose. Jack stepped closer.

'Let's have a look.'

Ben reluctantly removed the handkerchief and Jack peered at the injury.

'I'm not an expert,' he said, 'but I reckon it's broken. We'll drop the idiot at the station, let him cool off in a cell, then I'll take you to the minor injuries unit in Llandrindod.'

'There's no need,' Ben said and covered his nose again.

'There's every need. Get in the car while I secure the property. Keep your head back.'

Ben sat in the passenger seat and tried not to breathe in the alcohol fumes emanating from the prisoner. Jack reappeared, opened the back door, strapped the drunken man into his seat belt, then slipped behind the wheel and set off for the station.

Chapter eleven

Heidi and Stacey were about to leave the cafe when Stacey's phone rang. She removed it from her pocket and checked the screen before answering.

'Hi, Jack,' she said.

'Where are you?' he asked.

'Cardiff. Why? Something wrong?'

'I'm in Llandrindod minor injuries unit. Ben got smacked in the face. He's being X-rayed.'

'Shit! Is he badly hurt?'

'Doc thinks his nose is broken, but he's OK.'

'How did that happen?'

Jack sighed. 'We went to see Kitty's husband, Leo. He was as pissed as a fart, spotted us and started swinging his fists about. Ben was on the wrong end of a punch.'

'Are you OK?'

'I'm fine, and don't worry too much about Ben. He looks a bit of a mess but he'll be OK. I'll drop him at Noddfa when we're done here, but I reckon he'd be glad if you were home.'

'OK, we're leaving now.' Stacey put the phone back in her pocket. 'I need to go home. Ben's been hurt.'

'Badly?' Heidi asked.

'He's been hit in the face. Jack says he probably has a broken nose.'

'Let's get off then. We can look for Bilbo another day.'

They hurried back to the car, Stacey navigated through the Cardiff streets and turned onto the A470. She drove through Merthyr, onto Brecon and the A40, where she took the narrow road from Llywel across the ranges.

'Slow down a little, Stace,' Heidi said. 'There are heaps of sheep and lambs everywhere. Hit one and we'll be later getting to the cottage.'

'Sorry,' Stacey said and backed off the accelerator. 'I just want to be with Ben.'

'I know, but he's had a smack, he hasn't been shot.'

Stacey nodded and concentrated on the twisty mountain road. A little while later, she dropped down the steep section, drove past the village and pulled up in the drive. Jack's car was parked in the lane outside the cottage.

Stacey leapt out of her own car, not bothering to close the door, ran to the back of the building and into the kitchen. Jack sat at the table. Ben, a mug in his hand, sat in the carver next to the Aga. His face was bruised and a white dressing covered most of his nose.

'Oh my God,' Stacey said and dropped to her knees in front of him. 'How are you?'

'I'm fine,' Ben said. 'Don't fuss. Just a bit sore and a nasty headache, but I'll live.'

Stacey glanced up at Jack. 'Thanks for looking after him.'

He shrugged. 'No problem. The doctor said it's a straightforward break and no sign of any concussion. Gave him painkillers and advised he takes tomorrow off. I've cleared it with CS Warren.'

'I can't take time off,' Ben grouched. 'I'm in the middle of a murder investigation and we've got Phillips to interview.'

Jack snorted. 'He can wait. No way can we speak to him before he's sobered up and spending time in a cell won't hurt him. Ollie's gonna request an extension so there's no rush.'

'Yeah, but–'

'Ben,' Stacey said, 'just for once, do as you're told. Take some time. One day won't hurt.'

'You should listen to Stacey,' Heidi said. 'Trust me, you'll feel rough tomorrow, so stay at home and let her nurse you.'

Ben nodded but didn't look convinced.

'I'll get off now,' Heidi said, 'but if either of you need anything, call and I'll pop over.'

'We'll manage,' Stacey said, 'but thanks.'

'I'll go too,' Jack said. 'Anything happens you need to know about, I'll be in touch. Take it easy.'

'Yeah, I will,' Ben said. 'Thanks again for taking Phillips down so efficiently. Caught me by surprise.'

'It happens, guv.' Jack patted Ben's shoulder, brushed a kiss on Stacey's cheek and left with Heidi.

* * *

The next morning, after bruises had time to develop, Ben looked as though he'd been cage fighting. His head thumped and if he was honest, breathing was difficult. Stacey cooked a late brunch and as the weather was still warm and sunny, settled Ben on a lounger by the back door beneath a parasol. He wanted to protest but had to admit he felt pretty ropey and wouldn't have been much use at work; so he lay on the lounger and watched as Stacey weeded the vegetable beds.

'Jack said you were in Cardiff when he called yesterday. What were you doing there?'

Stacey got to her feet, wiped her hands on her trousers and sat next to him.

'I'm trying to write a feature about asylum seekers. I'd heard about a guy who cares for those who are waiting for the Home Office to decide whether or not they can remain in the UK. Heidi and I went to look for him.'

'Did you find him?'

'Not yet. How about your case? Any closer to tracking down Kitty's brother?'

'No, it's all very frustrating and we haven't made much progress. We do have the registration number of his vehicle now, but so far it hasn't been picked up anywhere.'

'Give it time.'

'Time is a luxury we can't afford. We don't know the killer won't strike again.'

'True, but you said early on this was a personal murder, that Haddon knew his attacker, so that's probably unlikely.'

'Maybe, but I can't take the risk.' He sighed and touched his damaged nose with his fingertips. 'We have Haddon's client list now, so that might shed some light.'

'Still think he lost someone a fortune?'

'It's possible, but until the accounts have been properly examined, we still don't know. Difficult to solve any crime without an obvious motive.'

* * *

Late in the afternoon, as the sun began to sink behind the mountains, the couple moved indoors. After supper, they watched a film together and opted for an early night.

Stacey lay in the darkness and sleep wouldn't come. Ben snored loudly, unable to breathe properly through his damaged nose, while Stacey fretted about his injury. Leo's unprovoked attack had unsettled her. It reminded her that policing was a dangerous job and she silently thanked the universe for Jack's timely intervention. A whole herd of "what if" thoughts stampeded through her brain and eventually she snuck out of bed and wandered downstairs. She heated some milk, made hot chocolate and sat at the table to drink. When it was finished, she crept back upstairs, slipped under the duvet and finally slept.

* * *

Jack arrived at eight the next morning. He gave his boss a visual once over and, satisfied he was fit enough for a day at the station, followed him out to the car. After they had left, Stacey rang Heidi with an update, then made fresh coffee and went to her office to work on the feature she was writing.

The window above her desk was open and she smiled, listening to a large flock of noisy sparrows fluttering and squabbling in the bamboo, as a warm breeze blew the scent of pine inside the room. The breeze set hundreds of granny bonnets waving and nodding as white-tailed bees jostled for space amongst the colourful flowers. Lost in the wonder of it, she jumped when there was a knock at the front door. Peering out at the lane she couldn't see a vehicle so got to her feet and padded along the hall. She opened the door and standing on the step was a young man, dressed in a dark hooded top and jeans. His hair was short, dark and unruly, eyes busy, flicking up and down the lane.

'Hello,' Stacey said. 'Can I help you?'

'Are you Stacey Logan, a reporter?'

'I am, yes. Who are you?'

'Rowan Gardiner. Kitty's brother. Let me in will you? I feel a bit exposed out here.'

Stacey opened the door wider. 'Go straight through to the kitchen.'

He slipped past her, she closed the door, dropped the latch and followed him to the back of the cottage.

'I heard people were looking for me. You and the police.' He shrugged. 'I need to talk to someone about what's been happening and chose the less scary option.'

'Who told you I was looking for you?' Stacey asked, warily.

'Sorrell got in touch. She told me about you and your mate's visit a couple of days ago. As it happens I was in the area so thought I'd take a chance and knock on your door. See where it takes us.'

Stacey nodded as though she knew what he was talking about.

'Fancy a cuppa?' she asked.

'That'd be great, ta.'

'Did you walk here?'

Rowan grinned. 'Not really. Tucked the van up one of the forestry tracks along the road – out of sight.'

Stacey sat at the table. 'I'm really very sorry about your sister,' she said.

Rowan nodded, closed his eyes, pinched the bridge of his nose and took several deep breaths.

'And your friend, Jonathon,' Stacey added.

'Yeah,' Rowan muttered, 'me too.'

The kettle boiled, Stacey made tea and placed a mug in front of the distressed man. He grabbed it and gulped.

Unsure of how to proceed, Stacey asked, 'Have you come to Wales to visit your parents?'

Rowan opened his eyes and frowned. 'Of course not. Why would I want to go there?'

'I don't know, comfort them maybe. You've lost a sister and they've lost a daughter.'

Rowan snorted. 'They weren't sorry to see me leave and probably won't miss Kitty that much. They weren't great parents, not very' –he searched for the appropriate phrase – 'hands on.'

'So why are you in Wales?'

'To collect my post from the lovely Miss Savage.' He smiled briefly. 'One of the people who told me I was a wanted man' – he swallowed hard – 'and about Kitty. I drove over to see Sorrell and Rebin too. Sorrell suggested I come here rather than wait to be nicked. She agreed I needed to talk to someone.'

'Well, you're in the right place. I'm a good listener.'

'There's one thing though.'

'What's that?' Stacey asked.

'You can't write about what I tell you. You can't print anything in the paper, and you can't tell anyone else I've been here.'

'I can go along with that, but I'd like to talk to my friend Heidi. She won't betray your confidence and is an excellent ally to have on your side. She can offer all kinds of help if needed.'

'Sorrell mentioned Heidi, said she was cool, so OK. I'm probably being paranoid but with Kitty and Jonathon both dead, I confess to feeling twitchy and not very safe.'

'I get that. I'd feel the same, I'm sure.' She smiled. 'You don't need to worry. Journalists protect their sources. Some go to prison rather than give a name to the authorities.'

'Are you saying you're one of those journalists?'

Stacey thought for a moment and grinned. 'Yeah, I reckon I am.'

Chapter twelve

Heidi yanked the wrought-iron bell pull which was hanging next to the incredibly glossy, black front door of the large, detached house just outside Abergavenny. Instead of the normal whitewashed, slate-roofed, Welsh architecture, its walls had been painted pink. Window frames and sills were picked out in white and made the structure look like an enormous dolly mixture.

Heidi took a few steps back and gazed at the front of the house and counted floors and windows. She heard a rattle behind the door and took two paces forward as it was opened by an elderly woman, wearing a floral day-dress, with low-heeled court shoes, and fingernails painted bright red to match a smear of lipstick. Her long white hair was piled into a bun on the top of her head.

The woman smiled. 'You must be Heidi Holtz,' she said. 'I must say, after speaking with you on the phone recently, you aren't quite what I was expecting.'

'Taller than you thought?' Heidi grinned. 'Don't worry. That's not the first time someone's said that. I know I look like a kid, but I've been through university and spent some time as a detective constable for the local force.' She leaned closer. 'Don't tell anyone, but I'll be twenty-seven next birthday.'

'Why did you leave the police?'

Heidi shrugged. 'Wasn't great at dealing with the red tape stuff. I'm so much more effective at getting things done from the outside. Not so many rules and definitely no stupid ones.'

Miss Savage smiled again. 'You and I should be a good match. There's afternoon tea in the library, second on the left. Do go in and make yourself comfortable.'

Heidi walked through the hall and into a large room, expecting to see the shelves full of matching leather-bound volumes. Instead, she gazed at shelves which held paperbacks by contemporary writers placed next to Dostoevsky, travel journals, modern history books, large hardbacks that described how to prune roses, others how to make longbows and spindle chairs.

'Oh, my word,' Heidi said as Miss Savage entered, speed-reading the spines. 'This is definitely my sort of library. You have some incredible books.'

'Every book I ever bought is here, together with all those given to me during my long life. It's my one weakness. I couldn't live without books.' She waved a graceful hand at more stacks on the floor and occasional tables that hadn't yet been assigned a home on the shelves. 'Now, sit. Very traditional tea – cucumber sandwiches, with fruit cake and stilton. Tea or coffee in the pots, please help yourself.'

'Looks marvellous,' Heidi said and sat at a round table, which was laid with pretty crockery and silver cutlery. 'Freddie loves afternoon tea.'

'Who's Freddie, my dear?'

'My father, Frederick Holtz. Has a pile in the Cotswolds and works in Whitehall.'

'Really? Doing what?'

'Never been too sure, to be honest. He doesn't talk about work at home.'

Miss Savage sliced the cake and filled the cups. 'I'm guessing you're here because you want to ask more questions about Rowan?'

'There is that,' Heidi said, 'but not entirely. I enjoy spending time with people who have brains and interesting stories to tell.'

Miss Savage laughed; a high-pitched, musical sound. 'Butter me up then get the thumbscrews out, is that it?'

'Not at all. I'm worried Rowan might be in some sort of danger and want to help him if I can.'

'What sort of danger?'

'Not really sure yet.' Heidi finished her sandwich and attacked the oozing chunk of stilton. 'Do you know why the police came to see you asking about him?'

'They didn't say much at the time. Can't say I like the police. Never done much for me in the past.' She hesitated then said, 'I know what happened to Rowan's sister and his best friend.'

'Did the police tell you they were dead?'

'No, but I hear things.'

Heidi raised her eyebrows. 'Jungle drums?'

Miss Savage smiled. 'Maybe.'

'Do you have any idea who might be responsible?'

'Not really, but all three spent the last few years working in a dangerous environment and no doubt upset people along the way.'

'What sort of people?'

'Smugglers, traffickers, the gendarmerie, the Home Office…'

'Fair few then,' Heidi said and refilled the delicate china cups. 'I thought they were helping in the camps, feeding and housing refugees.'

'There was more to it than that. There was a young woman. Yezda. Beautiful girl, highly intelligent and extremely tough. You would have liked her.'

'Would have?'

'She was Jonathon's lover and he was smitten. They met at university. When she upped and left, he took it hard. We were all very concerned about him.'

'We?'

Miss Savage waved a delicate hand and brushed the question away. 'He went to France to look for her, took Rowan with him. Didn't end well. They didn't find her. Rowan had a breakdown, Jonathon set up his firm. Things settled for a while.'

'What then?'

'Rowan recovered by which time Kitty was a convert and all three got involved again.'

Miss Savage struggled to her feet, a little unsteadily. Heidi stood and offered an arm.

'Are you OK?' she asked.

'Just tired. Didn't get my usual nap this afternoon.' Miss Savage smiled. 'I'm sorry, my dear, that will have to do for today, but you are more than welcome to call again. I've thoroughly enjoyed your company.'

'It's been good, thanks. I'll ring you soon. Would you like a hand upstairs?'

'No thank you. I have a daybed in here where I snooze. Do you mind seeing yourself out?'

'Not a problem.'

Heidi gave her host's painfully thin arm a gentle squeeze and walked out to the car. Before she drove away she tried calling Stacey but both her phones went to voicemail, so Heidi started the engine and headed for her flat in Brecon. Maybe Erica would be home.

* * *

Jack glanced up as Ollie brought Leo Phillips into interview room one. Ben sat in the incident room and watched a live feed from the camera in the room. Being the victim, he was unable to take part in questioning the prisoner.

Ollie switched on the recording device, logged date, time and those in the room and the interview began.

'Mr Phillips,' he said, 'the doctor has classed you fit for interview. Before we get into it, you have refused access to a solicitor. If you change your mind at any point, we'll pause and make sure you receive legal advice. Do you understand?'

Phillips nodded and swigged from a water bottle.

'The machine can't hear nods,' Jack said. 'You need to speak.'

'Yes then, I understand.'

'Maybe we could start with you telling us why you punched DCI James in the face, breaking his nose in the process.'

Phillips shrugged. 'I don't know. I was pissed. Can't remember much about it.'

'I suggest you gather your thoughts because that isn't good enough.'

'Can't help that, can I? Not if I can't remember hitting him. Like I said, I was proper pissed.'

Jack opened a file and removed a piece of paper. 'Not the first time you've done this is it? Conviction for drunken brawling a few years ago. Like to tell me about that?'

'Something and nothing,' Phillips muttered.

'If that was true, you wouldn't have a criminal record. What happened?'

Phillips smirked. 'I had too much to drink and things got a bit out of hand, that's all.'

Jack glared at the man. 'I'm glad you find this funny. Assaulting a police officer is a serious business. Tell me exactly why you ended up inside a courtroom.'

Phillips drank more water. 'It was a long time ago, OK? As far as I remember – all a bit fuzzy at the time – a loud-mouthed arsehole at the bar was giving Kitty the eye, trying to chat her up.'

'Was that all? He was looking at your girlfriend?'

'My wife! She was my wife!'

'So you smacked the arsehole about a bit.' Jack glanced back at the document from the file. 'Hit the bloke more than once it would seem, split ear, cut cheek, oh… and a broken nose. You've got form.'

'Just shut up, will you? It was a long time ago and I paid the price. All done and dusted. Now, I have a dreadful headache, been stuck in here too long and want to get home, so charge me or whatever and let me go.'

'Can't do that,' Jack said, 'not until I understand why you attacked my chief inspector.' He frowned. 'Breaking a senior copper's nose has consequences. Why did you punch him?'

Phillips massaged his temples and took a deep breath. 'I'm grieving, OK? Lost my wife in terrible circumstances while she was with another man, miles away from where she was supposed to be. Do you have any idea how that feels?'

'No, I don't. Tell me how it feels.'

'Like shit! Like I'm stuck in a cesspit. I'm not sleeping, not eating, just drinking myself into a stupor every day.' Phillips slammed his fists onto the table and leapt to his feet.

'Sit down!' Ollie roared before Jack could open his mouth. 'Sit down immediately or I'll cuff you.' Ollie got to his feet, handcuffs dangling from his hand. He took a step closer to the prisoner. 'I will not ask you again.'

Phillips shuffled back to the plastic chair and dropped onto it.

Jack nodded at Ollie and said, 'That's better.'

Phillips fixed Jack in his gaze. 'People die and it's always sad,' he said. 'We made an oath, "till death do us part". One of us would die first eventually, but not like this. I wasn't prepared, and for her to be found with someone else. I don't know whether I should carry on loving her, or hate her, and put a stop to this crushing grief. How could she?' His hands once again formed fists, but he worked hard at staying in his seat.

'Do you own a gun?' Jack asked.

'What? No.'

'Would you know how to shoot one if you did?'

'Done your homework I see. Yes, as you obviously already know, I shot pistols at university on their range.'

'Were you any good?'

'Not particularly, only ever a reserve for the team. Never shot in competitions.'

'And you're completely sure you don't have a gun at your house?'

'Absolutely. Haven't picked one up since I graduated.'

'So it wasn't you who murdered Jonathon Haddon by shooting him between the eyes?'

'No, it wasn't. I told you, I was at home that evening.' He groaned. 'This is getting silly. I'm sorry I punched your boss, but I definitely didn't shoot the guy who was with Kitty.'

Jack stared at the man, studied his body language and wasn't convinced. Anger radiated from Phillips at any mention of Haddon.

'OK,' Jack said, 'here's what we'll do. We'll go to your house, take a look around, more than likely confiscate your digital devices and have forensics take a look.'

'You can't do that,' Phillips said. 'I can't work without them.'

'We'll be as quick as we can. In the meantime, you'll come with us to witness the search of your property.'

'That's all a waste of time. I've told you. I don't have a gun.'

'We don't have much choice. Constable Langdon will take you back to your cell while we process the paperwork. Shouldn't take longer than an hour.' Jack hauled his large frame upright. 'Interview terminated 11.52am.'

Jack watched as Ollie escorted Phillips from the room, then searched out Ben in the incident room.

'What did you think of that?' Jack asked.

'Lot of anger,' Ben said, 'and probably has a problem with booze. Remember how he drank straight from the brandy bottle when we told him about Kitty? Grief, anger and alcohol are not a great combination.'

'You're not wrong. I'll round up a search team.'

Ben smiled. 'If we find a gun and it matches the ballistic report, we'll have this wrapped up by lunchtime.'

'Yeah, fingers crossed, eh?'

Chapter thirteen

While Ben and Jack, not having found a gun at Leo's property, attended magistrates' court to hear Leo plead guilty to assaulting a police officer, Stacey drove across the ranges to Brecon. The day was grey but mild, even on the mountain. By the time Stacey pulled up outside the basement flat Heidi and Erica shared, a fine misty drizzle filled the air dampening everything it touched. She walked carefully down the slick steps and discovered the door standing open.

'Hello?' she called.

'Come on in,' Heidi called back. 'I'm brewing some Arabic coffee. Thought we'd have a change.'

'Smells great.' Stacey perched on a high stool next to the breakfast bar. 'How's things?'

'Let's hear your news first.' Heidi jiggled the old-fashioned percolator and gave it a slap. 'Bloody thing always plays up.'

Stacey told Heidi about yesterday's surprise visitor, and once the coffee had brewed, Heidi recounted her visit with the nonagenarian living on the outskirts of Abergavenny.

'Miss Savage gave me a return ticket,' Heidi said with a smile, 'and I can't wait.'

Stacey chuckled. 'Seems you two hit it off.'

'We did. There's so much more to that elderly lady, she's like an iceberg.'

'Cold and frosty?'

'No, hidden depths. You'll have to meet her. I feel as though I've known her forever.' Heidi drained her mug and managed to squeeze some more from the pot. 'So,' she said, 'is Rowan planning to return any time soon?'

'Didn't make any plans for the foreseeable.'

'You got a contact number though?'

Stacey shrugged.

'OMG! You didn't. Did you forget to ask?'

'Of course not, but to be honest he was really twitchy. I thought if I was too pushy, he'd never get in touch again.'

Heidi made a rude noise and muttered, 'Call yourself a journalist?'

'Yeah, whatever. Sometimes contacts need a gentle hand so they'll feel comfortable talking about difficult issues. I'm sure he'll be back. He sought me out don't forget.'

'Maybe. Did you learn anything to help the investigation?'

'You were right about the network helping refugees, more details to follow I'm sure. He gave me the name of a Kurdish woman Haddon was in love with. Seems Rowan and Haddon went to Europe to search for her.'

Heidi nodded. 'Miss Savage mentioned her too. Called her Yezda, but didn't give her surname.'

'Neither did Rowan. He said his friend met her at Oxford.'

Heidi grinned. 'Can't think there'd be more than one Yezda beneath the Dreaming Spires. Work of a moment to wriggle inside their list of students past and present.' She snorted. 'You'd think a place like that would have better security.'

'If you do manage to uncover a surname, what then?'

'I'll run my search programs, might be able to discover a more recent location.' Heidi uncurled from the sofa and padded towards her desk. 'Anyway, now the police have gotten hold of a client list from Haddon's firm, I've been taking a nosy. At first glance everything looks kosher.'

Stacey followed her friend across the living room and peered over her shoulder at the computer screen.

'No angry clients who lost all in a crooked or ill-advised scheme?' she asked.

'Nothing obvious. As I'd already discovered, just about all of Haddon's clients were charities, from massively large, household names, to pretty small-fry organisations. No losses anywhere.'

'So the murderer isn't a client?'

'I didn't say that. I said no one lost money. I agree with Ben that Haddon was probably killed by someone he knew. Money isn't the only motive for murder.'

'I reckon it's Leo, Kitty's husband. Ben doesn't let on, but I know his nose is bothering him. He hadn't even spoken to Leo before the man punched him. Bloody psycho. Jealousy is a good motive, and if Kitty and Rowan were best friends with Haddon, surely Leo would have known him?'

'Did he say he did?'

Stacey shook her head. 'Ben said he claimed not to recognise Haddon, but if he is the killer, he's bound to have denied knowing him.'

'I'm not convinced,' Heidi said. 'I agree Phillips is a thug, but that's a long way from being a killer.'

'Ben did say the police searched his place and didn't find a gun.'

Heidi shrugged and cracked her knuckles.

'No clues then?' Stacey asked.

'Well, while I was digging around in Police Central, I came across mention of an envelope Haddon supposedly dropped off at Builth golf club the night of his death.'

'Interesting. What was in it?'

'I said, "supposedly". The boys in blue haven't found one.'

'We should go and look for it.'

'Waste of time. Ben's lot came up empty-handed. More than likely already picked up by the recipient. There's something else though that I found in the computers of Haddon, Watson and Willis.' Heidi tapped at the keyboard and a private message from Theo Watson to Dominic Willis appeared on the screen.

Stacey leaned closer and read out loud.

'"We've gotta get a grip on this, Dom. One of us should have a word with Jonathon, and soon. At this rate we'll end up broke. Have you seen how much he passes on to his pet charities? He's not earning any dosh for the company and you know as well as I do, we can't carry passengers in this game. The firm won't attract new clients if this continues. Suggestions?" So we're back to money again,' Stacey said.

'Not just money. Something far more important – reputation.'

'Did Willis get back to you after our meeting?'

'He did, recommended several investment schemes. Nothing very exciting and nothing dodgy that I can see.'

'Did he reply to Watson's message?'

'Yep. Told him he'd "sort it".'

'We should book that follow-up meeting. Maybe we can rattle him enough to tell us about the friction between the partners. There's always another side.'

'I agree we need to talk to more people.'

'Like who?'

'Felicity Savage told me Haddon and his friends upset a lot of people, including the Home Office.'

'Because they were smuggling refugees into the UK?' Stacey asked.

'Possibly, but it seemed a strange thing for her to say. Home Office, not police or the authorities. There are plenty of cases where UK citizens are sent to prison for bringing people in – some receive lengthy sentences. When Rowan was nicked a couple of years ago, a teenaged lad concealed in his van, his sentence was suspended and he was fined. Begs the question why.'

'Who do you suggest we ask?'

'Wouldn't hurt to give Freddie a ring. If there is more to this, he might be able to find out how much more. I'll make some calls, see what I can set up and message you.'

* * *

Ben pushed in through the back door of Noddfa, his hands full of carrier bags from the Indian restaurant in town. He found Stacey sitting at the table, laptop open in front of her.

'Sorry I'm so late,' he said. 'Couldn't get away before now.'

'Don't worry, it's not eight yet,' Stacey said and got to her feet. 'Hand over the bags and I'll dish out while you pop open a bottle of wine. This smells fab and I'm starving. How's your nose?'

'Not great. Painful and completely bunged up but I'll live. How's your day been?' Ben asked, fiddling with the corkscrew.

'So-so. Supermarket shopping and I popped in for a cuppa with Heidi.'

'I was surprised not to see you reporting on Leo Phillips' court appearance this morning.'

'Meant to go, but got a bit behind so Sam sent Andrew Carr, the cub reporter. How did it go?'

'The magistrate was reluctant. She felt the defendant should be shown some sympathy – having lost his wife – but in the end gave Phillips credit for pleading guilty and handed down six months.' Ben pulled out the cork and filled glasses. 'He'll be out in two, if he behaves himself.'

'Not your killer then?'

'No actual evidence to point that way but equally, nothing to prove he isn't. Doesn't have a great alibi.'

'Are you any further forward with the investigation?' Stacey asked as she put out the plates of food.

'Nope. Can't match the bullet casing with anything on record, and let's be honest here, the gun itself is probably at the bottom of the river, never to be seen again.' He sighed. 'Elsa Duffin found records of a call made to Haddon's phone a few minutes before he booked the taxi. Short call, less than two minutes.'

'Who phoned him?'

Ben grinned. 'Never as easy as that. Number withheld. If it was the killer, bearing in mind it's possible a professional might be involved, he'd have used a burner phone. Also probably at the bottom of the Wye.'

'Or she,' Stacey said.

'Yes, or she.'

'When you say "professional", do you mean hit man?'

Ben chuckled. 'Or woman. Your guess is as good as mine. It's the bullet to the head that bothers me. If you were armed with a gun there would be no need to get so close. It's a very cold killing.'

'So what's next for you tomorrow?'

'Pounding streets around Builth just in case we're missing a witness, and I want to visit Rowan's parents again. There's something not entirely right there but I can't put my finger on what. Maybe another chat will help. You?'

'Not sure yet. I'm working on a series for the paper about the refugee situation, so I'll either be at my desk, or if the sun shines, maybe an afternoon weeding carrots.'

Ben groaned. 'That sounds nice, gentle weeding in the sun. It's been a bit full on since the flood. All this work and we aren't any closer to finding the killer.'

'You'll get there, I'm sure you will. Something will turn up.'

'Yeah, hope so. Anyway, enough work talk. Eat up then we'll take a wander up to the ranges to shake down our dinner.'

'It'll be dark by then.'

'Full moon tonight, we can listen to the owls.' He grinned. 'If we're really lucky we might hear a nightjar on the edge of the forest.'

* * *

Ben arrived in the incident room just before eight the next morning. He headed for the coffee machine at the end of the room. Second rate as the brew often was, he needed the caffeine. Elsa looked up as he approached her workstation.

'Sir?' she said.

Ben stopped. 'Yes?'

'I've had the report back from the forensic accountants.'

'Anything earth-shattering?'

'I'm not sure.' Elsa flipped pages. 'Nothing was found that raised any flags. Haddon was squeaky clean. He made large donations to the smaller charities he advised but it's possible to trace where all the cash came from. No sign of unregulated activities, no tax evasion, no obvious theft of anything, and no money laundering.'

'A financial saint then?'

'Looks like it. He claimed tax relief on the donations – as he was entitled to do – then donated more.'

'So the report doesn't take us anywhere?'

'Not very far but it proves Haddon was a good guy who didn't deserve to be murdered. The killing may look like an organised crime execution, but that's unlikely as Haddon was no criminal.' Elsa turned more pages. 'There is one thing though.'

'Oh?' Ben pulled a chair close to Elsa's desk and sat. 'What?'

'As we know, Haddon advised charities. The accountant made a note about one of the largest he worked for. A Roof 4 All supports the homeless. Raises a lot of money, spends a lot too.'

'Speedboats and sports cars for the CEO?'

'No, sir. Small hotels which are converted into bedsits to take people off the streets.'

'So far, so good. How do they raise their money?'

'The usual. Private donations, national appeals, collecting tins, grants and a large network of charity shops.'

'So why did our accountant mention this organisation?'

'He said he couldn't prove anything beyond-all-reasonable, but also said the books didn't look entirely genuine.'

'Dodgy expense claims? That sort of thing?'

Elsa shook her head. 'No, it was more about individual entries. The actual numbers.'

'Sorry, Constable, I'm not with you.'

'The guy explained it like this. In a nutshell, humans aren't at all good at randomness – if that's the word. Our brains always look for patterns. Let's say you want to add a fictitious credit to the accounts, non-existent takings from a charity shop for example. No one would write something like £333.03 if they were falsifying the entry.'

'Still not sure I get it.'

'Odd numbers like that do occur, more often than you think, but never if someone is making them up.'

'That's very thin, even if our guy is correct.'

Elsa shrugged. 'I know, but he also said that turnover is well down during the last couple of years. That might be due to Covid, but he's convinced someone is skimming and being creative with the books to make everything match up.'

'OK, so what do you suggest?'

'Gotta be worth talking to Haddon's contact at the charity. The CEO is a woman called Natalie Turrell. The charity A Roof 4 All, is based in Bristol. Someone should pay her a visit.'

Chapter fourteen

That same morning, Stacey collected Heidi from outside her apartment in Brecon and drove along the A40 towards Abergavenny, while Heidi told her what she had discovered online.

'Yezda's last name is Karimi,' she said. 'I managed to find a record of her taking a ferry to Calais – walk-on passenger, no vehicle. Once she got to Calais she vanished. I can't find a single record of her at all. Nothing. I've been running photographs taken at the camps through my facial recognition program, an extremely long shot, but you never know. Stranger things have happened.'

'No sign of her returning to the UK?' Stacey asked, eyes fixed on the road.

'There wouldn't be, not if she was planning on finding her family and bringing them here.'

'Of course not, I'm not thinking properly. How do you think she was going to get them into the country?'

'Her only options would be a kindly charity worker prepared to take the risk, or people smugglers.'

'You mean travelling on one of those awful boats and risking death?'

'Either that or in a lorry.'

'People die in the backs of those too,' Stacey said.

'Yes, they do.'

Stacey nodded. She navigated through Abergavenny town centre and once on the other side, turned off the main road and headed towards Felicity Savage's quirky house, nestled deep in the countryside.

'I'm really looking forward to meeting your new friend,' she said. 'Why are we going to talk to her?'

'Like I said, there's more to Miss Savage than meets the eye. I'm convinced she is somehow involved with all of this. I think she knows what happened to Yezda and as I can't find out, we need to ask.'

A little while later, Stacey parked outside the dolly mixture house and Heidi jangled the bell. The shiny door swung open and Felicity Savage smiled at her visitors.

'Heidi! And your friend must be Stacey. Lovely to meet you.'

'Good to meet you too, Miss Savage,' Stacey said. 'Heidi has talked about you a lot.'

'Please,' the woman said, 'my friends call me Fliss. Now come on in and tell me what Heidi has said.' She took hold of Stacey's hand. 'I *really* hope some of it is bad.' She laughed. 'Let's go through to the library. Lead the way, Heidi dear.'

Heidi padded across the thick carpet, pushed open the heavy door and held it wide for Fliss and Stacey to enter. Stacey stared in astonishment at the groaning bookshelves, a broad smile on her lips.

'So,' Fliss said, 'I can see the pair of you are bursting with questions, so ask away.'

Heidi grinned. 'How long have you got?'

Fliss shrugged. 'As long as I'm awake. As you know, I tire easily these days.'

'We'd like to ask you about Yezda,' Stacey said. 'You told Heidi she travelled to France in search of her family.'

'That's right. She left the UK soon after she graduated from Oxford.'

'You also said that Jonathon Haddon and his friend Rowan Gardiner went to France to look for her.'

'They did, yes, but returned empty-handed.'

'You know Yezda don't you?' Heidi asked.

Fliss nodded. 'I met her when she was twelve. Somehow she'd managed to get herself to Dover. She was taken in by social services as an unaccompanied child and they stuffed her into a fairly ghastly children's home.'

'Did you work there?' Stacey asked. 'Is that how you met her?'

'Good Lord, no. I've always been too opinionated to work somewhere like that. I had a close friend who worked as a foster parent.' Fliss rubbed her eyes. 'Anni died a few years ago and I still miss her. We'd known each other most of our lives. Came to the UK together when we were young girls.'

'Came from where?'

'Germany. We were part of the Kindertransport scheme.'

'Goodness,' Stacey said. 'I suddenly have about two hundred more questions for you, but let's stick with Yezda for now. I'm guessing your friend gave her a home.'

'That's right. Yezda was a delightful girl – smart, polite, and so very pretty.' Fliss smiled. 'You should have heard her sing. Took my breath away.'

'How did she get to Oxford?' Heidi asked.

'Anni recognised how intelligent the child was, brilliant with numbers, so she encouraged her to learn, and after a lot of hard work, Yezda gained a scholarship.'

'Gosh, that's a story,' Stacey said.

'Yes, it is, and one you can't write about. Not yet, maybe never.'

'I understand. Do you know if she found her family?'

'Jonathon thought she had. He and Rowan searched the camps and showed her photograph around. A few people they spoke to were sure they had seen her.'

'Yet they didn't find her themselves?'

Fliss sighed. 'No, they didn't.' She closed her eyes and took a deep breath. 'The RNLI operating out of Dover found her. Yezda, her mother, father and younger brother are among the hundreds of poor souls who have died in the English Channel over the last few years.'

'Bloody hell,' Heidi said. 'Did Jonathon know about her death?'

'Yes he did and when he found out, his life changed forever.'

'How did it?' Stacey asked.

Fliss smiled sadly. 'This isn't my story to tell. You must speak to Rowan.'

'I don't have a number. Can you contact him?'

'The only way is when he comes for his post, but I will let him know you'd like to talk to him.'

'Does he come here often?'

'There's no discernible pattern, but as I said, I will let him know.'

* * *

Jack flipped down the sun visor as he drove onto the Severn Bridge heading for Clifton, north-west of the centre of Bristol. Ben stared out the side window at the muddy estuary beneath the graceful suspension bridge and chuckled.

'What's funny, guv?' Jack asked.

'When I was a kid we sometimes visited Weston-super-Mare and obviously drove over this bridge. The toll was ten pence but if you broke down on the crossing it cost ten pounds to get towed off.' He chuckled again. 'Every time we made it across, Da would mutter, "That's a tenner saved". He never said anything else the entire journey. Man of few words, my Da.'

Jack laughed.

Thirty minutes later he crossed Clifton Downs and parked within sight of a much older suspension bridge, built by Isambard Kingdom Brunel. Ben waved his arm towards the structure.

'That's where the first ever bungee jump took place, undertaken by members of the Dangerous Sports Club.'

'I love random facts,' Jack said. 'Shame I can't remember them like you do.'

'Not very useful though, is it?'

The men strolled through the narrower streets of Clifton Village. Expensive food shops jostled with alternative health centres, antique and craft shops, bars and bistros. The appropriately named Brunel House, offices of A Roof 4 All, were in the centre of an elegant terrace of tall, multi-storey buildings. Jack walked up a short flight of stone steps and held the door open for his boss.

The reception was small. A number of black-and-white photographs of homeless individuals hung on the walls. The receptionist glanced up and smiled.

'Good morning,' she said. 'How can I help you?'

Jack displayed his warrant card. 'We're here to have a word with Natalie Turrell. She is expecting us.'

'I'll give her a call. Please take a seat.'

A few moments later a door opened and a dumpy woman, dressed expensively and adorned with flashy jewellery, probably in her late thirties, stepped into the room.

'Morning, gentlemen,' she said. 'I'm guessing you're here to talk about Jonathon Haddon?'

'Yes, that's correct,' Ben said.

'Come in then and we'll get this over with.'

The detectives entered her office and took seats opposite the desk. Natalie settled on a leather swivel chair.

'I heard about Jonathon's death,' she said. 'Utterly ghastly business. Shot between the eyes the papers said. Are there gangsters in Wales?' She paused. 'Maybe there are, all those Welsh-Italian coffee and ice cream shops. Sounds like gangsters to me. Is there a Welsh mafia where you come from?'

Ben held up a hand to stop the verbal diarrhoea in mid flow. Jack snorted, wandered over to the window and gazed down at the busy street.

'Great location this,' he said. 'I'm guessing the rent is pretty high.'

Natalie smiled. 'I wouldn't know,' she said. 'I don't pay any.'

'Really? How does that work?'

'I own the building and live on the upper floors. Made sense to install R4A on the ground floor, precisely to avoid paying rent. More funds available to help those in need.'

Jack didn't give up. 'Properties in Clifton are really expensive. Your mortgage payments must be enormous.'

'Now you're being impertinent, Sergeant. For your information, the building has been in family ownership for years. I own it outright.' Natalie folded her arms defensively. 'I have to say, it feels as though you are accusing me of something, can't make up my mind what though.'

'I'm sorry,' Ben said, 'but we are investigating a particularly disturbing murder and to do that we need to examine all angles.'

Natalie shrugged. 'So let's get on with it then.'

'Can you tell us how long Jonathon Haddon worked as your financial adviser?'

'Nearly five years now. I engaged him soon after I set up R4A. The charity received a large donation–'

'How large?' Jack asked.

Natalie frowned. 'Half a mill. The first building was already undergoing conversion and no other suitable properties were on the market. Rather than have such a large amount sitting idle, I contacted Haddon, Watson and Willis for advice.'

'I see,' Ben said, 'and that's how you met Jonathon?'

'Yes. We got on well and he's been very useful. These days charities must do all they can to maximise their income.'

'How would you describe your relationship?' Jack asked.

'Purely professional.'

'But you liked him?'

'What wasn't to like? He was bloody good at his job and worked hard for his clients. He only advised charities, that's why I chose his firm.'

'Did you know he'd spent time in the refugee camps in France?' Ben asked.

'Yes, I heard about that. He had a lot of pet charities. A good man. I was very upset to hear he had been killed. The world will miss Jonathon.'

'Can you tell us where you were early morning of the 15th of May?'

'Oh my God.' Natalie sniggered, an unattractive sound. 'This is a new one on me. Never been accused of murder before.'

'We're not accusing you of anything,' Ben said. 'Checking alibis is what we do; it's a useful way of eliminating people from the investigation.'

'Whatever.' Natalie turned to her computer, tapped the keyboard and peered at the screen. 'That was a Sunday,' she said and tapped some more. 'I went to the Old Vic Theatre the evening before – a production of *Salad Days* – followed by a business dinner on the floating restaurant in the docks.'

'What time did that finish?' Jack asked.

'Around eleven thirty, then I went home to' – she pointed at the ceiling – 'my apartment upstairs.'

'Were you alone?' Jack asked.

'I must say, you are really beginning to irritate me. Yes! I was alone.'

Jack nodded and scribbled in his notebook. 'What was your motivation for setting up the charity?' he asked.

Natalie smiled. 'The usual. I've lived a good life and wanted to put something back.'

'Ms Turrell,' Ben said, 'do you know of anyone who would have reason to kill Jonathon?'

'What sort of a question is that? Of course not. As I told you, he was a good man. Good men don't tend to attract enemies.' Natalie got to her feet. 'Now, I've been very patient but must call this to a halt. I have a meeting in Bath at three o'clock and really can't be late.'

She moved from behind her desk and opened the office door. Ben and Jack stood and buttoned their jackets.

'Thank you for your time,' Ben said. 'We'll be in touch if we need to.'

The detectives left the office, walked through the small reception area and out to the street.

'Time for lunch before we head back?' Jack asked.

'Why did you wind her up?' Ben grumbled. 'There was no need. Treat people better and they'll tell you more.'

'Not always, guv. Strikes me as a hard woman that one. Obviously not short on funds to be able to own a place like that. I'd be interested to know what salary she draws from the charity.'

'Thank God you didn't ask her. We can find that out easily enough by checking with the Charity Commission.'

'I'll be on to Land Registry,' Jack said. 'She can't be more than forty. How is it possible she owns that place free and clear?'

'Now you're jealous.'

'Not true. I have everything I want in Wales. I love the cottage on the Epynt, sharing it with Julie and the kids. There isn't enough money in the world to replace my life.'

'So why did you give her such a tough time?'

'Cos I don't like her. As I said, a hard woman. Not someone who you'd think would run a charity for the homeless. I don't buy her "want to put something back" line, not for a second.'

Ben sighed. 'We'll check her out when we're back in Wales.'

'So,' Jack said, 'lunch?'

'Go on then, we have to eat, but don't pick anywhere too posh.'

'Don't worry about the bill. I'm happy to pay.'

'It's not that, but the way my face looks, I'm not sure we'd get in.'

Chapter fifteen

Stacey slammed the driver's door, started the engine and pulled away from the pink house. Heidi waved out of the window and tried not to spill a small pile of books from her lap.

'Do you think Fliss will speak with Rowan?' Stacey asked. 'Let him know we need to talk to him?'

'Why wouldn't she?'

'Oh, I don't know, the whole thing seems a bit Secret Squirrel to me. She must have a phone number for him.'

'Why must she? Think about it, Stace. We accept something's going on but don't know who all the players are – or even what they're up to.'

'Why would that prevent Fliss ringing Rowan?'

Heidi chuckled. 'You've been at this long enough. Mobiles can be traced, and there's a good reason Rowan is keeping his head down. Sister and best mate dead? You said yourself he was twitchy when you saw him.'

'Yeah, I suppose. Drives me mad I can't put things together, all these little pieces of random information. Like trying to complete a jigsaw without looking at the front of the box.'

'Hmm,' Heidi said, riffling through the books she'd borrowed from Fliss.

'What did you pick out?' Stacey asked.

'A rare book on early computing, one on the Kindertransport scheme, something about Jacqueline du Pré, and a book of knots.'

Stacey laughed. 'None of those go together.'

'That's the idea of books, they don't have to.'

A white van suddenly careered around a sharp bend, followed by a second. Stacey took evasive action, steered left and surfed halfway up a steep verge, before dropping back to the tarmac with a clunk. The pile of books on Heidi's knees, scattered to the floor.

'What the hell?' Heidi said and craned her neck to look at the vans. 'Turn around, Stace. Right now. I really don't like the look of this.'

'Are you sure?'

'Of course I am. Look! Gateway! Turn there and go back.'

Stacey stamped on the brakes, her old car shuddered to a stop on the loose gravel, and after a few frantic moments, she managed to get it pointing in the opposite direction. She hit the accelerator and drove after the vans as fast as she dared.

'Those vans are owned by Immigration,' Heidi said. 'Bet you a quid they're on their way to Fliss' house. Get a move on, can't you? The vans are as wide as the lane. Nothing can get past them.'

Stacey concentrated on the twists and turns of the narrow lane, cow parsley and foxgloves whipping the sides of the car. Seconds later, she pulled to a halt behind the vehicles which, as Heidi had predicted, had come to a stop outside the pink house.

Heidi flung open the passenger door. 'Bring your cameras,' she ordered and dashed towards the front door, which was wide open, a uniformed man standing beneath the bell pull. He spotted Heidi.

'Hey,' he said. 'Stop! You can't go in there.'

Heidi ran faster, ducked low at the last moment and left the guard snatching at air.

'Fliss!' she yelled. 'Where are you?'

A female officer emerged from the library.

'What's all this noise?' she demanded.

'Out of my way,' Heidi warned. 'I'll knock you over if I have to, so move.'

The woman moved and Heidi ran through the door. She spotted Fliss sitting in a leather armchair. A pair of male officers stood over her and made the old lady look even smaller than usual. Heidi marched closer and glared at the men.

'Move back! Right now!'

The female officer joined the group and snapped, 'Just who the hell do you think you are? This is an ongoing situation. You need to leave.'

'Not a chance in hell. How dare you terrorise an elderly woman.'

'If you refuse to leave, I will have you removed.'

'Try it,' Heidi said. 'Trust me when I say that it would not be a clever career move on your part.'

The French window at the far end of the room swung open and Stacey, camera in hand, stepped inside. She lifted the Nikon and fired a clutch of shots before anyone moved. A tall officer strode towards her, arms outstretched. Stacey pulled out her press pass and held it high.

'I don't know what's going on here,' she said, 'but I suggest everyone calms down.' She walked closer to the easy chair, nodded at Heidi and smiled down at Fliss, then looked back at the woman in uniform. 'So, tell me why you're here?'

'None of your concern. This is an operation in progress. You can't be here.'

Stacey chuckled. 'You'll have to do better than that. Miss Savage is our friend and we aren't going anywhere. Who are you and what do you want?'

'Some ID would be useful,' Heidi growled.

Reluctantly, the woman displayed a warrant card. Her name was Vivien Woods, a senior enforcement officer.

'I have a warrant to search the property,' she said.

'What are you searching for?' Heidi asked.

'We've received a report there are illegal immigrants living in this house.'

'Who made the report?'

'I don't have to tell you.'

The woman held out a document which Heidi scanned.

'Stacey, wait here with Miss Savage. Don't leave her, OK? I'll show this bunch around – make sure they don't make a mess.'

'There's no need,' Woods said.

'Yeah right.'

Heidi squeezed Fliss' shoulder and led the way from the library. The tall officer remained, but he moved away from the chair and stood next to the door. Stacey perched on a footstool and bent close to her friend.

'Fliss,' she whispered. 'Sorry, but I have to ask. Is there anyone here?'

'I don't know,' Fliss whispered back. 'There *might* be.' She glanced at the guy by the door. 'I'll explain later – if I get the chance of course.'

* * *

Jack drove up the hill, through Bwlch, then turned right and followed the lane towards Llangorse Lake. Arriving at the Gardiners' house, they saw only one car parked in the drive. Jack pulled up in the lane close to the verge, the detectives stepped out and walked up the front path, as Geraldine Gardiner appeared on the step.

'Good afternoon, madam,' Ben said. 'Can you spare us some time for a chat?'

'What's the point?' Geraldine asked. 'Haven't you said everything you need to already?'

'We were passing. Wondered how you and your husband were coping?'

'How do you think? My husband is out, arranging Kitty's funeral. Leo can't do it, can he?' She glared at them. 'You shouldn't have locked him up, not at a time like this.'

'He entered a guilty plea to wounding a police officer,' Jack said. 'The court had little choice.'

'He was distressed. He'd just lost his wife and wasn't thinking straight. People in distress shouldn't be treated like that.'

'May we come in?' Ben asked. 'Rather than stand on the doorstep?'

'I suppose,' Geraldine said, 'but don't think you're getting tea.' She turned away from the open door and headed towards the kitchen.

Ben and Jack followed her along the hall. Geraldine took a seat at the table, ripped tissues from a box and dabbed her eyes.

'On our last visit,' Ben said, 'we offered you the services of a police liaison officer, which you declined. It's OK to change your mind if you think having someone here would help.'

'We'll deal with this on our own, thank you. Having one of your lot hanging around the place won't change anything. Kitty's dead and nothing will bring her back.' A sudden rush of tears appeared and Geraldine ripped more tissues from the box. 'Have you anything new to tell me?' she asked. 'Have you tracked down her brother yet?'

Ben shook his head. 'Not so far, but we are looking for him. We want to talk about his conviction a couple of years ago.'

'Thought you'd bring that up and I don't know what else I can tell you. Raymond was furious when he found out; there was such a row, it went on for days.'

'Is that why your son moved out?'

Geraldine rubbed her eyes. 'The straw that broke the camel's back. Kitty took her brother's side and the family fractured beyond repair. Rowan left for good about a week later and hasn't been home since.'

'Were there problems before that?' Jack asked.

Geraldine nodded. 'It all started when Rowan and Jonathon travelled to France to look for the Yezda girl. Raymond told them not to go but they didn't listen. By the time they returned, Rowan was ill – I told you Kitty cared for him – and as soon as he recovered, he got even more deeply involved with the whole asylum seekers nightmare.'

'Do you know why your husband didn't support your children?' Ben asked.

'Because they were breaking the law, meddling in something that was nothing to do with them. It's not like they could make a significant difference.' She sighed. 'As I said, the family fractured. We spoke to Kitty occasionally, but I haven't seen Rowan since he left.' She hauled herself upright. 'Now, I'd like you to leave. Raymond will be home soon and he won't be happy to see you here.'

Ben nodded and the detectives got to their feet.

'OK,' Ben said, 'we'll leave you in peace, but if you want to talk, or think of anything that might be useful, please get in touch.'

The woman nodded, ushered the officers to the front door and showed them out. They walked through the pretty front garden, planted with bright begonias, and got in the car. Jack turned the vehicle around and set off towards the main road.

'That didn't go well,' Jack said. 'It's difficult to understand why she isn't more helpful. After all, we are only trying to discover why her daughter died.'

'I reckon she's browbeaten,' Ben said. 'I thought so on our first visit, and she definitely wanted us out of the house before her husband returned.'

His mobile rang and he dragged it from his pocket.

'DCI James,' he answered.

'It's me,' Stacey said. 'Something's come up and I won't be home tonight.'

'What's happened? Are you OK?'

Stacey sighed heavily. 'I'm fine. Heidi and I got caught in the middle of something and we can't leave, not yet.'

'Where are you?'

Stacey took another deep breath. 'Abergavenny. We were visiting Miss Savage when a squad of immigration enforcement officers raided her home. They've left now but she's obviously upset and Heidi's spitting feathers.'

'I can imagine, but what on earth are you doing there?'

'Following my story. I can't really talk now, but I'll ring this evening. Will you be at Noddfa?'

'Should be, but I told you not to get involved with this. Why don't you just come home?'

'I can't leave Felicity. As I said, she is pretty upset. We'll speak later, I promise.'

Stacey disconnected the call. Ben huffed and tucked his phone away.

'Trouble?' Jack asked.

'Don't ask. Get us back to the station. We have to hope the rest of the team has been more productive than we have. We're getting nowhere fast with this investigation.'

Chapter sixteen

Fliss and Heidi sat at the table in a large kitchen while Stacey rummaged in the larder, and a chest freezer in the utility room, looking for something for supper.

'Did you have a meal planned, Fliss?' she asked. 'I've found some mince and could rustle up a bolognaise.'

'You really don't need to bother,' Fliss said. 'You've both got homes to go to. I'll be fine on my own.'

'Nonsense,' Heidi said. 'A bit of company never goes amiss, besides, you should tell us why the enforcement officers turned up earlier. Do you hide refugees in your home?'

'Oh, dear,' Fliss groaned and took a deep breath. 'The honest answer is yes, sometimes.'

'When Stacey asked you if there was anyone here, you said there *might* be. The heavy brigade didn't find anyone, so I don't understand your earlier comment.'

'Sounds like I've lost it, you mean?' Fliss said. 'Well, I haven't. Nothing wrong with my brain. Thing is, sometimes people do stay here, those who need to keep to the shadows. Good people, with families some of them, whose only crime is to *be* here.'

'Surely you know when someone is hiding in your home?'

'Not always. We decided it was better for me if I knew as little as possible. I'm not routinely told when a guest is due.'

Having got the tomato sauce underway, Stacey sat at the table. 'You must let them in when they arrive,' she said.

Fliss shook her head. 'At the back of the house is a stairway that leads from a single-story extension – the old boot room – up to the attic. I leave the outside door unlocked so people can come and go as they please. The door into the house is always locked so I'm quite safe.'

'You're taking a huge risk though,' Heidi said. 'The authorities won't go easy on you just because you're old.'

Fliss made a rude noise. 'Do you think they worry me? After what I've lived through in my long life. I don't think so.' Fliss patted Heidi's hand. 'Thank you, my dear, for dealing with them so effectively, but I'd have got there in the end. Caught me on the hop that's all. I'm a tough old boot.'

Heidi grinned. 'Never doubted it for a second.'

'Do you ever meet those you shelter?' Stacey asked.

'Sometimes, but only when I bump into someone in the garden.'

'So refugees are delivered then collected a little while later. Is that right?'

Fliss nodded. 'I don't even have to feed them. There's a small kitchen up there and as I said, no one stays for long.' She chuckled. 'They are usually here avoiding Immigration – ironically.'

'Bloody good job the attic was empty,' Stacey said.

'Quite.'

Stacey got up from the table, stirred the tomato sauce, tasted it carefully, and hunted in overhead cupboards for suitable herbs.

'What's Rowan's part in this?' Heidi asked. 'You should tell us. Be easier to help if we know all of it. Not only that, we need to find out who shot Jonathon and lock them up. They can't be allowed to kill anyone else.'

'I agree, but I'm not sure how you'd catch the perpetrator.'

'Why is that?'

'Bound to be one of the people smugglers. They don't often travel to the UK. They make their money in France.'

'Why do you think a people smuggler did this?'

Fliss sighed and wiped her eyes. 'After Yezda died, Rowan and Jonathon were determined that anyone involved in the filthy business should be caught and punished. They were both information gathering and passing on what they learned to the government. That's why Rowan received such a light sentence when he was caught taking people across the border.' She sipped from a glass of water. 'I think one of the bad guys tracked down Jonathon.'

* * *

Ben arrived at Noddfa after seven. He let himself in through the back door, dropped a thick file on the table, took off his jacket and put the kettle on. He opened the fridge, discovered some leftover soup and put it on the Aga to heat, then sat in the carver while he waited for supper and opened the file.

The first thing he saw were photographs of the victims from the showroom. He winced at the sight of the hole in Haddon's forehead, a trickle of blood marring his pale skin. He looked again at Kitty, lying face down in muddy water, blue dress sparkling in the low light. He placed the pictures on the table and began reading through the staff's statements. The kettle boiled. He made tea and returned to his seat.

After the statements, he reread the reports collected during the investigation. Pathology reports, DNA results, forensics, and of course the autopsies. He scrubbed at his face wishing he could see just a single decent clue, something tangible he and the team could work with.

He left his seat again, filled a bowl with soup, hacked a chunk of bread from a homemade loaf in the larder and began his meal. He wasn't hungry but knew he should eat, so forced the food down. He wondered how Stacey was and what she had got herself involved with. He didn't like the sound of immigration officers – or the fact he was spending the evening alone.

He wiped a bread crust around his bowl and crammed it into his mouth. Stacey's laptop rested on the table and he dragged it towards him. Opening the screen, he discovered the device was in snooze mode, so he woke it up and began researching the refugee situation.

After an hour or so, he shut the laptop, groaned and worried about Stacey. If she wasn't in danger from whoever had killed Haddon, then she was surely in danger from the authorities. He knew she wouldn't drop the story – she never did – but reporting what was going on wouldn't make her popular. He couldn't make up his mind whether having Heidi on her side was a good or bad thing either.

He got to his feet and washed the bowl, then he poured himself a whisky, retreated to the living room and switched on the television. He needed some downtime, but couldn't focus on anything. Eventually he gave up. He made sure the cottage doors were locked, turned off the lights and went up to bed. Maybe he'd be able to work out something after a good night's sleep.

* * *

Stacey was up early the next morning. After a quick splash in the bathroom, she went down to the kitchen in search of coffee and found Fliss, already sitting at the table, wearing an extravagant, blue silk dressing gown, covered with hummingbirds and bougainvillea flowers. She looked up as Stacey entered and smiled.

'Good morning, dear. Did you sleep well?' she asked.

'I did, thank you.' Stacey replied. 'Did you have a good night?'

'I always sleep well. Never been one for tossing, turning and worrying.'

The door opened and Heidi appeared. She smiled and plonked herself next to Fliss. Stacey poured boiling water into a cafetiere, carried it to the table and placed it in front of her friend.

'Just what I need,' Heidi said. 'Everyone OK this morning?'

'We're fine,' Fliss said. 'Would you like breakfast before you leave?'

'I'm not sure we are leaving,' Heidi said. 'I don't intend going anywhere unless I know things are good here.'

Fliss patted Heidi's hand. 'Things are good here. You really don't need to worry about me.'

'I'm not convinced. You're miles from anywhere. How do you cope out here on your own?'

Fliss laughed. 'I'd never have put you down as a fusser. One thing I am sure of is you hate anyone fussing over you.'

Heidi shrugged and began fiddling with a bright pink paper serviette she took from a pile on the table.

'I could stay,' Stacey said. 'Not a problem. I'd be here when Rowan pops in.'

'There's no need for either of you to stay,' Fliss said firmly. 'I've had a couple of exciting days and could do with some solitude. I'm very well adapted to living alone.'

'Make sure you ring me if you need anything,' Heidi said and handed over a beautifully crafted lotus flower.

'I will, I promise, but I want you girls to promise me something very important.'

'What's that?' Heidi asked.

'That you'll take care of each other, especially if you keep digging around in this murky business.'

* * *

Ben sat at his desk in the incident room, discovered a couple of painkillers in one of the drawers and dry-swallowed them. He'd had a bad night, not dropping off until nearly five, only to wake again suddenly after an hour, with a headache from hell. He waited while the team settled around the large table and massaged his temples.

'You OK, guv?' Jack asked quietly and placed a mug next to his boss.

'Just a headache. Right then,' Ben said, looking up. 'Where are we on this? Any clever insights? New clues? Anything?'

'Well,' Elsa said, 'I've been digging into Natalie Turrell's background to see if her story checked out.'

'Did it?' Jack asked.

'The property ownership did. The place has been in the family for years as Natalie said, but it isn't free and clear.'

'That's interesting. A recent mortgage?'

'Three years old, an eye-watering £475k.'

'Blimey, that'll set her back a fortune every month. Presumably she's paying herself a hefty salary from the charity to finance the loan?'

Elsa nodded. 'A hundred and sixty thou a year, but also draws benefits.'

'Expenses? That sort of thing?'

'Some of that, but she charges the charity a large rent for the lower floor, then plays around with the utility bills so she pays the smaller share.'

'What does she spend her money on?' Ben asked. 'Apart from the mortgage.'

'Don't know, sir. So far I haven't been able to find any flash cars, no fancy boats and no property other than the place in Bristol. It's possible she invested in bitcoin, but no way to prove that.' She slid some printed pages across the desk. 'Here's a summary. I'm no accountant, but it all smells dodgy to me.'

'Have you spoken to the forensics guy about this?'

'Yeah and he's having another look, together with accounts for R4A held with the Charity Commission.'

'OK, good.' Ben looked across the table at Ollie and Tegan. 'I want you two in Abergavenny. You need to speak to Miss Savage again. We really must find Rowan Gardiner and she's the only link with him we have.' He sighed heavily. 'Stacey and Heidi were there yesterday and got tangled up in a raid by Immigration.'

'Bloody hell, sir, what went on?' Ollie asked.

Ben grinned. 'I haven't spoken to "the press" this morning, so don't have any more information. For all I know, the pair might still be there. Stacey told me they intended to stay the night.'

He turned to look at Kevin Biggs and raised his eyebrows. 'Have you made any progress at all?'

'Not much,' Kevin admitted. 'Spoke to the showroom staff and those at the hotel for a second time, also chatted to the cabbie. No one had anything to add. Had a bit of luck looking for the Yezda woman. Got her surname from the university she attended and managed to discover she took a ferry to France, just like Theo Watson told you.'

'Any record of her returning?'

'Not so far, sir, but I'm looking.'

'Did you get a chance to go over to Hay to take a look at Haddon's place?'

'Due to meet the local cops there this morning. As you know they've already been in and seem to think we are accusing them of not doing their jobs. Not looking forward to it.'

Ben grinned. 'I'm sure your sparkling personality will get you through.'

'What about us, guv?' Jack asked.

'Case review, look through everything. I'm beginning to lean towards Haddon's murder being due to the refugee situation, rather than the financial angle.'

'So you're back to considering a hit man?'

'Do you think that?'

Jack shrugged. 'Anything's possible.'

'We'll keep it in mind.'

Ben's mobile chirped, he checked the screen and read a text from his partner. He looked up as Tegan and Ollie were leaving the room.

'It's OK, guys, the press have left Miss Savage's place.' He glanced back at Jack. 'The sleuths will be at Noddfa tonight, and it appears that we're invited to supper.'

Chapter seventeen

Later that evening, once supper had been finished, Ben got up from the table, collected a bottle of wine from the larder and filled glasses.

'Right then,' he said, sitting back down. 'You two need to tell me exactly what went on in Abergavenny yesterday.'

As though delivering a police report, Heidi recited the salient points surrounding the visit from immigration enforcers, and the fact that Felicity Savage had admitted hiding refugees in her home.

'No sign of anything when we were there,' Heidi said. 'I escorted the officers around the place, they found no one and I saw no sign that anyone was hidden there.'

'I don't understand why such an elderly woman is involved with this,' Jack said. 'Whatever happened to a gentle retirement?'

Heidi chuckled. 'Fliss is definitely not the sort for that. I'm pretty sure she could have seen off those louts without my help.'

'We thought it would be a good idea to stay the night,' Stacey said. 'Make sure she really was OK and not just saying she was. She is in her nineties.'

'Did she tell you why she has anything to do with it?' Jack persisted.

Heidi placed one of the borrowed books in front of him on the table.

'What's this?' he asked.

'A book about the Kindertransport scheme run just before the start of the Second World War. Felicity Savage, and a friend she named as Anni – now deceased – were among the nearly ten thousand children rescued from Europe in 1939. She empathises with refugees fleeing from war and death as she and her friend were forced to.'

'I watched something about that on telly,' Jack said. 'Must have been dreadful, sending your children away knowing they'd be safe, but that you might never see them again.'

Stacey took up the story. 'The girls were placed in a farm Llanwrda way. They'd told the authorities they were sisters and couldn't be separated. They were believed and took their foster parents' surnames – easier than sticking with German names, as the countries were about to go to war.'

'No wonder she's so tough,' Ben said, 'having to live through something like that at a young age.'

'That's not the end of the story,' Heidi said. 'After the war they learned, like so many others, they were the only members of their families to survive the Holocaust.'

Ben breathed heavily and rubbed his eyes. 'Never far away is it?' he asked. 'Man's inhumanity to man. Were they well treated on the farm?'

'Yes,' Stacey said. 'They were taken in by a childless couple, the Savages. After the girls had adjusted from living in an increasingly dangerous Germany, to the green softness of Wales, they really took to rural life. Fliss spoke of her foster parents with tears in her eyes.'

'At least there was a happy ending,' Jack said.

Heidi grinned. 'It got better. The couple adopted the girls and they grew up. Felicity became an activist and

Anni fostered other children. When the Savages died and left the farm to the girls, it was sold and they bought the dolly mixture house. They lived there together until Anni passed a few years ago.'

Jack sipped from his wine glass. 'Nice things worked out well for them. I'm sure all the refugees weren't as lucky.'

Ben removed a cork from a second bottle of wine and refilled their glasses.

'OK,' he said, 'we've established why she wants to help, but what is the extent of her involvement? Must be major if Immigration paid her a visit.'

'As far as I can see, she provides a dead letterbox,' Heidi said, not catching anyone's eye.

'Gotta be more than that,' Jack said. 'Immigration must have had a solid tip to turn up *en masse*, warrant in hand. Are you sure she wasn't hiding anyone?'

'Like I said, I didn't see anyone and the officers left empty-handed.'

'Did the old lady say anything about Haddon and his friend Rowan?'

'A little,' Stacey said. 'She believes a people smuggler, one of those selling places on crappy blow-up boats, might have shot Jonathon.'

'Any reason she'd think that?' Jack asked.

'She was a little sketchy but mentioned something about the lads passing on information to the authorities about gangs operating on the French coast.'

'Actually,' Heidi said, 'I've been talking to my father, as he's Mister Government. He's planning to come over to my place for lunch in the next few days. Might be a good idea for you to be there. What he has to say could be useful to your case.'

* * *

Stacey got up with Ben the next morning and after he left for the station, she set to catching up with chores. The weather was breezy but sunny, so she stripped the bed and stuffed the sheets in the washing machine. Having been so caught up with the refugee case everything had got behind, especially the housework and gardening.

She scrubbed the flagstones in the kitchen and by the time the washing was done, the fridge and Aga had received a once-over. Stacey loaded up the wicker laundry basket and went outside to pin sheets on the line. She took deep breaths of clean mountain air and remembered to count her blessings, mainly that she lived in a safe and beautiful place, and had no reason to run for her life.

A robin perched on the fence just a few feet away from the washing line, and a male blackbird sang stridently from the top of the apple tree. The lure of the garden was strong, so Stacey went inside, made coffee, and carried it to the bench next to the back door. She closed her eyes, turned her face towards the sun and revelled in the warmth, allowing the natural mountain sounds to fill her senses. The quiet background buzzing of bees nipping in and out of foxglove flowers and sheep calling on the ranges was suddenly obliterated as the landline rang. Stacey nipped into the kitchen and snatched up the handset.

'Morning. Stacey Logan.'

'Oh… uh… hello. It's Sorrell from Aberglasney. We met recently.'

'Hi, yes I remember. How are you and Rebin?'

'OK I guess, it's just…'

'What's wrong? Can I help you with anything?'

'I wondered whether you'd mind if we drove over to see you.'

'Has something happened? You sound upset.'

'That's because I am. I really need someone to talk to, but I don't have to come over. I don't want to disturb you.'

'You won't. I'll be really happy to see you. If you leave soon it'll be lunchtime when you arrive. I'll rustle up a meal.'

'Thank you so much. We'll leave now.'

Sorrell disconnected the call and Stacey heard dead air. She wondered what had upset the young woman and began making pastry to line a caramelized onion and pepper quiche – a safe option in case her visitors were vegetarian. A little over ninety minutes later, she heard the sound of an engine in the lane, wiped her hands and walked out to the front of her cottage.

The doors of an old 4x4 opened and Sorrell and Rebin climbed out.

'Hello,' Stacey called. 'Found me OK then?'

'No problem,' Sorrell said. 'Llanagethin is the only place to go after you've turned off the main road.'

'Hello, Stacey,' Rebin said. 'I brought Rufus. Can I get him out of the car please? He's hot in there. He's got his lead on.'

'Of course you can. Bring him in and we'll give him a bowl of water.'

'Thanks,' Rebin said, opened the back door of the truck and his pet jumped out, tail wagging.

Stacey smiled at Sorrell. 'It's nice to see you. Are you OK?'

Sorrell frowned. 'Not really,' she said.

'Let's go in and start lunch, you can tell me what's happened over food.'

'Thanks for this. I really appreciate it.'

'No need to thank me, now let's eat. I missed breakfast and I'm starving.'

* * *

Ben was about to leave the station through the main doors in search of some fresh air when the desk sergeant looked up.

'Sir?' he called.

Ben turned back. 'Yes?'

'DS Trent just rang, said to hang onto you. He's on his way down.'

'Did he say what he wants?'

'No, sir. Just for you to wait.'

A few moments later, Jack shoved his way through the heavy fire door.

'Good,' he said, 'you're still here. Kevin Biggs has been in touch.'

'Problem in Hay-on-Wye?'

'No, on his way home. He stopped off for lunch in a pub on the Erwood road.'

'And?'

'While he was at the bar waiting for his food, a woman came in from the car park. There was a 7.5-ton truck parked behind the building and she said she could hear banging from inside. Kev went out and sure enough, the woman was right,' Jack said. 'Kev went straight back inside, nicked the driver and made him open the back. He found people inside, guv. We need to get there fast.'

Jack turned and dashed out of the station, Ben on his heels. They got in the car, Jack fired up the engine and set off along the road from Builth, which ran alongside the river towards Erwood. Not being the best passenger in the world, Ben held tightly to the grab rail and stared through the side window at the water. He could still see remnants of the recent flood, debris wrapped around trees edging the river, a fence lying flat, large branches dumped in the middle of fields. The landscape was in recovery though, vegetation and grass regrowing. He gently touched his damaged nose, pleased that also seemed to be in recovery.

A few miles later, Jack swooped in through the wide entrance of the Cooper's Arms and pulled up close to a white panel van. Three marked police cars were already in attendance, together with a first response vehicle and a smattering of ambulances. A small crowd of customers stood close to the pub, peering and pointing. Another small crowd of distressed individuals sat on the dusty ground, paramedics checking them over. Jack opened his door.

'I'll deal with this lot, guv,' he said, nodding at the spectators. 'You go and find Kevin and send me a couple of uniforms over.'

Ben nodded and strode towards the truck as a pair of dark blue vans pulled into the car park. Undertakers, Ben thought and swallowed hard. As he walked closer, he heard sobbing, a child whimpering and a quiet desperate wailing. About twenty people, nearly all Middle-Eastern-looking, sat on the tarmac. Some had silver rescue blankets wrapped around their bodies, some were struggling to breathe, others gulped from water bottles, some vomited, others were praying or thanking God, Ben couldn't tell which. He spotted Kevin Biggs walking towards him. The man looked dreadful, pale and shocked, and was trembling slightly.

'Thank fuck you're here, sir, I– oh, sorry.'

Ben waved away the apology. 'What can you tell me about the situation?' he asked.

'Managed to find a guy who spoke good English.' Kevin indicated a tall man who looked to be in his early forties. 'He told me he was from Afghanistan. He has a woman with him, his wife, and his young son…' Kevin gulped. 'The boy is dead, sir.'

Ben took a deep breath. 'Is the child the only casualty?'

'No, sir. Looks to be seven dead – including the boy. Twenty-three still breathing but paramedics say that may change. Some are in a bad way.' Kevin looked directly at his boss. 'I'm struggling a bit, sir. Never dealt with anything like this before.'

Ben patted the man on his shoulder. 'You're doing well, Kevin. Now take me to the driver.'

The prisoner, a man in his twenties, dressed in jeans and a black vest, was locked in one of the patrol cars. His hands were cuffed behind his back and a uniformed officer stood guard, leaning on one side of the vehicle. Jack – having dispersed the crowd of rubberneckers – snatched open the back door, leaned inside and glared at the young man hunched uncomfortably on the vinyl seat.

'Did you know they were in there?' he snarled and moved closer. The captive flinched as he felt Jack's breath on his face. 'Did you know, you bastard?'

'Sergeant,' Ben warned and placed an arm on Jack's arm. 'You need to step back.'

'No,' Jack said, 'I need to get answers from this... vermin.'

'Move back. We'll get answers the right way.'

Jack angrily shook off Ben's hand. 'He better not get away with this. Not a chance he walks.'

'He won't. We've got him banged to rights.' Ben gently nudged Jack another few feet away and lowered his voice. 'We need him to talk and he won't do that if you frighten him half to death. Look at him, Jack. He's not the mastermind, he's a delivery boy. We've got to do this right. No mistakes.'

He glanced up as Carrie Salmon arrived and steered her truck towards the rear of the large car park.

'I'll stay here,' Ben said. 'You go and keep Carrie company, make notes of her early findings.'

Jack nodded, his shoulders dropped and he trudged across the tarmac as though he was wearing lead-filled diver's boots. Ben took a deep breath and turned back to the young man in handcuffs.

Chapter eighteen

The patio behind Noddfa was warm in the sun and as the small group ate lunch, Sorrell told Stacey that she had received a visit from immigration enforcement officers. From what she said it was clear the raid mirrored the one in Abergavenny and Stacey could tell the younger woman was really rattled.

'They were searching for Bilal – obviously,' Sorrell said. 'They looked at Rebin as though he shouldn't be here either.' Rebin got up from the table and went to throw a ball for his dog at the far end of the garden. Sorrell lowered her voice. 'I'm terrified they'll take him away from me.'

'I'm sure they can't do that,' Stacey said. 'You told me Rebin was born in Carmarthen hospital. He's a UK citizen surely?'

Sorrell nodded and swiped her eyes with one of her sleeves. 'What you say is true, but my heart struggles to believe it. I've already lost my husband.'

Stacey reached across the table, covered Sorrell's hand with one of her own and squeezed.

'They've been before,' Sorrell said, 'and each time it happens I feel like I'm melting, dissolving on the spot. I find it difficult to think straight sometimes but try to keep positive for Rebin.' She smiled sadly. 'He's such a happy, clever little boy, spitting image of his father, and I know this is having a dreadful effect on him.'

'Do you ever see Bilal?' Stacey asked.

'Not as much as we used to. We started out living together and worked through the system, trying to claim asylum. It can take years to be granted the right to remain. While the application is being processed, those applying aren't allowed to work. If they do and are caught, they are removed from the country or held in one of the ghastly immigration centres.' She sighed heavily. 'We didn't want that to happen to Bilal when his application had run its course and he was refused.'

'Can you tell me where he is?'

Sorrell shook her head. 'Don't ask because I won't tell you. Others are at risk and I've only just met you.'

'I understand,' Stacey said. 'So what happens now?'

'I honestly don't have a clue. I'm not sure I want to go back to the house. Not yet. They might come back.'

'Could you stay with family? Somewhere the authorities wouldn't find you?'

'Mum and Dad moved to Australia a few years ago.'

The women fell silent and watched Rebin play with his dog. Barks and high-pitched giggles floated across the vegetable garden as he repeatedly threw a tennis ball and Rufus sprang enthusiastically after it. Sorrell closed her eyes and Stacey spotted a single tear run down a pale cheek.

'How about a few days here?' Stacey asked.

'You'd let us stay with you?'

'I don't see why not. I have two spare bedrooms and everyone says a change is as good as a rest. You could certainly do with one of those. No one would look for you here. Why would they?'

'I really can't impose,' Sorrell said. 'It's an incredibly kind offer though, thank you.'

'You wouldn't be imposing. I'm not an idiot and wouldn't invite you to stay unless I wanted to help.' Stacey smiled. 'There's one thing though, my partner is a copper; chief inspector actually.'

Sorrell shook her head and her dreadlocks swung like bell-ringers' sallies.

'I can't see how that would work. Wouldn't he inform the authorities we are here?'

'Why would he? Neither you nor Rebin have broken any laws. I'll speak to him. It'll be fine, I know it will.'

Sorrell didn't look convinced.

'Ben's a good guy. Not only that, but my friend Heidi knows one of the best lawyers in the country. He might be able to help you. Look on it as a mini holiday.'

Sorrell sighed. 'It does sound tempting.'

'Then that's what we'll do.' Stacey got to her feet. 'Coffee first, then I'll drive you to your place.' She took hold of Sorrell's hand. 'I promise I'll do all I can to help you. You'll be safe here.'

* * *

After too many hours spent in the car park of the Cooper's Arms, Ben and Jack were finally able to leave. The survivors discovered in the refrigerated truck had been taken to Hereford County Hospital for treatment, the dead were on their way to the county morgue, and SOCO were swarming over the vehicle. Groups of uniforms stood around protecting the scene; others questioned the landlord, his staff and customers about events leading up to the gruesome discovery. The driver had already been taken to the police station and Jack was itching to face him in the interview room.

The detectives remained silent on the journey back to base, both shocked and upset by the dreadful scene they had witnessed. Knowing they had hours of work ahead of them before they could clock off, Ben sent Stacey a text saying he was working late and would stay the night at his place.

After parking the car behind the station, Jack led the way upstairs to the incident room. The place was empty apart from Elsa who was sitting at her workstation, eyes glued to the computer screen. As soon as she saw the officers enter, she walked over to the coffee machine, filled two mugs and carried them to the end of the long table. Ben glanced up and smiled his thanks.

'How are you, sir?' Elsa asked. 'Neither of you look great if I'm honest.'

'If *I'm* honest, I don't think we are. That was probably the worst call-out I've ever experienced,' Ben said. 'I'm assuming the prisoner is safely locked up?'

'Yes, sir, but you should take a moment before you tackle him. I've spoken with CS Warren and brought her up to date. She said to contact her immediately if there's anything you need.'

'Thanks,' Ben mumbled and gulped from his mug. 'Any word from Ollie and Tegan?'

'No, sir.'

Elsa returned to her desk and was soon rattling her keyboard again.

Ben looked at Jack. 'How are you doing?' he asked.

'Ah, you know. Shocked and furious. I won't ever forget the sight of that poor little boy lying dead on the ground. I didn't think his mother would ever let him go. If that had been my son, I'd never recover. I know I wouldn't. How has this dreadful crime come to Powys?'

'Maybe it's always been here and we haven't picked up on it. Hiding in plain sight.' Ben groaned and scrubbed at his face. He drained his coffee. 'OK then, let's get downstairs and find out what the driver knows. Try to keep a lid on your anger, Jack. Like I said earlier, we need to extract information from this guy. If you come on heavy the kid will get himself a brief who will, no doubt, advise him to keep his mouth shut.'

'Yeah, I get it, guv, but don't expect me to wear kid gloves. We have to do whatever it takes to make him talk.'

Ben nodded, got to his feet and the officers went downstairs to the custody suite in the basement of the station. They settled themselves in interview room one and, a few minutes later, the custody sergeant delivered the van driver. Jack waited until the young man had taken his seat then switched on the recording machine and stated date, time and those present in the room. Ben began the interview.

'I'd like you to confirm your name and address,' he said, 'for the benefit of the recording.'

'Dave Milton,' the young man muttered. 'I live at number twenty, Beechwood Glade, Newport. I'm twenty-six.'

'Who do you work for?'

'Registered with an agency. They send me on driving jobs.'

'What was your destination today?'

'A firm in Dover, Long Logistics. I took an early train to the east coast and picked up the truck on an industrial estate.'

'Where were you told to drive it?'

'Another industrial estate in Newbridge-on-Wye.'

Jack couldn't remain quiet any longer. 'Did you know there were people in the back of the truck?' he growled.

'What? No of course not!'

'I don't believe you.'

Milton shrugged. 'I guess that's your problem, mate, cos I'm telling the truth.'

Jack glared at the prisoner. 'I am *not* your mate and your story doesn't add up. Why on earth would you be sent all the way to the coast to bring a truck to Mid Wales?'

'How would I know? I just go where I'm sent and do what I'm told.'

Jack pulled a phone from his pocket. 'I am showing Mr Milton a picture taken this morning next to the truck he was driving.'

Jack swiped the screen and held the device in front of Milton's face. The image depicted the body of the young boy, lying on gravelly ground, head resting in the lap of his mother who was obviously weeping. Milton looked away.

'Look at it!' Jack hissed. 'You did this. You are not only responsible for this child's death, but the deaths of six other people.'

Milton shook his head. 'No, not me. I haven't killed anyone. I told you, I didn't know there was anyone in the back. I'm just a driver. I pick up what I'm told and never open the trucks. They're all sealed with security tags.'

'I still don't believe you,' Jack said.

'Can't help that, can I? Speak to the agency, they'll tell you.'

'I fully intend to.'

'Are you known to us?' Ben asked.

'Don't know what you mean,' Milton said.

'Have you got a criminal record?'

Milton looked down at his hands and nodded.

'What for?'

'Drugs,' the man muttered. 'I used to deal weed but packed it in after I got nicked.'

Ben nodded. 'OK, this is what's going to happen. We will give you a drugs test, then you can wait in a cell while we verify what you've told us.'

'Nah, can't do that. Gotta get home to the missus – she's expecting.'

Jack leaned across the desk. 'Should have thought about that before you started moving refugees halfway across the country.'

'I didn't know they were in there!' Milton yelled.

'So you say. I still reckon you're a lair. Be warned, if we discover your story doesn't check out, the next time we meet I won't be anywhere near as tolerant.'

Jack ended the interview, slapped off the recording device, got to his feet and stuck his head out of the room.

'Sergeant,' he shouted. 'Put this one back in his cell and arrange a drugs test.'

As soon as Milton had been removed, Ben and Jack went upstairs to the incident room and began trying to verify what the man had told them.

Chapter nineteen

Once the car had been loaded with Sorrell and Rebin's belongings, and an elderly neighbour had agreed to keep an eye on the chickens, Stacey made sure her passengers were belted in and set off along the narrow lane towards the main road. She had just reached the T-junction when her mobile chirped. She glanced at the screen and read Ben's text informing her he wouldn't be home that night.

'Problem?' Sorrell asked when she saw Stacey frown.

'Ben – he's busy at work and won't be coming over this evening.'

'At least I don't have to worry about him.'

Stacey chuckled. 'I've already told you there's no need. You'll see when you meet him.'

The roads were quiet, the lull before the tourist summer storm, and within an hour Stacey parked in the drive at Noddfa. She left the car, unlocked the front door and her guests began unloading bags from the boot and carrying them upstairs. Sorrell had decided her son would share a room with her so Rebin dragged Rufus' bed upstairs and put it against the wall beneath the window. The dog was clearly excited and belted up and down the stairs, checking out all the other rooms.

Sorrell went down to the kitchen and dropped on the carver next to the Aga. She rubbed her face.

'I can't remember ever being so tired,' she said.

'Well now you can have a rest,' Stacey said, 'and stop worrying, for a few days at least.'

A shadow appeared in the open doorway. Sorrell's head shot up, eyes momentarily wide and fearful until she recognised Heidi.

'Afternoon,' Heidi said as she stepped inside the kitchen. 'This is a nice surprise. Good to see you.'

'You too.'

'Sorrell and Rebin are planning to stay for a few days,' Stacey said. 'They had a visit from immigration enforcers and just need to have a bit of a rest.'

'That's interesting,' Heidi said. 'Do you think it was the same bunch?'

'Sounds like it.'

'What do you mean the same bunch?' Sorrell asked.

'Felicity Savage also had a visit.'

'Fliss got raided? Oh God. Is she OK?'

'She's fine,' Heidi said. 'How do you know her?'

'Everyone knows Fliss,' Sorrell said as though that explained the situation. 'Did Immigration find… uh…'

'You mean did they find any refugees? No they didn't. Stacey and I were there when the thugs came knocking. Fliss didn't have to deal with them on her own.'

'I'd like to know what prompted the raids,' Stacey said. 'Someone must have said something, especially as they knocked on Sorrell's door too. Be good to know if the raids were connected.'

Sorrell sighed. 'Yes, it would, but the chances of finding out are less than zero.'

'Not necessarily,' Heidi mumbled. 'Where's your boy?'

'Outside playing with the dog. We're planning a trip to the river before supper.'

'Where's Ben?'

'Work,' Stacey said. 'Sent me a text to say he won't be home tonight, busy he said.'

'Same as Erica. She's on nights this week. Got room for one more?'

Stacey smiled. 'Always room for a little one.'

'Yeah, yeah, laugh it up, longshanks.'

Rufus suddenly burst through the open door, spotted Heidi and skidded to a halt, claws sliding on the stone floor. He sat and Heidi rubbed his head then she took a seat at the table.

'At least you're quiet today,' she said and the dog wagged its tail.

Rebin, looking for his pet, ran into the kitchen.

'Hello, Heidi,' he said. 'Do you live here with Stacey?'

'No, matey, I don't, but I'm going to stay the night.'

The boy nodded, then he gave his mother a quick hug, clicked his tongue at the leggy mongrel and the pair headed back to the garden.

'What do you want to talk about?' Stacey asked.

'I think I know what Ben is working on,' Heidi said.

'Really? What?'

Heidi took a deep breath. 'I picked up some chatter online regarding a truck load of refugees discovered somewhere near Erwood. Seems there have been some deaths.'

* * *

The interview room door swung open and Dave Milton was ushered inside. Ollie settled him at the table and took up his position by the door as Jack switched on the recording machine ready for the next round of questions. Jack sat next to Ben and grinned. Milton lowered his eyes.

'I want to ask you about the truck,' Jack said. 'I'm convinced you knew you weren't delivering chilled food because the refrigeration unit wasn't turned on. Didn't you ask yourself why you were being paid to drive an empty truck all the way from Dover to Mid Wales?'

'I've already told you I didn't know those people were inside.'

'Yes, you did and I told you you were lying. You also told us you didn't look inside because the doors were securely sealed and tagged. Why would an empty truck be sealed like that?'

'Dunno, mate. I'm just the driver.'

Jack slapped the top of the table, the sound ricocheted around the room and made everyone jump.

'Let me tell you what I know. How would that be?'

Milton shrugged and folded his arms. 'Whatever.'

'Here goes then. Firstly, the agency you named has never employed you, never even heard of you. Second, the DWP *does* know you. They have confirmed you claim Universal Credit and housing benefit, including council tax rebate. And thirdly, your previous conviction was in fact for dealing coke and DMT, not as you told us for weed.' Jack glared at the man. 'You must be addled if you didn't think we'd find that out. You need to start talking, lad, or I'll add manslaughter charges to your rap sheet.'

Milton shrugged again. 'Up to you to prove it and convince a jury. I'll take my chances.'

Jack laughed. 'You're an idiot, you know that don't you? When a jury sees that photo of the poor little dead boy, they'll find you guilty in a heartbeat. You don't stand a chance and are looking at a long prison sentence.'

Milton said nothing.

'You need to realise how much trouble you're in,' Ben said. 'If you help us with this, tell us what you know, it will help your case. We will make sure the court knows you were cooperative.'

Milton sighed. 'How many times do I have to tell you? I didn't know there was anyone in the truck. I was paid to drive from Dover to Newbridge where I was told to leave the vehicle outside a unit on the industrial estate.' He smirked. 'Course, I can't tell you anything about that cos I never got there.'

Jack leaned across the table. 'I'm beginning to lose patience with you,' he growled. 'Tell us who paid you.'

'What are you going to do? Beat it out of me?'

Milton leaned back in his chair, balancing on two legs. Jack stretched out one of his own legs, tucked a toe beneath the seat of the plastic chair and lifted, it tipped and Milton fell backwards to the floor. A loud clatter filled the air and the prisoner yelped.

'For the tape,' Jack said, 'the prisoner leant back too far in his chair and toppled it.'

'I confirm that is what happened,' Ben said.

Milton scrabbled to his feet and glared at Ollie leaning on the wall next to the door. 'He pushed me over,' Milton said. 'You saw that. He fucking pushed me. I might have cracked my bloody skull open.'

Ollie grinned. 'I saw you lean back too far. I did not see anyone push you.'

Milton flopped back on the chair. 'You know what?' he said. 'I've had enough of this. You shouldn't be talking to me without a solicitor. It's wrong. Against my human rights.'

'You were cautioned on arrest,' Ben said. 'Furthermore, you were offered a solicitor on two separate occasions. You refused, saying you didn't need one because you hadn't done anything wrong. You have the right to change your mind so, would you like a solicitor present?'

'Yeah, I would.'

'One of your own?'

'Don't have one.'

'OK, we'll find you a duty solicitor.'

'Might take a while,' Jack said, 'but there's plenty we can do to fill the time.'

'Oh, so now you're gonna take me to a cell and taser me repeatedly, say I was kicking off.'

Jack chuckled. 'Don't be daft, you watch too much telly, boy. No, we'll charge you for benefit fraud and driving under the influence. Your drugs test showed three different illegal substances in your system.' He chuckled again. 'No chance you'll get bored, not unless we can't get hold of a brief before the morning.'

'I demand my phone call!' Milton said. 'Right this minute! I need to ring the wife, she's about to drop any day now and I should be there.' He caught Ben's eye. 'Can't you charge me and give me bail? Sharon gets really stressed without me. You need to let me go home.'

'No can do,' Jack said. 'This interview isn't over by a long shot and now you've slowed things down because you want a brief. Interview suspended at 19.45.' Jack switched off the machine and smiled at his prisoner. 'Hope you sleep as well as I will tonight. You're gonna have a hectic day tomorrow. A manslaughter charge awaits you, that's heavy… *mate*.'

Ollie escorted the prisoner back to his cell while the relevant tests were set up. Half an hour later, Milton was given access to a phone and made a five-minute call to his wife which – to Ollie's ears – sounded like five minutes of an angry wasp buzzing down the line. Ben and Jack climbed the stairs to the incident room and once again discovered Elsa alone, her workstation lit by a single Anglepoise lamp.

'You still here?' Ben asked.

'I'm not a ghost, sir.'

'You should have left a while ago.'

'Thought I'd hang around in case you needed someone to make coffee and surreptitiously add a tot of something stronger.'

Ben smiled. 'We definitely need someone to do that. Thanks.'

'How did it go?' Elsa asked as she filled the coffee machine.

'Slowly,' Ben said. 'Milton seems to think we'll believe the rubbish he spouts, even though we've pointed out the folly of his ways. We have enough evidence to charge him for multiple offences and with a little more, he's looking at manslaughter charges. If there's a God in heaven, Milton's definitely going down; for a long stretch.'

* * *

While Stacey and Sorrell began preparing toad-in-the-hole for supper, Heidi sat at the table and showed Rebin how to make an origami bird. The boy watched carefully, his nose nearly touching the tabletop, and copied the folds Heidi made in the paper. After a few wrong turns, and some help, Rebin managed to produce a slightly wonky crane.

'Now,' Heidi said, 'if you pinch its chest and gently tug the tail up and down, it will flap its wings.'

Rebin fiddled then laughed when he achieved the desired result.

'Mummy, look! Look at my bird.'

Sorrell examined the paper sculpture. 'You're such a clever boy,' she said.

'Can we make another one, Heidi?' Rebin asked.

'How about a hopping frog?'

'I like frogs. Will it really hop?'

'If we make it carefully.' She handed the boy a square of paper. 'Are you watching?'

Rebin nodded, his upturned nose only a couple of inches away from Heidi's nimble fingers. With supper in the Aga, Stacey and Sorrell sat at the table and watched the masterclass.

'How did you two meet Fliss?' Sorrell asked.

'We were looking for Rowan Gardiner,' Stacey said. 'He uses her address to receive post. As we couldn't find him, Heidi got in touch with Fliss and we went over for a chat.'

'And you're sure she's OK after being raided?'

'She's fine. In her own words, "a tough old boot".'

Heidi looked up from her paper folding. 'She seems to think that people smugglers were responsible for Jonathon's demise,' she said, hoping Rebin didn't know what the word meant. 'Sorrell, if you know where Rowan is you should tell us. If Fliss is right…' She didn't finish the sentence.

Sorrell nodded. 'I get it. I'm fairly sure he went back to the camps in France. That's where he said we was going last time I saw him. As you say, and if Fliss is right, France is not the place to be.'

'Mid Wales neither as it turns out,' Heidi muttered.

'Do you really have no way of contacting him?' Stacey asked.

'I know some of the other charity workers in Europe, I can try to get a message to him but no guarantees. Even if I do manage to speak to him, I'm not sure he'd return. Helping those in need is like a drug to him, more so since Jon and Kitty.' She lowered her voice. 'This business your partner is involved with, do you think it's connected?'

'Possibly,' Heidi said. She placed a finished paper frog under Rebin's nose. 'Watch,' she said, then pressed an index finger on the tail of the model and it obligingly hopped forward. Rebin laughed.

The boy collected the paper animals and lined them up on one end of the table.

'I want to show them to Daddy.' He glanced up at his mother. 'It's been ages since we saw him. I miss him soooo much.'

Sorrell ran a hand through his brown curls. 'Me too, lovely boy. I promise we'll see him soon.'

Stacey opened the oven door and removed a beautifully risen Yorkshire pudding, stuffed with chunks of locally made sausages. She placed it on the table together with roast potatoes and a dish of broccoli and carrots. While Sorrell loaded up the plates, Stacey made a jug of thick gravy.

'I'm hungry,' Rebin said. 'Give me lots.'

'Say please,' Sorrell said.

'Please.'

Chapter twenty

The incident room was empty and quiet. Elsa had clocked on early and was digging through various bank accounts and credit cards held by Natalie Turrell, CEO of A Roof 4 All. After an hour or so she got to her feet, made coffee and spent a few minutes gazing out of the window. Too much screen time induced a kind of seasickness. Finally tearing herself away from the view, she walked back to her desk the long way round, flopped on the chair and refocused her eyes on the screen.

A credit card transaction suddenly jumped out of a page of other entries. Natalie had made a payment of ten thousand pounds to a Bristol casino. Elsa leaned back in her chair and chuckled. She'd put a month's wages on the fact that her subject was a problem gambler. Widening the search she uncovered online gambling accounts which also led back to Natalie. Elsa compiled a list and began to think the money raised by remortgaging the property in Clifton had been frittered away – all of it. As far as she could see, Natalie Turrell was broke.

Elsa cleared the screen and began checking the woman's alibi for the night Haddon had been shot. *Salad Days* had indeed been performed at the Bristol Old Vic, but there was no sign Natalie had bought a ticket. It was possible someone else had paid but that would be impossible to prove. She turned her attention to the floating restaurant in the docks and again couldn't discover a booking in the subject's name. Elsa checked her watch and saw it was just before seven. Hoping the forensic accountant was already at his desk, she dialled his number. She had some new questions for him.

Half an hour later, Ben walked into the room.

'Good Lord, Constable Duffin,' he said. 'Don't you ever go home?'

'I work better when the office is empty,' Elsa said. 'Find it difficult to concentrate with everyone making a racket.'

'I can sympathise with that. What are you working on?'

'Natalie Turrell. I reckon I've found out what she spends her money on.'

'Have you?'

'Pretty sure. She's a gambler – casinos and online poker. I've calculated her losses over the last year or so and she's running at an average of around £10k a month.'

'Bloody hell, that's a lot of money. Does any of it come from the charity she runs?'

'I'm not sure yet but the forensic guy is checking. I spoke to him just before you came in and he's gonna take another look. He wondered if that's why the charity's income is down during recent years.'

'What made you look in that direction?' Ben asked.

'I spotted a large payment to a Bristol casino from Turrell's personal credit card.'

Ben raised his eyebrows. 'How did you manage that?'

'I… uh… had a few lessons… from Heidi Holtz.'

'Ah, I see. Be careful, Elsa. Heidi isn't a copper any longer. You are.'

'Yes, sir. There's another thing. Turrell's alibi. I can't verify her trip to the theatre or a late dinner at the docks. She didn't book either, but you'd think she'd buy a drink in the interval or during the meal. She didn't use her bank card at all that night' – she smiled – 'apart from buying a tank of fuel at a service station on the outskirts of Bristol.'

'You're wondering whether she bought the fuel to drive to Builth.'

'Can't prove it but it's worth considering, don't you think?'

'I do, yes. Let me know as soon as the accounts guy gets back to you.'

'I will and I'll instigate a search of ANPR. Maybe we can pick up her car on this side of the bridge.'

'You've done well, Elsa. Keep at it but make sure you knock off early tonight. Can't afford to have you off work because you've overdone things,' Ben said, 'or because you've bent the rules too far.'

'Yes, sir.'

The door to the room opened and Tegan walked in with Ollie.

'Morning, sir,' Tegan said. 'Heard you caught a bad one yesterday.'

Ben grimaced. 'Bloody awful, but with luck we'll learn something useful from the driver. We've been granted an extension so as soon as the duty solicitor arrives, Jack and I will have another crack at him. How did you get on with Felicity Savage?'

Ollie snorted. 'She wasn't much different from our first visit, other than a bit grumpier. Well pissed off about the intrusion of immigration officers and utterly convinced someone tipped them off. She referred to the complaint as malicious. Got me thinking though.'

'What about?'

'Who made the call? Must have come from someone either in the know, or with a grudge. Unlikely to be someone involved in saving souls.'

'We asked around locally,' Tegan said, 'in case anyone knew what was going on, but no one admitted knowing anything. I even called Immigration, but they refused to tell me anything other than confirm they were operating in the area. They referred to the tip-off as "a report from a member of the public".'

'Be good to know who that was,' Ben said. 'I'll see what I can find out. They might be a bit more forthcoming if I ask.'

Jack arrived as the desk phone rang. He picked it up on the way past, listened then replaced the handset.

'That was Hereford hospital,' he said. 'We have permission to interview some of the survivors from the truck.'

'That's good news,' Ben said. 'What about Dave Milton?'

'I checked with the custody sergeant on the way in. Duty solicitor can't get here until mid-afternoon.'

'That gives us plenty of time. Go grab a car, Jack. I'll meet you out front.' He looked back at his team. 'Tegan, have a word with CS Warren. I want to know who made the complaint to Immigration. Ollie, speak to SOCO. Find out if they've discovered anything useful in the truck. Jack and I will be back after lunch, we'll catch up then. If you run out of things to do, help Elsa tracking Turrell's car. She'll update you.'

'Yes, sir,' they said as he left the room.

* * *

Jack took the wheel as usual and joined the A470, heading towards Hereford. Ninety minutes later, he pulled into the hospital car park and together the detectives walked in through the main entrance. After a quick word with a woman on reception, they took the lift to the top floor and were directed to a side ward. They paused outside, took a breath, then Jack rapped gently on the door and pushed it open quietly.

A brown-skinned man was sitting next to a bed containing a woman lying beneath white, hospital sheets. Spotting the detectives, he began to stand.

'Please, don't get up,' Ben said, displaying his warrant card. 'We met a couple of days ago.'

'I remember,' the man said.

'How is your wife, sir?' Ben almost whispered.

'Better. Not healed, but better. She is sleeping.' He gently pushed a strand of hair from her forehead. 'There is a room, for families,' he said. 'We should go there.'

'Of course. Please, lead the way.'

The tall man led them a few yards along the corridor and inside a sparsely furnished but relatively clean room, with a water dispenser and a kettle. The group sat, Ben and Jack together on one sofa, the man taking a seat opposite.

'We are investigating what happened to your family, and the others,' Ben said. 'I need you to answer some questions, if you feel up to it.'

The man nodded slowly. 'I will answer.'

'Could you begin by giving us your names?'

'I am called Afran. My wife is Naza. My son…' He gulped. 'He was called Zoran. Our family name is Ahmadi. We are Afghani Kurds.' He glanced towards the door, obviously anxious to return to his wife.

'We'll do our best to be as brief as we can,' Ben said. 'Once you have been allocated somewhere to live, we'll speak again.'

'We will get a house?'

'Not right away, probably a hotel room while the local authority – the council – looks for something more permanent.'

Afran nodded, a look of acceptance or resignation on his face, Ben couldn't be sure which. What he was sure of was the crushing sadness he saw swimming in Afran's deep brown eyes.

'Can you tell me, sir, what is your wife being treated for?' Jack asked.

'Hypothermia, dehydration and very low blood sugar, so the nurses tell me.'

Jack smiled. 'Your English is very good. Do you know how long you were inside the lorry?'

'Too long. Many hours. It was very hot, the air too thick to breathe. My son was young. He was not strong and could not survive. My wife will have a sick heart for the rest of her days.'

'We are truly sorry for your loss,' Jack said. 'I have a son, about the same age as your boy.' Jack reached out and took the grieving father's hand. 'I promise to do my best to catch those responsible.'

'Thank you. Now ask your questions. I need to be with Naza.'

'Start by telling us about your journey across the Channel,' Ben said. 'How you came to be in the truck.'

Afran nodded. 'I worked for ten years as an interpreter for the British Army. Life was dangerous but I earned money and the army protected me. I meet Naza, we married, had a son then...' He seemed to run out of words.

'Then what?' Jack asked.

'The Americans and the British went home, and left us behind. We went to the airport. They would not let us through the gates.' He covered his face. 'We saw people hanging onto and falling from airplanes.' He swallowed hard.

'Were you cleared to travel?' Ben asked.

'We had the papers but couldn't give them to anyone, so we started walking. We heard boats from France would take us to the UK.'

Jack scribbled constantly.

'I know this is difficult,' Ben said, 'but it's vital. We need as much information as possible. It will help the investigation.'

'The death of my son cannot go unpunished.'

'I'm with you on that,' Jack said. 'So, did you find a boat in France?'

Afran nodded. 'It was towards evening when we left the shore, but not dark. The boat was overloaded, I knew that, but the water was calm, the weather warm, so we took the risk. We kept Zoran between us. Safe.' He smiled, just a flicker at the memory of his son. 'We crossed the sea. It took ten hours, and we were cold and frightened. On the British beach were men. They said that for more money they would take us away from the coast. Hide us. Safer inland they said. I paid a man and we got inside the truck at about five o'clock.'

'Bloody hell,' Jack said. 'You were in there for hours!'

Afran nodded again. 'It was hot, no water or proper toilet and too many people. Every hour it got worse. I tried to make everyone lie down, rest, breathe slowly, but some panicked because of the dark.' He wrapped his arms around his middle and bent over until his forehead nearly touched his knees. 'My son had asthma and struggled from the beginning. We had medicine to help him, but we dropped the inhaler and couldn't find it again. He lived a while longer after that then… he died.'

'Once again,' Ben said. 'I really am very sorry this awful thing has happened. I'll try not to keep you long so you can get back to your wife. Do you know what nationality the people who sold you places on the boat were?'

'Maybe Romanian, or somewhere else in Eastern Europe.'

'Did you see any westerners?'

'No, only in the camps. Young people, feeding us, building temporary shelters, but not with the boats.'

'OK, so when you landed, what happened then? Who met you on the beach?'

'A white, British man said he had a truck parked near the beach. We ran, climbed in, he took money, then shut the doors.'

Jack removed a photo of Dave Milton from his inside pocket and held it out. 'Was this the man, sir?' he asked.

Afran peered at the picture and shook his head. 'Not him. The man on the beach was older, fatter, shorter than me and losing his hair.'

'Did he tell you his name?'

'No, and we didn't see him again. It was a long time before the engine started; hours. When it did, we took heart to be on the move but the journey was also long. Many stops.' He turned his face to the ceiling. 'I thank God you found us before we had all died.'

Chapter twenty-one

After an early dog walk through one of the forestry plantations, and a quick paddle in the river, Rebin and the women returned to Noddfa for brunch.

Stacey was just about to drop a couple of links of pork and leek sausages into the pan when she heard a knock at the front door. She moved the pan off the hotplate and walked along the hall. Opening the door, she discovered Frederick Holtz on the step.

'Stacey!' he said. 'Good to see you. It's been a while.' He leaned forward and brushed a kiss on her cheek.

'You too,' she said. 'What are you doing here?'

'I was invited for lunch at my daughter's place in Brecon, then late last night she changed the venue to Noddfa. I hope I'm not intruding.'

'Not at all. Heidi – who didn't inform me about the change of venue – is out on the patio with a young woman called Sorrell and her son Rebin.' She smiled. 'You've timed your arrival perfectly. I'm about to cook brunch, are you hungry?'

'I can always make room for a fry-up.'

Freddie walked through the kitchen and out to the garden.

'My darling girl,' he said as he emerged into the sunshine, 'seems you forgot to tell Stacey I was coming.'

'Got a lot on my mind,' Heidi said. 'Glad you could make it though. Meet Sorrell and her little boy, Rebin.'

'Freddie,' Stacey called. 'Coffee?'

'Please.'

Stacey went back inside, put the sausages in the pan and refilled the coffee machine, while keeping an ear on what was being discussed on the patio. By the time coffee had brewed and she carried the pot outside, Heidi was telling her father about the case, from Haddon's death, the Immigration raids and finally to the recent discovery of a truckload of desperate souls.

Stacey returned to the Aga, added bacon and button mushrooms to the pan, chopped chives for the scrambled eggs, and began toasting thick slices of bread. Sorrell appeared in the doorway.

'Would you like a hand?' she asked. 'You can't go on cooking for us.'

'I enjoy it,' Stacey said, 'but you could start ferrying stuff to the garden. That would be a great help.'

A little while later, full plates were carried out of the kitchen and the meal began. Rufus sat beneath the table, nose on Rebin's knee, and Stacey saw the boy slip the odd morsel to his friend.

'This is just what I needed,' Freddie said. 'Today is turning out exceedingly well, I must say. Country drive, good company,' – he smiled across the table – 'new friends, and as always, delicious food. Where's Ben?'

'Work,' Stacey said. 'I heard Heidi tell you about the truck. He'll be dealing with that for the foreseeable I'm sure.'

'Yes, awful business' – Freddie nodded at Rebin – 'but let's not spoil this wonderful feast, we'll talk later.'

Rebin was spearing mushrooms and popping one at a time into his mouth. As he chewed he played with a paper frog, tried to get it to hop across the table. It bounced towards Freddie's plate who turned it around and hopped it back. The boy giggled.

'Did you make the frog, Rebin?' Freddie asked.

'Yes, but Heidi helped. We made flappy birds too. I'm going to keep them safe so I can show Daddy.' He shovelled scrambled egg into his mouth and simultaneously flipped the frog back. 'We haven't seen Daddy for a long time. Mummy says he's working but I don't think that's true.'

'Don't you? Why not?'

'Well…' Rebin said. 'We have a friend called Rowan and one night I was looking out the window. I like stars.' Rebin cut a piece of sausage and peered at it. 'I saw Daddy get in Rowan's van and I heard Rowan say he would hide Daddy.' Rebin dropped the sausage and Rufus snapped it up. 'I think Daddy is a spy. When we used to go to see him, Mummy said we had to make sure no one was following our car.'

Freddie smiled.

'I can see you're being very brave and taking good care of your mother. Your father will be proud of you. You know, I might be able to help.'

'Really? How?'

'Can't make any promises but I work in London and I'm pretty sure that's where most spies work. When I get back to my office, I'll see if I can find him for you.'

'Thank you, soooo much.'

'Be warned though, if he's on a mission it might take a little while so you will have to be very patient.'

Meal over, Freddie insisted on washing up, while Heidi and Stacey dried and put away. Sorrell stayed in the garden and kept an eye on her son.

'That's quite a story Sorrell told,' Freddie said, swirling plates in foaming water. 'If what she says is true, there must have been some mistakes made with her husband's asylum claim. I have a friend in the Home Office. I'll ask her to have a rootle around, see what she can turn up.'

'What about the other stuff?' Heidi asked. 'Haddon and Rowan working as a two-man undercover team and passing info to your lot in Whitehall?'

'That will entail more asking around. Discovering the right person to speak to will be the first challenge, but I will do my very best.'

'You always do, Pa. Thanks.'

* * *

At the end of the day the team gathered in the incident room and settled at the table. Ben stood at its head beneath the board displaying details of the growing investigation.

'Here's where we're at,' he said. 'After consideration, the discovery of the truck containing refugees is officially being linked to the deaths of Jonathon Haddon and Kitty Phillips. I am liaising with CS Warren who has oversight of the case. At this point, we are not handing it to the NCA.'

He glanced around the room and saw heads nodding in agreement.

'Afran Ahmadi, a survivor from the truck, told us the people who made it across the channel were met on the beach at Dover by a group of white men. One individual, who took money from the refugees before shutting them inside the vehicle, Afran described as around 5'6", middle-aged, overweight and beginning to lose his hair. We showed him a picture of the guy we have banged up downstairs and he didn't recognise him.'

'What's happening with Milton, sir?' Tegan asked.

'The duty solicitor advised him to give a no comment interview and that's exactly what he did. No matter, we have enough for several charges including manslaughter. You and Ollie are taking him to court in the morning. Not a hope he'll get bail.'

'Good,' Tegan said.

'When you're back from court,' Ben said, 'paperwork. Find me connections to the main players. There must be some. Next up, Elsa has made great strides investigating Natalie Turrell. It looks likely that Turrell has a gambling problem – lots of money draining away from her accounts and credit cards. Added to that, her alibi can't be verified.' He glanced at his constable. 'Any luck with ANPR?'

'Not yet, sir,' Elsa said. 'Still looking.'

'OK. As of now' – Ben looked around the room – 'Turrell is a person of interest. Kevin, I want you to work with Elsa. Draw up the necessary digital search warrants and specifically look for any contact with Jonathon Haddon outside their professional relationship.'

'Yes, sir.'

Ben sipped from his mug. 'I am fairly convinced that Felicity Savage has a part in this, not least because of her link to Rowan Gardiner, brother of Kitty and friend of Haddon. I do not understand why we haven't picked up Rowan's vehicle. Not a sign of it anywhere and it's imperative we speak to him.'

Elsa snorted. 'Should have thought about it before,' she said. 'I bet he went back to France and that's why the cameras on this side of the Channel haven't nabbed him. I'll check all border crossings.'

Ben rubbed his face and groaned. 'We need to make faster progress on this.'

'I'll dig into the history of the vehicle used to transport the poor sods to Mid Wales,' Kevin said. 'Older van, multiple registered keepers…' He shrugged. 'Might turn something up.'

'OK, good idea,' Ben said. He glanced at the clock above the incident board and saw it was approaching seven o'clock. 'Twelve hours is enough, troops. Go home, all of you. Rest, eat and be back in here at seven tomorrow.' He looked at Elsa. 'Not before, Constable, you're turning a nasty shade of grey.'

'Yes, sir.'

Ben turned away and put his jacket on.

'What will we be doing, guv?' Jack asked.

'Coming up with good ideas overnight and acting on them in the morning – hopefully. See you tomorrow, Sergeant.'

Ben patted Jack on the shoulder, walked downstairs to his car, started the engine and began the drive towards the Epynt Mountain and Noddfa.

* * *

The weather was changing. Grey, heavy-looking clouds jostled for position above the ranges and the air felt wet as a rare humidity settled on the hills. Ben drove slowly through the narrow lanes and as he pulled up outside the cottage, he heard the distant grumble of thunder and fat raindrops began to patter on the roof of his car. He grabbed his jacket, together with a bundle of files from the back seat, and nipped up the front path to the door. Slipping his key into the lock, he was surprised to hear a dog barking in the hall. He cracked open the door and heard Heidi yell from the kitchen.

'Rufus! Shut up!'

Ben opened the door a little wider and saw a black mongrel skitter over the flagstones in the direction of the kitchen.

'Evening, Heidi,' he said. 'Have you bought a dog?'

'Not likely. Why would I want a dog? Stacey has a couple of houseguests. The mutt belongs to them. Let's step into the living room briefly and I can update you.'

'Now I'm curious,' Ben said and did what Heidi suggested.

A short while passed before they entered the kitchen. Sorrell looked as though she wanted to bolt, but Rebin marched straight up to Ben.

'Hello,' the boy said. 'I'm called Rebin and my mummy is Sorrell. Are you Stacey's boyfriend?'

Ben smiled. 'I'm fairly sure I'm too old to be called a *boy*friend, but I do live here with Stacey. My name is Ben.'

'You weren't here last night. Were you at work? Are you a spy? My daddy's a spy and a man from London is going to look for him.'

Sorrell stretched out a hand and gently pulled Rebin towards her. 'Shush now, sweetheart,' she said. 'Remember how we have to be quiet while we're staying here?'

Stacey left the Aga, gave Ben a quick hug and plonked a kiss on his cheek.

'Missed you, Sherlock. Are you OK after yesterday?'

'Holding up and I missed you too.' Ben delivered a kiss of his own.

'Supper soon, shepherd's pie.'

'Sounds perfect.'

Heidi poured a stiff measure of whisky and pushed it across the table.

'Looks like you could do with that,' she said. 'Bad business.'

'How did you hear about it?' Ben asked.

'Don't be daft,' Heidi said on her way to the larder in search of wine. 'Let's concentrate on a bit of R and R for you. We'll discuss it later.'

After they'd eaten, Sorrell carried her son up to the spare room, tucked him in and walked back downstairs.

'Heidi's told me what's happening with you, Sorrell,' Ben said. 'I'm sorry things aren't great at the moment.'

Sorrell shrugged. 'Shit happens.' She sipped from her glass. 'You'd think I'd be getting used to it by now, that was our third visit.'

'Stuff like that never gets any easier. I hear Freddie Holtz is on the case.'

'Yes, he said he'd ask around. Kind of him.'

Ben smiled. 'Well, if you've got Heidi and her father on your side I'm sure things will improve.'

'I'm very grateful to all of you.'

Stacey poured more wine and sat at the table. 'So,' she said, 'what's happening to the guy you nicked who was driving the truck?'

'Court in the morning,' Ben said. 'Benefit fraud, driving under the influence and multiple counts of manslaughter. He'll be banged up in Cardiff jail by teatime.'

'I'd better turn up for the hearing this time,' Stacey said. 'Sam's been grumbling, called me a slacker.'

Heidi snorted. 'And you're bothered?'

Stacey shook her head. 'Not much, I can handle Sam. How are the survivors doing, Ben? Do you think there's a chance any of them would talk to me?'

Ben sighed heavily. 'Maybe – I'll have a word.'

'That'll be great, thanks.'

Ben yawned. 'It's no good, ladies. I'm shattered and have another early start in the morning, so I'll go on up and will try my very best not to wake anyone when I leave for work.' He got to his feet, plonked a kiss on top of Stacey's head and headed upstairs.

Chapter twenty-two

Soon after Ben left Noddfa the next morning, Stacey also got up, crept downstairs, made coffee and carried it to her office. She switched on the computer and gazed out of the window above her desk as it booted up. Yesterday's thunderstorms had moved on and the sun was out. Droplets of water still clung to the leaves of the bamboo, light filling them with rainbows. The resident sparrows, feathers fluttering, landed on the graceful nodding stems and the raindrops finally made it to earth.

Stacey opened a file Heidi had compiled the evening before, using images gathered from social media. Bystanders who witnessed the discovery of the refugees had captured the event on their smartphones and posted them on the internet. Stacey scrolled through the pictures and watched short snatches of video.

One picture caught her attention. It showed a refrigerated truck parked behind the Cooper's Arms. At the rear of the vehicle were two men. She recognised the older man as Kevin Biggs, a copper from the station, and guessed that his companion – younger, black vest, tattoos and jeans – was the driver, just about to drag open the doors. She leaned back in her chair, pleased she hadn't missed the shot. Now she knew who she'd be looking for when she arrived at court.

Heidi, barefoot and dressed in an oversized rugby shirt, appeared in the doorway. 'Hi,' she said, 'you're up early.'

'I was checking out those photos you put together.' Stacey pointed at the screen. 'See the driver? Where did this footage come from?'

'CCTV camera on the back of the pub.' Heidi stretched. 'Thought you'd like that. Now you can report the whole incident even though you weren't actually there. That'll shut your editor up.'

'Hopefully. What are you planning to do today?'

'Need to go home. I miss Erica and would like to be there when she gets up today. Cook her a meal and enjoy some time together.'

'Things are OK between the two of you aren't they?'

'Of course. Why would you think they aren't? Getting married is one of the best things I've done so far.'

'Just asking. I wonder, would you mind staying here until I get back from court to keep Sorrell company? Dave Milton's bound to be first up so I should be back before one.'

'No problem. I'll sit on the patio and work on my tan.'

'Make sure you don't burn.'

'I'm not an idiot,' Heidi huffed and went upstairs to get dressed.

* * *

After a couple of hours wading through the mountain of paperwork the current investigation had generated, Ben was thankful for the distraction when Chief Superintendent Warren pushed open the door of the incident room. He got to his feet.

'Morning, ma'am,' he said.

'Morning, Ben. Good to see you and your team are putting the hours in. Any progress?'

'Not as much as I'd like. The discovery of the truck has added a new dimension. We have the driver at least. He's in court this morning and bound to be remanded. I'll give him a couple of days before I tackle him again. Time in HMP Cardiff may encourage him to be a little more talkative.'

'We can but hope. Don't forget, if you need more staff, I should be able to arrange a couple of uniforms.' She placed a hand on the pile of paper. 'They could help with the grunt work.'

'Thank you, ma'am. I think we're OK for now. As you've seen, I have a good hardworking team.'

The senior officer nodded, grey bob bouncing. 'As you know I'm keeping NCA away, but that can only last for so long.'

'I understand and I'm grateful.'

'As we discussed, I put in a call to Immigration and they've given me the name of their informant. One Raymond Gardiner.'

'Bloody hell. The father of one of the victims, Kitty Phillips.'

'Gardiner's information resulted in two raids. One at the home of Felicity Savage, the other at a property near Aberglasney, home of Sorrell and Rebin Moradi.'

'I met Sorrell recently,' Ben said without adding details. 'I wonder how Gardiner knew about her.'

CS Warren chuckled, a deep throaty sound. 'I'm sure you and DS Trent will discover the connection when you speak to the man.' She stepped closer and lowered her voice. 'I must say, I am very impressed with Constable Duffin. Her updates are concise and her investigative skills impressive. Keep an eye on her, Ben. Detective material if ever I saw it.'

'I will, ma'am, thanks.'

'Right,' she said, 'must get on, but don't forget, if you need anything, you know where I am. Any developments make sure I'm informed.'

'Of course, ma'am.'

After the chief super left the room, Ben shrugged into his jacket.

'Did you catch all that, Jack?'

'Yes, guv. Let's get over to the Gardiners' and lean on Raymond. I always knew there was something off there.'

Jack left in search of a car. Ben walked across the room and stood next to Elsa.

'Any new revelations, Constable?'

Elsa looked up at her boss and grinned. 'Yes, sir. Just received confirmation Natalie Turrell's vehicle crossed the Prince of Wales Bridge a little before midnight the night Haddon was shot.'

'Any sign of its destination?'

'Motorway to Swansea but no sightings after that. Not so many cameras in the sticks but her car was definitely in Wales that night.'

'Anything from your friendly accountant?'

'He's calling in after lunch to talk me through what he's discovered.'

'Excellent. You and Kevin keep on with the paperwork. I can't see that we'll be that long.'

Elsa nodded and turned back to the screen. Ben left the room and ran downstairs to the car park where he found Jack waiting for him in a dark blue Mondeo. Ben got into the passenger seat, Jack started the engine and set off towards Bwlch and Llangorse Lake. As usual, Jack drove with a heavy foot and less than an hour later pulled up next to the verge outside the Gardiners' place. He turned off the engine and glanced at his boss.

'How do you want to play this, guv?'

'Start gently. Depending on how the conversation pans out, that might change. We mustn't forget Gardiner has lost his daughter in distressing circumstances and his son is missing.'

Jack nodded. The detectives left the car, walked through the garden packed with flowering bedding plants, and rang the bell.

* * *

The brief court appearance of David Milton was short and disappointing. Ollie and Tegan had obviously delivered him early so Stacey wasn't able to snatch a photo as he was being escorted inside the building. She'd watched the young man carefully as he stood in the dock and stated he was innocent of all charges against him. As Ben had predicted, Milton was remanded and as soon as he'd been removed from the courtroom, Stacey slipped out. She took the opportunity and walked through Brecon towards the offices of *The Mid Wales Times.*

Reaching reception, she nipped through the foyer and ran upstairs to the editor's lair at the top of the old building. His door stood open, and Stacey saw him hunched over his desk. Sam looked up and frowned.

'Well, well,' he said, 'made it to court then?'

Stacey dropped on the visitor's chair. 'Said I would. As soon as I get home I'll knock up a piece and send it through. Not much to say really – Milton went not guilty and was remanded.'

'So do you have anything for me?'

'Honestly, Sam, life isn't all about work you know. How are you getting on clearing up after your house was flooded?'

Sam groaned. 'The wife's sister has extended her stay and has convinced Mrs Jenkins nothing but a new kitchen will do.' He rubbed his eyes. 'Good job the insurance is picking up a good portion of the bill. Now do you have anything or not?'

Stacey smiled. 'A big story, but much more work needed.' She dropped a flash drive under Sam's nose. 'There are some disturbing pictures on there – not sure the paper can print many of them. They show the truck which was being used to move refugees. As you know, the driver was the guy in court.'

'I'll take a look. When do I get words to go with them?'

'Soon, but I'm sure this event has something to do with the shooting of Jonathon Haddon.'

'That's quite a leap, but I guess I can see where you're coming from. Too much of a coincidence for two such awful crimes to happen in Powys within days.'

'Exactly! I just can't spot the link. The police seem to be struggling as well.' Stacey got to her feet. 'Sorry, boss, can't hang about, I've got guests. Popped in to drop off those photos and make sure you know how hard I'm working for you.'

'Yeah, I get it. You've never disappointed in the past, it's why I keep you on.'

'Bloody hell. Thanks – I think. What brought that on?'

Sam grinned. 'I can be nice. Get the article to me by five and I'll have a look through.'

Sam rammed his glasses on the end of his nose and turned his attention back to the mound of correspondence. Stacey took the hint, left the office and collected her car from the edge of town.

Twenty minutes later she turned onto the range road, crawled up the hill from Llywel and wound down her window. The sky and air were clear, she slowed and gazed at the wild land stretching as far as the Beacons. Sheep and their growing lambs wandered about on the warm tarmac, while kites and buzzards swirled lazily in the thermals, sun catching their feathers as if lit from inside. She pulled over to allow a long army convoy to pass and thought about the refugees in the truck – what they would have given for a breath of mountain air.

Chapter twenty-three

Raymond Gardiner frowned as he opened his door and saw the detectives on the front step.

He nodded. 'Gentlemen, I hope you have some news for us.'

'Better to talk inside, sir,' Jack said.

Gardiner opened the door wider. 'We're in the sunroom at the back of the house. Down the hall and keep on through the kitchen.'

'Thank you, sir,' Ben said.

He followed the directions and found himself inside a bright and airy room; a stunning vista of the lake stretched away in front of him. Geraldine was sitting on a cane sofa upholstered in a bold, flowery print, a glass of orange juice resting on a side table.

'Good morning, Mrs Gardiner,' Ben said and took a seat on her right.

Jack perched on a second, two-seater sofa, Ray on the remaining vacant chair.

'Would you like some tea,' he asked.

'No thanks,' Ben said. 'We'd like a chat about some phone calls you made recently.'

'Phone calls you say? Who am I supposed to have called?'

'Immigration Enforcement, two separate calls.'

Raymond didn't seemed concerned and readily admitted he had contacted the agency.

'I was doing my civic duty,' the man blustered. 'The lines are there to gather information the authorities use to carry out their jobs. The police, DWP and the tax office all have phone lines. I can't see the problem. As I said, I was doing my duty so I don't really understand why you are quizzing me about those calls.'

Geraldine placed a hand on her husband's forearm.

'Ray, take a breath. Don't get so worked up. You know it isn't good for you.'

He pushed her hand away and glared at the officers. 'I don't see how this has anything to do with the matter in hand, namely my murdered daughter and my absent son.'

'You really should calm yourself, sir,' Jack said. 'We just want to ask about the content of those calls and why you made them.'

Raymond huffed loudly. 'I told you, to report law-breaking.'

'What sort of law-breaking?'

'I provided details of two properties where I believed illegals were living.'

'Can you give us those addresses?'

'I don't know the actual addresses and postcodes so I told the call handler where the properties were situated.'

'Care to enlighten us?' Jack asked, pen poised above his notebook.

Raymond sighed heavily.

'Would someone please tell me what this is all about?' Geraldine asked. She glanced at her husband. 'Why didn't you tell me you'd made calls to those people?'

'Those people?' Raymond snapped. 'You mean enforcement officers who uphold the law.'

Geraldine returned her gaze to the floor and removed a tissue from her sleeve.

'Tell me where the properties are,' Jack persisted, 'and the names of the residents.'

'I was assured my reports would be confidential.'

'We're investigating a series of serious crimes, not least the death of your own daughter. If you don't start talking, I'll nick you for obstruction and we'll continue this conversation at the station.'

Raymond glanced at Ben who said, 'He means it.'

'No wonder you lot attract such a bad press these days...' Raymond said. 'OK. Felicity Savage, she lives in a large house near Abergavenny, and Sorrell Moradi. She has a smallholding a mile or so from Aberglasney Gardens.'

'Why did you suspect these women were hiding illegal immigrants?' Ben asked while Jack scribbled more notes.

'It was a pretty safe bet. Rowan visited Fliss regularly to collect his post and was previously convicted of smuggling an illegal migrant into the country. Kitty joined the crazy venture and – in part because of Fliss – I am missing both my children.'

'You called her Fliss,' Ben said. 'Do you know Miss Savage?'

'Oh, yes, I know her. We go way back. Just before the start of the war my great aunt and uncle took her in with another girl.'

'Doesn't sound as though you were close,' Jack said.

'Of course we weren't close,' Raymond spluttered. 'We were at war with Germany, and they were German.' He made a rude sound. 'They weren't even family but the farm was left to them. Blood is thicker than water – or should be.'

'By rights,' Geraldine said, 'Ray's father was next in line for the farm as his aunt and uncle had no children of their own. He didn't take it very well.'

'No one would,' Raymond said, 'and I was right not to trust that old witch. She stole our children from us, brainwashed them; her and Jonathon Haddon. He's as guilty of that as she is.'

Jack raised his eyebrows. 'Where were you the night he was killed?'

Raymond laughed nastily. 'So now you think I was somehow responsible for the death of my own daughter? Well, you're barking up the wrong tree and I have to say, I don't appreciate your tone.'

'How does Sorrell fit in?' Ben asked.

Raymond blinked, he hadn't expected the change in direction. 'She came here once before Rowan left home,' he mumbled. 'Brought her family with her, a mixed-race boy and an Asian-looking man she described as her husband. I could tell he didn't belong here, so I rang Immigration.' He lowered his head. 'I hoped if they searched her house, they would find Rowan.'

'Surely,' Ben said, 'if you're related to Felicity, you could have phoned her directly and asked if she knew where your son is?'

'I told you, we had no contact.'

'You should have called her,' Geraldine said, 'not reported her. Surely it's time to bury the hatchet? Rowan could be in danger and I'm so afraid for him. I cannot lose another child. It would kill me.'

'Oh, for goodness sake! He'll be in France hanging around with all those useless hippy do-gooders, wasting his life.'

'Shut up!' Geraldine snapped. 'You never listened to a word our children said did you? Too wrapped up in the ancient feud with Fliss to even notice them most of the time. All you do is moon around playing hard done by and I'm sick of it.' She took a deep breath. 'If you *had* involved yourself with their lives, taken an interest… well, part of this mess is your fault. You've been a terrible father and a crap husband.' She got to her feet. 'I've had enough of this. Help the police, Ray. Help them to find Rowan. I don't want to speak to you again until I know my son is safe.' She glanced at the detectives. 'I'm sorry, but I can't stay in the same room as him.'

Geraldine picked up her cardigan from the back of the sofa and stalked out of the sunroom, leaving an uncomfortable silence behind her. Ben and Jack shared a look.

Jack turned a page in his notebook and asked, 'OK then, Mr Gardiner, we'll crack on. Do you know if Rowan volunteered at a specific camp in France?'

* * *

After Heidi had left to spend some time with Erica, Stacey took her guests to a different stretch of the river further away from the village. The afternoon sun was hot but next to the water, where it threaded its way through a thick stand of conifers, the air was cooler. Rufus splashed in and out of the pools, leaping back onto the bank to shake vigorously, Rebin squealing with delight. Stacey walked on until the group reached a lazy bend in the river, its banks thick with brambles, ferns and wild raspberry canes. Pushing her way through a thick patch of valerian and creeping buttercups, she emerged on a wide, pebbly beach, a fallen trunk a perfectly placed seat for a view of the river.

'This is just beautiful,' Sorrell said. 'Did you put the log here?'

Stacey laughed. 'No way, that probably weighs at least a ton. Nature created this little patch of heaven without any help from me.'

She sat on the moss-covered seat and Sorrell perched next to her.

'I know Rebin loves his pond,' Sorrell said, 'but my favourite is running water, seems more alive somehow.' She took a deep breath. 'Bilal would adore this place.'

'You'll all have to visit, when you're back together again.'

'I'm beginning to doubt that will ever happen.' Sorrell wiped her eyes. 'We were so sure at the start that all would be well. All those months, all those shitty forms and interviews, what a waste of time.'

'Don't,' Stacey said. 'Don't undo the good we've done, and don't give up hope.'

Sorrell nodded and smiled as Rebin joined his dog, swimming in one of the deeper pools, splashing and laughing as brightly coloured salmon fry zipped past his nose. She picked up a shard of blue and white pottery, a sign of long dead generations of hill farmers, and asked, 'Did you ever manage to catch up with Bilbo?'

'Unfortunately not. Heidi and I spent a day in Cardiff a while back and came close to tracking him down but got called away. Leo Phillips smacked Ben in the face and broke his nose.'

'Rowan wasn't keen on Leo. He told me once that he tried to talk his sister out of marrying him.'

'Do you know why?'

'I'm not entirely sure but the man was always a bit quick with his fists. Rowan can't stand violence of any sort.'

'No news about him from your mates in France?'

'Not so far. Most of the folk I know are in Calais, but there are many camps.' Sorrell removed her boots and socks and crept carefully over the sharp stones towards the water. She glanced back over her shoulder. 'How about we go to Cardiff in the next day or two? I'm sure it would be useful for you to talk to Bilbo about what he does – for your article. I have a load of stuff to take to him and really ought to make sure the chicken sitter is still happy to look after my flock.'

'Great idea. I'd definitely be up for that. It's a date.'

Chapter twenty-four

Jack started the car and pulled away from Gardiner's house. Ben put his head in his hands and groaned.

'Bloody hell, Jack, this is such an awful mess. Why on earth didn't that man tell us about his connection with Felicity Savage? And all that shit about her "being dead to him".'

'I feel sorry for his family,' Jack said. 'His poor wife.'

Ben nodded. 'Give me a straight answer,' he said. 'Do you think Raymond shot Jonathon Haddon?'

Jack's forehead creased in a deep frown. 'I can't, guv, but I suppose it's possible. A case could be made.' He pulled up at the junction, indicated right and checked the traffic.

'Turn left,' Ben said.

Jack didn't question his boss but checked his rear-view mirror and changed direction.

'Go on then,' Ben said. 'Make the case.'

'OK, how about this. No love lost between Raymond and Haddon, that was obvious. He also mentioned that in his opinion Felicity had stolen his children. Contacting Immigration was an act of revenge, maybe so was killing his son's best friend.'

'Not sure that works. His daughter also died.'

'Carrie Salmon was sure Kitty's death was an accident. She thought if the killer had known Kitty was in the showroom, she would have been shot too. Raymond didn't see her and believed she was miles away in Cardiff.'

'Hmm.'

'Where are we headed, guv?'

'Felicity Savage's place.'

Jack nodded and stayed on the A40 towards Abergavenny.

'How would Raymond know Haddon was in the showroom?' Ben asked.

'Maybe he rang him at the Caer Beris and arranged the meet.'

'Still can't make it work. The place was locked up tight according to the manager. Haddon got in using Kitty's keys and her father thought she was in Cardiff.' Ben punched the dashboard and made Jack jump. 'I'm clutching at straws. We've got nothing but dead bodies.'

'I reckon,' Jack said, 'we need to put pressure on the main players, give them a shake and see what drops out. Nick them and interview them under caution, at the station. People like Raymond and Leo Phillips often crumble if they think they're being ganged up on.'

'Yeah, it sometimes works like that. Who else would be on your list?'

'Natalie Turrell obviously. If Elsa can turn up something useful in the accounts, it'll be a righteous nicking.' Jack chuckled. 'Ms Turrell won't like seeing the inside of a cell.'

'OK, I agree. It's a fair plan. We'll get on with it tomorrow. The list should also include Watson and Willis. Interview them simultaneously, that way they can't confer–'

'And we can have some fun.'

Ben smiled. 'Take the next left, Sergeant.'

* * *

Ben arrived at Noddfa soon after six and brought a fish and chip supper with him from the pub in Llanwrtyd. With the weather being so hot, he wanted to keep Stacey away from the Aga. The group ate from the paper outside on the patio.

'So,' Ben said, 'I'm guessing you all had a good day.'

'We had a fab day,' Sorrell said. 'I love my place, but Stacey's mountain is just so quiet and incredibly beautiful. No traffic noise at all.'

'How have you got on today?' Stacey asked.

As Ben scrunched his food wrapper into a greasy ball, he told Stacey how he and Jack had visited the Gardiners and called in on Felicity Savage.

'Raymond Gardiner made the calls to Immigration?' Sorrell asked, voice full of anger. 'God, he's a piece of work. I met him once and can't say I was impressed.'

'How was Fliss?' Stacey asked.

'Real character, isn't she?' Ben said. 'She gave us tea and was more than happy to chat about her past, not so forthcoming about the present.' He chuckled. 'When I asked why she hadn't told us that she was distantly related to Rowan she said it was because we didn't ask.'

The landline rang. Stacey went inside the cottage and picked up the handset.

'Hello. Stacey Logan.'

'It's me,' Heidi said.

'Hi. Did you manage some quality time with Erica?'

'Yeah, it was nice. Have you got anything on tomorrow?'

'Nothing so far. Why?'

'I've been chatting to my dad and he's passed on a snippet of information relating to smuggling gangs. Wondered if you fancied following up on it with me in the morning.'

'I'd be up for that. Where are we going?'

'I'll fill you in tomorrow. Pick you up at nine. Make sure you're ready.'

As always, as soon as Heidi had said what was needed she hung up. Stacey put down the phone and returned to the sunny patio.

'Sorrell,' she said, 'I have to go out tomorrow, Heidi's on a mission. Will you and Rebin be OK here on your own? I'll leave a key so you don't have to hang around all day.'

'We'll be fine. Might pop over to my place, make sure the chicken sitter is happy to do a few more shifts. I'll pick up the stuff I've got for Bilbo, cut down on the travelling when we go to visit him.'

Ben nodded. 'I think Stacey mentioned Bilbo.' He turned to his partner. 'Where are you going tomorrow?'

Stacey shrugged. 'Heidi was vague as usual.'

'Just make sure you don't get into anything risky. I'll say it again, this is a dangerous business and I really don't want it to end in tears.'

* * *

The next morning, Heidi arrived outside Noddfa bang on time and spotted Stacey sitting on the low wall outside her cottage.

'I've set up a meeting,' Heidi said as she pulled away, 'in Reading.'

'Reading? Who are we meeting?' Stacey asked.

'A man who knows a man.'

'That makes it clear then.'

'Look,' Heidi said, 'I'll be honest, this could be a bit dodgy. You can bail anytime you like and don't need to be involved.'

'OK, so stop the car.'

'What?'

'Stop the car. If you don't tell me immediately what's going on, I'll bail now.'

Heidi sighed but pulled into a gateway. 'Pa heard a whisper about a possible criminal network operating in the UK, with links to France, Belgium and Iraq. People smugglers.'

'Iraq?'

'That's sometimes where refugees pay for their trip. The money is held – or the debt if they can't pay – and not released to others in the line until their customers reach the UK. The individuals who haven't paid become indentured workers – slaves in other words.'

'So who exactly are we meeting in Reading?'

'I don't have a name, just a location. Someone who's up for earning a few extra quid in exchange for information.'

'Shit.' Stacey rubbed her face. 'This doesn't sound dodgy. It sounds downright dangerous. Does Freddie know you're intending to do this?'

Heidi shrugged. 'I guess, he gave me the info after all.'

'Did he mention Bilal?'

'One thing at once, OK? We need to concentrate on today. So… are you with me or against me?'

'I want to say I'm with you, but I'm not sure I'm brave enough.'

Heidi put the vehicle in gear and pulled back onto the lane. 'Let's see how we go then shall we? Remember, you can bail at any point. There's something else.'

'Oh? What?'

'Tuck your cameras out of sight and don't try to sneak one in with you. I'm pretty certain we'll be searched.'

'Really?'

Heidi nodded.

The journey along the M4, east towards Reading was uneventful. There were a few hold-ups, but as each mile rumbled beneath the tyres, Stacey's anxiety notched up, even though Heidi had told her she was sure they'd be safe. The man they were going to meet had been told that Stacey was an author who was writing a book concerning the migration of people and seemed pleased for the opportunity to give his side of the story. Stacey wasn't sure, not in the slightest. If the man was involved with sending refugees across the Channel in unsafe boats, he was bound to be a hard bastard and they were always dangerous.

'How much further?' she asked.

'Satnav says twenty-five minutes. How are you feeling?'

'Not great. I'm wondering if guns might be involved. Since my brush with Alice Fox, when she nearly blew my head off with a shotgun, I'm not keen.'

'Understandable. I'm sure he won't have a gun but agree his minders might.'

'You're doing a really crap job at selling this to me.'

'You can wait elsewhere if you like and if I'm not back in an hour, you wave the red flag and contact my dad.'

Stacey thought for a minute. 'I'm not sure how much use I'll be, but think I need to be with you.'

'Make your mind up time, sister,' Heidi said.

Stacey hesitated then said, 'With you.'

Heidi smiled, and a few miles later, turned onto a large industrial estate.

'Keep your eyes open for unit thirty-nine,' she said, 'somewhere at the rear of the plot. Nothing on you? No sneaky spy cameras?'

'Nothing.'

Heidi drove into the car park, spun the truck one hundred and eighty degrees, then reversed, back bumper against the wall of a block building, the bonnet lined up with the exit. An advantage if they needed to make a swift getaway.

They left the vehicle and walked towards a scruffy, olive-coloured door, set in the wall next to a large, metal shutter. The moment Heidi raised her fist and hammered on the door, Stacey knew she had left it too late to back out, and she took a couple of deep, steadying breaths.

The door opened and a man's face appeared. He looked them up and down suspiciously before waving them in. Two more men were waiting inside, both dressed in dark clothes, wearing black boots and sunglasses, hardly appropriate in the low light. One sported a thick, gold ring in his ear. They both had handguns, tucked in the waistbands of their trousers, grips in plain sight, like a warning. Stacey swallowed and concentrated on keeping her breath steady. One was small and wiry, like a fox, the other very large, tall, with a broad chest and long arms. The smaller man looked Middle Eastern, the giant was white British.

The small man stepped forward. 'We need to search you.'

Stacey held out her arms and gritted her teeth as he ran his hands over her body and forced them into the pockets of her jeans, and tried not to shudder. She watched as he conducted an identical search of Heidi, who – Stacey could tell – was doing her best not to headbutt the little man.

'They're clean,' he said. 'Take them in.'

The large man nodded, put a hand on both women's shoulders and marched them towards a door at the back of the unit. He knocked, opened the door and pushed them inside.

'Visitors, boss.'

A dark-skinned man sat behind a scruffy metal desk. Two more unfriendly-looking types stood behind his chair. The giant nudged the women towards a pair of seats facing the desk. Stacey hadn't expected so much security and worked hard at not looking intimidated. Heidi had made it seem like they were meeting an informant, but this guy was definitely in charge.

'Thank you for agreeing to talk to us,' Heidi said.

The man laughed. 'Money is always an incentive and of course the promise of your confidentiality. Be sure you don't betray my trust.' He turned his attention to Stacey. 'I'm told you are a writer. Maybe I have read one of your books?'

Stacey concentrated on producing something akin to a smile. 'Unlikely,' she said, 'unless you're academically interested in the migration habits of *Homo sapiens*.'

'I'm an expert in migration. It's what I do.' He chuckled again. 'I don't need to read a book about it.'

'I've been told you would be happy to answer some questions?'

'That's correct, but first the fee.'

Heidi rummaged in her jacket and handed over an envelope, which he slipped into a drawer.

'Ask away then, *writer*.'

Stacey nodded and took a breath. 'Can you tell me how many refugees you have sent across the Channel in the last two weeks?'

'None last week, the weather was bad. The week before, two hundred and ninety passengers.'

'Why do you do this? Smuggle people.'

'If I don't, others will. Many people wish to come to UK. They believe they will be safe and nearly all can speak your language. They don't know French, or German.' He laughed. 'They think the English will be friendly, welcoming.'

'There are legal routes. They could apply in a third country. There are government processing centres.'

The man snorted loudly. 'Nothing of that works. The British government do not want migrants and make the process purposely difficult.'

'What happens when they arrive on the British coast? Assuming they haven't been spotted.'

'They are moved inland.' He grinned. 'Scattered like grass seeds on the wind.'

'Some operators don't offer life-vests to save on costs and increase profits. Is that what you do?'

He shrugged. 'If I have vests, I offer vests, but I am not concerned. People do not refuse to get in a boat if they don't have a vest.'

Stacey paused, constructing the next question in her head. 'It has been said that people like you charge migrants five thousand pounds for a place. If you did transport two hundred and ninety in the last couple of weeks, you have netted well over a million.'

He laughed. 'The money is not mine alone, many people must be paid from funds I collect.'

'Do you believe you are helping people?'

'Of course. They want to live in the UK. It is as difficult to stop them leaving Europe as it is to prevent swallows leaving Africa.' He laughed again and spread his arms wide. 'All want to live in UK.'

'I want to ask about the children,' Heidi said. 'In recent months, thirty-two people died when one of the boats took on water and sank. Five of the dead were children. Does that upset you?'

The man glared at her and got to his feet.

'This is enough,' he snapped. 'I answer no more. You can leave now, but don't forget to keep your word. I will hold you to your promise. Break it and you will pay a heavy price. Now – go!'

The women got to their feet and without looking back left the office. They were returned to the main door of the unit and ejected by the minders. Heidi stomped to the truck and unlocked the doors, they got in and she pulled out of the car park.

She looked at Stacey and grinned. 'That went better than I thought it would. You OK?'

'Better now I'm not in that office. Put your foot down and get us away from those terrible people.'

'My pleasure,' Heidi said and headed for the M4.

'I know I can't report the location, or anything about the individuals at that meeting,' Stacey said, 'but shouldn't we tell someone those guys are there?'

'Very little point, they won't be there for long. Anyway, making and then breaking promises given to gangsters is an incredibly bad idea.'

'They can't be allowed to keep on doing this.'

'They won't. Remember where the tip-off came from. That crew is already being watched I'm sure.'

'I hope you're right.'

'I'm always right. Now let's get back to yours, I'm bloody starving.'

Chapter twenty-five

Ben had made the decision that the first of the main players to be interviewed under caution would be Natalie Turrell and Raymond Gardiner. Watson and Willis could wait, and Leo Phillips wasn't going anywhere until he had completed his prison sentence. Two uniformed officers were sent to Bwlch to arrest Gardiner, while Ollie and Tegan made the trip to Bristol. As Ben waited for the first of his interviewees to arrive, he listened carefully as Elsa talked him through what the forensic accountant had managed to glean from Turrell's financial records.

'Like I said, sir, she has a gambling problem – big time. Debts all over the place and no sign of the cash she raised remortgaging her place.'

'Any concrete evidence she's been fleecing R4A?'

'Many misdemeanours. I told you about the juggling of bills, well, she claims for just about everything, not just loading debits under the heading of entertaining.'

'So you mean vehicle costs, travelling expenses, that sort of thing?'

Elsa nodded and grinned. 'And her clothes, shoes, holidays listed as "research" – every trick in the book. We've got her on that, but that's not the best.'

'Don't keep me in suspense.'

'OK, two things. She keeps the Gift Aid generated in the shops for herself, it never hits the books, and two large government grants totalling over two hundred grand have disappeared without a trace.'

'Bloody hell.'

'Begs the question, sir, did Haddon find out? If he did, maybe he blackmailed her and rather than pay up, she killed him.'

'Your theory certainly comes under the heading of motive. Get in touch with Tegan. They won't have made it to Bristol yet, so tell her to seize Turrell's books and look for a gun at her property.'

'Will do, sir.'

'Where's Kevin Biggs?'

'The Ahmadis are being discharged from hospital. Because they had travel documents from the UK, they were jumped up the list. Amazingly, they've been given a one-bedroomed flat in a tower block in Cardiff.'

'What does that have to do with Kevin?'

'He's driving them there. He's still really rattled by what happened and wanted to do what he could to help. Not only that, but he thinks they may have more information and hopes they'll talk during the journey.'

'Good idea, but he really should have run it past me first.'

'Yes, sir.'

Ben got to his feet. 'Gardiner will be here soon. Jack and I will be busy with him for a while. Bit of luck by the time we're done, Turrell will be waiting for us. Tell Sergeant Trent I'm in the custody suite – and well done, Constable. You've put in some good work on this case.'

Elsa blushed. 'Thank you, sir.'

* * *

The interview with Gardiner turned out to be a complete waste of time. He had refused access to a solicitor and even though Jack pressed him, the man didn't change his story. Without any actual evidence against him, Ben had no choice but to release him under investigation. Gardiner was so angry Ben pitied the uniformed officers tasked with driving him back home.

Upstairs in the incident room, Ben and Jack grabbed a quick lunch of sandwiches from the local bakers and topped up on caffeine.

'That was rubbish,' Jack grouched. 'Couldn't squeeze anything new out of him. No sign he was anywhere near Builth the night of the murder, and nothing dodgy in his background. Not even a speeding fine.'

'Worth a try though,' Ben said.

'Let's hope we make more progress with Turrell.'

'Bound to. We have plenty of evidence against her. Might not be able to pin Haddon's death on her, but she can't wriggle away from the fraud she's committed.'

'Tegan find a gun?'

'No, but she got hold of the charity's books together with personal financial records. The lovely Ms Turrell is waiting downstairs and has a solicitor on the way.'

Jack shoved the last of his sandwich into his mouth and washed it down with the remainder of his coffee.

'Better get to it then, guv.'

The detectives walked down to the custody suite and into the interview room. Natalie sat at the desk, a uniformed female officer keeping her company.

'I really don't appreciate being dragged here like this,' Natalie said as they entered. 'You're overstepping the mark. My solicitor agrees and will point out the error of your ways when he arrives.'

'Won't have long to wait,' Jack said. 'He's upstairs booking in.'

'Wasting my time,' she grumbled. 'I have much more important things to do than this.'

There was a tap on the door and the custody sergeant showed a smartly dressed, good-looking man inside the stuffy room.

He glanced at the detectives. 'Gentlemen,' he said. 'I'm Mark Jacobs.' He offered his hand to Natalie. 'Good afternoon, Ms Turrell.'

He sat next to his client. Jack switched on the recording device, stated date, time and listed those present in the room, including the lawyer.

'Let's make a start then,' Ben said and looked at the prisoner. 'Would you please state your full name, address and date of birth?'

Natalie glared across the desk but complied with his request.

'Thank you,' Ben said. 'You have been arrested on suspicion of fraud. Is there anything you would like to tell us before we begin the interview?'

Natalie smirked. 'Only that you're making a huge mistake and will regret making it.'

Ben nodded and opened a file. 'A forensic accountant has examined your books and your personal tax affairs. He has uncovered discrepancies we would like you to explain.'

'Discrepancies? Like what?'

Ben talked her through the expenses she had claimed incorrectly and Natalie brushed his queries aside. She referred to "accounting errors", "inexperienced bookkeepers", and eventually, grudgingly admitted to the odd mistake.

'Difficult to keep personal and business separate sometimes,' she said. 'I live such a busy life.'

'These things do happen, Chief Inspector,' Mark Jacobs said, 'and can be easily rectified by discussing the matter with HMRC. By all means charge and release my client, but I'm sure this won't get to a courtroom.'

'Maybe you're right, but we're not done yet.'

Jacobs raised his eyebrows and watched Ben flip through documents in the file, slip one out of the stack and look up at Natalie.

'Ms Turrell, do your shops claim Gift Aid payments?'

'Yes of course. If the goods donated were gifted by taxpayers. We claim twenty-five pence for every pound taken, in this case raised at the point of sale.'

'Who pays you the money?'

'I claim the allowance using records of sales from the shops and the HMRC pays it.'

Jacobs cut in, 'It will be claimed under GASDS, the Gift Aid small donations scheme.'

'Thank you for clarifying that, sir,' Ben said. 'The problem we have is that the payments are being made to your client's personal account and do not appear to have been transferred to R4A's balance sheet.' He turned his gaze back to Natalie. 'Can you explain this, Ms Turrell?'

'Not just like that. Not without looking at the books. Sounds like an accounting error to me.'

Jack chuckled. 'A very long running and serious error,' he said. 'Not a single penny of this money has reached the charity since it was originally formed.'

Natalie's eyes widened and Jack thought he detected a slight pinking of her cheeks. She glanced at her adviser.

'I agree with my client,' Jacobs said. 'Without access to the books and sufficient time to examine them, she cannot be expected to comment. My advice would be that you release her under investigation, and I am sure we can clear this matter up.'

Natalie visibly relaxed until Jack said, 'We're still not done.'

Jacobs sighed heavily. 'Then move things along, will you?'

Jack grinned, removed a second sheet of paper from the file on the table and placed it in front of his prisoner.

'R4A was awarded two large government grants which seem to have vanished completely. Use them to service your gambling debts, did you?'

'How dare you!' Natalie shouted, getting to her feet.

'I'm calling a halt to this,' Jacobs said. 'I need time to confer with my client.'

'Knock yourself out,' Jack said. 'Interview terminated at 15.29.'

The detectives made their way back upstairs to the incident room and saw Kevin Biggs at the far end, fiddling with the coffee machine. He gave it a sharp slap.

'Bloody thing,' he muttered. 'About time we got a new one.'

'Be a good idea,' Jack said. 'How did you get on today with the Ahmadis?'

'OK I guess,' Kevin said, pouring water into the machine, only for it to trickle back out onto the hotplate. 'I give up,' he said and flopped on a nearby chair. 'Mrs Ahmadi looks better, but still weak, and they're both obviously in mourning. Difficult to get them to talk.'

'Elsa told me they have been given a place in Cardiff,' Ben said.

Kevin nodded. 'In a tower block. Nothing inside at all. No carpets, curtains, furniture, not even a mug, nothing.' He rubbed his face. 'I nipped out and bought some food, sandwiches and stuff they didn't need to cook. Didn't feel good leaving them there, they looked so bloody lost.'

'What happens now?' Jack asked.

'Their application will begin. Hopefully they'll be allowed to stay as Afran worked for the army, but the woman from the council said nothing is a given. She's going to contact local charities who might be able to help supply the basics.'

'Where is their son?' Ben asked quietly.

'At the morgue. Not likely to be released for the foreseeable. Part of the parents' distress is down to not being able to bury him.'

'Did they have any further information about their journey to the UK?'

'Not really, but they said it took every penny they had to make the trip and they left relatives behind. Afran hasn't been able to contact his mother for days and that's not helping matters.'

'You did good, Kevin, but next time don't go off reservation without speaking to me first.'

'No, sir.'

Ben removed his wallet, pulled out some notes and offered them to his officer. 'Go and buy a new coffee machine and then knock off early. You look done in.'

Kevin got to his feet and rummaged through paperwork on his desk before holding out a cardboard folder.

'From the garage,' he said. 'SOCO's report on the van. Still waiting on DVLA.'

'Leave it with us and we'll see you first thing tomorrow.'

Kevin left the room, and Ben opened the folder and scanned the report. The document mentioned scratches on the inside of the doors, smears of blood and five fingernails discovered near the opening. An overflowing chemical toilet was tucked in a corner. Ben shuddered and forced himself to keep reading. A quantity of human waste had been found on the floor, personal items scattered amongst it. The report contained a list, items of clothing, a couple of broken smartphones, a teddy bear, plastic bags of food and… an asthma inhaler. Ben groaned.

Jack caught his eye. 'Anything useful?' he asked.

'Pretty much what you'd expect, none of it pleasant. Take a look.' Ben tossed the report across the desk.

'Yeah, will do. What are we going to do about Natalie Turrell?'

'Apply for an extension, hold her overnight and conduct another interview first thing. I think you were right about shaking her up. She looked distinctly rattled when I mentioned the missing government money. Elsa wondered whether Haddon found out about it and had blackmailed Natalie.'

'No reason why that couldn't be possible.'

'So you think she could have shot her financial adviser between the eyes?'

Jack shrugged. 'Didn't have to be her. She could have paid someone to do the dirty.'

Ben nodded and got to his feet. 'Right, I'll pop down and let the custody sergeant know we plan on keeping her in. You arrange the extension then we'll clock off. Early start again tomorrow, Jack. Pass the word.'

'Yes, guv. See you in the morning.'

Chapter twenty-six

Sorrell knocked on the door of a Victorian end-of-terrace house on the edge of Cardiff just before ten the next morning. She had timed her trip into the city perfectly and managed to avoid most of the rush hour traffic. Stacey was pleased her friend had offered to drive. Yesterday's trip to Reading had been stressful and she was still suffering the after-effects.

After a short wait the door was opened by a man leaning on a stick. He looked to be in his early sixties with ginger hair, a couple of missing teeth, his beard liberally sprinkled with white. Recognising Sorrell he smiled expansively, blue eyes bright and lively.

'Hello, my lovely,' he said and dispensed a quick hug. 'Good to see you. Come in for a cuppa.'

'Hi, Bilbo,' Sorrell said and returned his hug. 'Meet my new friend, Stacey Logan, I mentioned her recently. She's a white-hat journalist.'

'I remember,' Bilbo said and held out a welcoming hand. 'Good to meet you, Stacey Logan, please come in.'

The smiling man stood to one side and waved his guests inside, high-fiving Rebin as the boy passed.

Sorrell led the way through a hall made narrow by towers of boxes, large and small, and supermarket bags-for-life stuffed full of what looked to be clothes and bedding. Like the hall, the kitchen was also crammed with bags, boxes and larger plastic cartons. Stacey saw some were filled with food.

'Find yourselves a seat,' Bilbo said, as he threaded his way to a gas cooker and filled a kettle. 'I make no excuse for the state of the place. These are all donations.' He smiled again. 'Sometimes it's worse.' He set up mugs and asked, 'Did you bring your load over, Sorrell?'

She nodded. 'Tents and sleeping bags mainly – courtesy of a tatter at Glastonbury – some food, and one of my local charity shops passed on bed linen and curtains which didn't sell.'

'Marvellous. I can always find a home for curtains and sheets. As it happens' – he poured boiling water onto teabags and handed Rebin a glass of milk – 'I need to make an urgent delivery this morning.' He glanced at Stacey. 'A married couple, rescued from the truck discovered near Erwood, have been granted emergency accommodation. You covered the story I believe.'

'I did, yes,' Stacey said. 'Such a terrible thing to have happened.'

'Yes, it is. Fancy coming out with me this morning? I need to drop off some food and other supplies along the way but I haven't loaded the van yet. An extra pair of hands never goes to waste.'

An hour later, Bilbo's van had been packed until no space remained. Stacey climbed in the passenger seat and Bilbo set off, Sorrell and Rebin followed in their old 4x4. The roads were busy but passable. The first stop was outside what looked to be a squat – a run-down, three-storied property, not far from the centre of the city.

'Just dropping off some food and a couple of boxes of T-shirts, donated by a local clothing manufacture. Great guy, big supporter. He said the shirts are slight seconds, but I can't find anything wrong with them and certainly better than going without.'

'Do asylum seekers live here?' Stacey asked, peering up at the tall building and snapping a couple of shots with her point-and-shoot camera.

'No, street people – alcoholics and junkies mainly. They doss here. I'm nearly always given more than enough supplies for the refugees and these folk need to eat like anyone else.'

'Aren't there any night shelters in Cardiff?'

'Of course, but to use them you need to be clean. For some, that's impossible. You can wait in the van if you like, I won't be long.'

'Wouldn't dream of it. I'll give you a hand.'

Another broad smile crinkled Bilbo's face. 'Cool. I was hoping you'd offer. My back ain't that great these days. One thing though, leave your camera here OK?'

'No problem,' Stacey said. She tucked the device beneath an *A to Z* of the city and opened the passenger door.

* * *

A night in the cells hadn't agreed with Natalie Turrell. She looked tired, hair unkempt, and without makeup her skin was as pale as paper. She had changed out of the red business suit she had been arrested in, and was wearing a long-sleeved, navy-blue T-shirt and grey jogging bottoms, no doubt brought in by her legal adviser. The spike heels had been replaced by an expensive pair of trainers. She was brought to the interview room by a female officer, where Ben, Jack and Mark Jacobs waited. Jack switched on the recording device and the interview resumed.

'Morning, Ms Turrell,' Ben said. 'I hope you managed to get some sleep. I've been told you refused breakfast.'

'Is that what it was?' Natalie huffed. 'I'm not sure I saw anything edible.'

Ben glanced at Jacobs. 'Have you had sufficient time with your client, sir?'

'For now, Chief Inspector. I'll let you know if I would like more.'

Ben nodded. 'Before we begin, Ms Turrell, have you anything to say following your interview yesterday?'

She sighed. 'My solicitor and I have already told you, we are unable to answer your questions without access to my records.' Natalie folded her arms. 'As my request has been denied, I have nothing further to say.'

'I would like to register my dissatisfaction,' Jacobs said. 'My client should not have been held overnight because of what is basically a financial irregularity.'

'You have just done that,' Ben said, 'but I would like to remind you that a large amount of money is involved. I am concerned your client may be a flight risk. Nearly half a million pounds is missing from a charity, and we must take this matter seriously.'

Jacobs shrugged. 'As I've already said, Ms Turrell could be released on police bail, and we can deal with these anomalies in a more civilised manner.'

Jack snorted. '"Anomalies", eh? Not what the forensic accountant called them. "Blatant fraud" were the words he used.'

'He's entitled to his opinion.'

'Yes, he is,' Jack said, 'but we'd like to talk about something else today – a new line of inquiry.'

Without waiting for Jacobs to comment, Jack opened a cardboard file and removed a black-and-white photograph which he slid across the table towards Natalie. The image depicted a stretch of nearly empty motorway, obviously captured at night.

'What's this? Natalie asked.

'A picture taken by the ANPR system. Automatic number-plate recognition. Don't you recognise your own car?' Jack tapped the photo with an index finger. 'Check out the time, just over an hour before Haddon was shot and interestingly, taken this side of the Prince of Wales Bridge.'

Natalie sighed heavily. 'And?'

Jack grinned. 'That was the evening you told us you'd visited the theatre, enjoyed a late dinner at the docks and went home to bed. We can't prove any of that, but we *can* prove that at approaching midnight that night, you entered Wales.' Jack leaned back in his chair. 'Did you forget about the trip?'

'I don't appreciate your tone,' Natalie said.

'And I don't appreciate you lying to me,' Jack snapped. 'Why did you drive to Wales?'

'Maybe to aid my digestion after a late dinner and unwind after a busy day.'

Natalie smirked and Ben watched as she played verbal chess with his sergeant. Jack opened the file again, took out a piece of paper and placed it in front of Natalie.

'Card receipt,' he explained. 'You buying fuel on the outskirts of the city – CCTV at the service station confirms this – just after eleven. The play at the Old Vic finished a little before ten. What did you have for dinner? Hot dog from a van in the car park?'

Natalie's face lost its smirk. 'It is possible I lent my car to a friend. I often have, many times.'

'So, did you?'

'Can't be sure without access to my diary.'

'Oh come on, Natalie. We're talking about a couple of weeks ago, not a couple of years. I'll ask again, did you lend your car to a friend the weekend Jonathon Haddon was murdered?'

'I can't remember.'

'I don't believe you.'

'Sergeant,' Jacobs said, 'my client has already said she can't remember and needs to check her diary. Again, I respectfully suggest you release Ms Turrell under investigation. With access to her records, I am sure we can clear up these matters.'

'Glad you're sure,' Jack said, 'cos I'm not.'

'Seems we've reached an impasse.'

'Not at all.' Jack grinned. 'I anticipated your client's need for her diary. As we speak, the document is being couriered from Bristol. Should be here within an hour or so. Don't worry though, we have plenty to discuss before it arrives.'

* * *

Bilbo made several stops as he trundled around the city streets. At some locations he unloaded bags and boxes from his van, at others he picked up household items. It was nearly two o'clock when he pulled up outside a residential tower block, desperately in need of restoration.

Bilbo turned off the engine and stepped out of the van as Sorrell pulled into a space next to him. He walked closer to her vehicle.

'Sorrell,' he said, glancing at Rebin, then shifting his gaze to the tower, 'probably be best if you and Rebin sit this one out… given the circumstances.'

'Yeah, I get it,' she said. 'If you do need a hand…' She waved a mobile phone in the air.

'Will do but we should be fine, none of this stuff is particularly heavy. You up for this, Stacey?'

'I reckon. Hope the lift works. Which floor are we aiming for?'

'Five.'

'I really hope the lift works.'

Bilbo and Stacey carried the furniture through the main doors and were pleased to discover at least one lift was functioning. They got out on the fifth floor. A few yards along the hall, Bilbo put down their burden and knocked on a red, plywood door. A few moments later it was opened and a deep brown eye peered through the gap.

Bilbo switched on his megawatt smile.

'Mr Ahmadi? My name is Bilbo and I'm from a local charity. The council contacted me and said you could do with some bits and pieces.' Bilbo held up some form of identity card and pointed at the sofa. 'This turns into a bed and I have a table and chairs downstairs. Shall we bring this inside?'

The door opened a little wider to reveal a tall, brown-skinned man. 'We have no money to pay,' he said.

'No need to, friend,' Bilbo said. 'Everything has been donated by good people who just want to help. My companion is Stacey. She's helping me with the lifting today.'

Finally the man seemed convinced. He opened the door and Bilbo and Stacey carried the sofa bed inside a tiny living room. The floor was bare concrete and, beneath the window, a woman in a headscarf sat cross-legged, back against the wall, hands clasped tightly in her lap, eyes staring at nothing, her body rocking gently.

'My wife, Naza,' the man said. 'She is still not well.' He gulped a breath. 'I am Afran. We lost our son, Zoran.'

'We are deeply sorry for your great loss,' Bilbo said. 'The council told us what has happened.' With Stacey's help, he positioned the sofa against one wall. 'We have some more stuff for you in the van.'

'I will come,' Afran said. 'Your friend can stay with my wife, maybe help her off the floor. I cannot be long. She does not like me to leave her.'

'Right then, we'll get on with it. OK with you, Stacey?'

'I'll be fine.'

After the men had left, Stacey crouched on the floor next to the grieving woman, gently unclasped her hands and took them in her own.

'I'm a friend,' she said. 'Can you speak any English?'

The woman nodded slowly. 'A little, my husband teach.'

'That's good, I can't speak your language at all. Did the hospital give you any medicine? Are you taking it?'

The woman shrugged so Stacey mimed putting a tablet in her mouth and swallowing. She held up a thumb and

Naza returned the gesture. Stacey got to her feet, walked closer to the second-hand sofa bed, pine-framed with a folded, navy-blue futon resting on top.

'This makes a bed,' she said. 'Watch.' Stacey pulled out the frame and adjusted the buttoned mattress. 'You should lie down. The floor is cold and hard.' She stretched out a hand to Naza who took it and allowed herself to be helped upright. She only needed to take a couple of steps before Stacey lowered her onto the bed. 'There are blankets and pillows downstairs, we can make this better.'

'Is already better, thank you.'

The front door opened. Afran stepped into the room, a table grasped in his long arms, two wooden chairs tied to the top. He placed it carefully beneath the window, then turned and spoke to his wife in what Stacey guessed was Persian. He knelt next to her and brushed a tear from her cheek with the ball of his thumb. She spoke, voice strained, more tears stacking up behind the first.

Afran stood. 'Naza says to thank you for the things and she is sorry she cannot make you tea.'

'Not a problem,' Bilbo said. 'I have one more load downstairs, including a camping cooker with three rings and a gas bottle. Tell your wife I'll make tea. Come on, Stacey, just one more run.'

Chapter twenty-seven

When Natalie's diary was eventually brought to the interview room, it didn't help her case. Entries for the week in question made no mention of her lending a car to a friend. The claimed trip to the theatre, followed by dinner on the floating restaurant weren't recorded either. According to the diary, she'd had nothing booked on the night in question. Jack was delighted and pressed her hard until eventually, Mark Jacobs called a halt.

'Gentlemen,' he said, 'we have reached the point where you either charge my client or release her. I'm not convinced you have presented enough hard evidence for a charge to be levelled against her.'

Jack leaned back in his chair. 'We have enough,' he said. 'For a start your client has not been truthful, she cannot explain why her vehicle was in Wales that Saturday night, and has failed to prove it was driven by someone else. That doesn't look good in an investigation like this.'

'I don't agree,' Jacobs said. 'She should be released.'

'I'm afraid I'm not going to do that,' Ben said. 'If Ms Turrell cannot clear up the outstanding issues now, I will charge her with fraud and the possible involvement with the death of Jonathon Haddon.'

Natalie leapt to her feet. 'No way! I didn't kill Jon. Why would I?'

'Because he caught you with your fingers in the till,' Jack said.

'You're mad. I'm a successful businesswoman–'

'With a gambling problem,' Jack muttered.

Natalie surged ahead. 'Successful people like me don't shoot other people.'

'You were in Wales. Tell me what you were doing here.'

'I've already said, I don't remember.'

'Not good enough.'

'Last chance, Natalie,' Ben said. 'Talk to us or you will be charged and we will take you to court tomorrow.' He glanced at Jacobs. 'Obviously we'll oppose bail.'

Natalie flopped back on her seat. 'Help me, Mark,' she said. 'Earn your fee.'

'I'm not sure I can, not unless you fill in the gaps. My advice would be to answer their questions. If you go to court, you will be remanded.'

'But I can't remember,' Natalie wailed. 'How can I tell them what I don't know? What I do know is I didn't kill Jon. You must believe me.'

'Then prove it,' Jack growled.

Natalie put her face in her hands and began to sob.

'OK then,' Ben said. 'We've gone as far with this as we can.' He addressed Jacobs. 'Your client will be charged, held overnight and presented at court in the morning.' He got to his feet. 'You may like some time with Ms Turrell before we find her a cell. Knock on the door when you've finished. Interview suspended at 17.26.'

* * *

The phone rang just as Stacey switched off the hall light and was about to go upstairs to bed. Tutting to herself, she turned the light back on and went to the office to answer it.

'Hello, Stacey Logan.'

'Hi, Stace, it's Erica. Sorry it's late but is Heidi with you?'

'I haven't seen her today, I was in Cardiff. Is everything OK?'

'I guess.' Erica sighed heavily. 'Yes, I'm sure it is but I haven't heard anything from her all day. She's not here and hasn't left a note.'

'I haven't spoken to her either. Have you called Freddie?'

'Too late to bother him now. This is Heidi all over. Said she'd be here when I came home from work, but there's no sign of her. No bloody supper either and I'm starving. I'll have to nip out for a takeaway. If you do hear from her, ask her to call me.'

'I will. How are things with you? It's been ages since we've caught up.'

'Yes, it has. Work has been full on and I'm always knackered working shifts. Get used to one set of unsociable hours, then ten days later everything changes. The drive to Swansea isn't helping.'

'Put in for a transfer.'

'I have but it's taking too long. Ignore me, Stace. I'm being a grump.'

'Are you sure you're OK?'

'Fine, it's just' – she sighed – 'I worry when Heidi isn't where she's supposed to be. It's always in the back of my mind she'll go walkabout again, like she did before. She says she won't, but we both know Heidi.'

'Things are different now though, you're married.'

'As I said, ignore me. Just text if you hear anything.'

'I will, you too. Try to sleep well.'

Stacey hung up the phone, hoping Heidi would arrive home soon. She switched off the lights and crept upstairs, anxious not to disturb her houseguests.

* * *

As usual, since the case had begun, Ben was up early. Stacey got up with him. He snatched a quick coffee then left her to pad about the kitchen in her pyjamas and ease into the day. She walked across the cool quarry tiles, opened the kitchen door, and propped it open with an old potato weight. The weathermen had predicted a heat wave, temperatures above thirty-five degrees, but this early the mountain air was cool.

Stacey sat on the bench by the back door to drink her coffee, and a couple of minutes later, Sorrell joined her.

'It's a beautiful morning,' Stacey said. 'Gonna be hot later.'

'That's why I'm up early. It's time Rebin and I went home. I've really enjoyed my time here, you've been a lifesaver, but I've got stuff to do. Can't hide away forever.'

'I've enjoyed your company, all of you. Come back anytime.'

'Such a kind thing you did.' Sorrell squeezed Stacey's hand. 'You'll certainly see us again, and don't be a stranger at my place either.'

A sharp click from the side gate made Stacey look up and she saw Erica striding along the narrow path.

'Erica. Everything OK?'

'Heidi didn't come home last night and Freddie hasn't heard from her.'

'She not answering her phone?'

'Would I be here if she was answering her bloody phone?'

'No, sorry.'

'The day before yesterday, Heidi told me she was intending to spend the day with you, something about a story you're writing. Where did you go?'

'Reading,' Stacey said and tried to swallow the bad feeling that had suddenly clogged her throat.

'What the hell is in Reading?' Erica asked.

'I thought she'd have spoken to you about the trip.'

'Spit it out, Stace.'

'Freddie gave her a tip and on the back of that, she set up a meeting… with people smugglers.'

'What?! Oh my God! Why on earth are you messing about with gangsters? Does Ben know what you've been up to?'

'Not about Reading.'

As though noticing Sorrell for the first time, Erica glared at her and asked, 'Who the hell are you? What have you got to do with this?'

'My name is Sorrell, and I have nothing to do with this.' She got to her feet and glanced at Stacey. 'I'll leave you to it. I've got packing to do.'

She left the bench and went in through the back door. Erica dropped into her place and rubbed her face.

'Sorry, Stace. There was no need for that. I apologise to you and your mate, but you need to tell me everything you can about Reading. Something bad has happened to Heidi. I know it has and I need you to help me find her.'

'OK. Give me five minutes to get dressed and we'll get on the road. Have you got a work car?'

'Yeah, an unmarked.'

'Then you drive and I'll make phone calls.'

Chapter twenty-eight

Stacey shot indoors and dressed quickly, spoke to Sorrell, and grabbed a kit bag and some bottles of water, then she followed Erica to her car and strapped herself in. Erica turned the vehicle around and drove up the steep lane to the ranges on her way to the M4. Stacey dialled the first number on her mental list – Andrew Carr, cub reporter for *The Mid Wales Times.*

'Andrew,' she said when he answered. 'Drop everything and get to Brecon Magistrates' Court.'

'Stacey?' a sleepy voice mumbled. 'I'm on a day off.'

'Rubbish! Journalists don't have days off. Anyway, you'll thank me. Ben told me the police have charged a suspect, connected with the recent murder case, with fraud. I haven't got a name which is why you need to be at court as soon as possible.'

'Blimey, thanks,' Andrew said. 'How come you aren't covering it?'

'Can't get into it now, just don't let me down.'

'I won't. I'll ring you later.'

Stacey cut the call and dialled another number as Erica raced down from the ranges and onto the A40.

'Holtz,' said a deep voice.

'Freddie, it's Stacey. I'm with Erica and we're on our way to Reading to look for Heidi at the industrial estate you told her about.'

'Slow down, Stacey,' Freddie said. 'I don't know anything about Reading.'

'Heidi told me you'd given her a tip-off about a gang of people smugglers. She said she'd set up the meeting on the back of your info, and a couple of days ago we met a shady bunch of characters in a unit outside town.'

'Did you say people smugglers?'

'Yeah. Six guys. Five heavies, at least two with guns, and one boss-type.'

'I didn't give Heidi any tip-off.' Freddie snorted loudly. 'Why does she have to be such a loose cannon?'

Stacey knew he didn't expect an answer and remained silent, allowing the man to process what she had told him.

'OK,' he said. 'Give me the address. I'm in London so I'll drive to Reading and meet you outside the estate on the road. I doubt the gang will still be there, but we need to take a look. You and Erica must not go to the unit on your own. I'll probably arrive first and I'll wait for you.'

The line disconnected and Stacey glanced at Erica whose eyes were fixed on the road as she sped towards the motorway.

'Did you hear all that?' Stacey asked.

Erica nodded. 'Now ring Ben.'

'No, not yet. We should wait until we've met Freddie, listened to his take on the situation.' Stacey groaned and rubbed her face. 'I didn't tell Ben about the trip to Reading earlier in the week.'

'Whatever,' Erica said as she joined the slip road, 'but you'll have to tell him eventually.'

Stacey nodded slowly. She knew that what Erica had said was true and found the realisation difficult. She pushed the thought to the back of her mind as Erica switched on the blue lights and gained speed as she shot along the M4. The pair didn't say much during the journey.

Erica concentrated on the driving, while Stacey fretted angrily over Heidi, wondering why her friend had made up the story about Freddie's involvement, and where the information had actually come from.

Two hours and thirty-eight minutes later, Erica turned off the motorway and a couple of miles further on, pulled into the road leading to the industrial estate. Parked a hundred yards from the entrance, was a smart VW camper van, with blackberry-coloured paintwork and darkly tinted windows. As Erica drew closer, a hand stuck out of the driver's window and waved her down. She pulled up next to the van and Stacey opened her window.

'Hi, Freddie,' she said, 'like your wheels.'

'Not mine,' he said. 'Park up, get in the van and tell me everything you can remember about your previous visit.'

A couple of minutes later, Erica slid open the side door of the camper and was surprised to see three, fairly large men, dressed in khaki, squashed together on the back seat. Anxious not to draw attention, she slipped inside, knelt on the floor and pulled the door closed. Stacey got into the passenger seat.

'Mates of mine,' Freddie explained. 'We go way back and it's useful to have mates in a crisis.'

Stacey wasn't sure what "way back" meant as Freddie was at least twenty years older than any of his companions.

'Tell us what you know about unit thirty-nine,' the man in the middle of the seat said. 'Everything you can remember.'

Stacey turned to peer through the front seats and described the position of the unit on the estate, the car park, the men she had seen inside and the boss. The man questioned her about the internal layout.

'Come on,' Erica said, 'we're talking ourselves to death. We should be breaking the door down.'

'Erica,' Freddie said, 'I don't really need to remind you that this is not a police operation. My friends like to be discrete. They'll take a look while we wait here and if we're needed, they will let us know.'

'I'm going with them,' Erica said. 'I am a copper after all.'

'Please, my dear. Allow the lads to assess the situation first.'

'I'll give them five minutes,' Erica huffed. 'We don't hear anything in five minutes I'm definitely going in.'

The man on the back seat smiled and muttered, 'Give us a fighting chance, love. Make it ten.' He opened the side door, he and his companions stepped out and shut the door behind them.

'Who are those blokes?' Erica asked.

Freddie turned in his seat, caught her eye and grinned. 'Not sure I saw anyone… being I'm not here myself.'

'But–'

'Let's wait to see what they find inside the place.'

Erica picked herself up off the floor and dropped on the empty bench seat.

'Heidi drives me bloody nuts,' she said.

Freddie chuckled. 'She has that effect on many people. She's always been independent and a touch headstrong, but bending the truth is a new one.'

'Do you think she's been snatched by the people smugglers?' Stacey asked.

Freddie sighed. 'I sincerely hope not, but we can't deny it is a possibility. These individuals are dangerous.'

Nine minutes passed before one of the men returned and tapped on the driver's window.

Freddie buzzed it down. 'Anything?' he asked.

'Nothing obvious, sir. Place is empty. Come and take a look.'

He got in the camper and Freddie drove to the back of the site pulling up outside unit thirty-nine. Stacey shuddered, remembering being searched and meeting the man she thought of as the boss. How quickly he had turned angry. She climbed out of the van and followed the others through the olive-coloured door. The group walked along the corridor to the end office where the other men waited. Freddie looked around the room, he opened the drawers of a metal desk, searched a pair of ancient filing cabinets and finding nothing, he rubbed his face.

'We'll go back to the van,' he said. 'You three take a wander around, chat to people in other units, see if you can winkle anything out and make it quick.'

Freddie and the women returned to the van, Freddie drove it out of the industrial site and parked next to the pavement by the main gate.

'What do we do now?' Erica asked. 'Where do we look for Heidi?'

* * *

Having instructed Ollie and Tegan to escort Natalie Turrell to court, Ben contacted HMP Cardiff to request a visit with Leo Phillips. The request was granted, so leaving Elsa to run the incident room, he and Jack went downstairs, found a car and began the drive to the city.

The weathermen had been right to warn about the coming heatwave. Even at ten in the morning the temperature was on the rise and Ben fiddled with the air conditioning. As they travelled through the Beacons towards Merthyr Tydfil, the expanses of brown mountain grass seemed to shimmer in the unbroken sunshine.

'Hope nobody is lighting disposable barbeques up there,' Ben grumbled. 'Wouldn't take much to set this lot alight and if it got into the peat, or the forestry plantations, it could burn for weeks.'

'I'm hoping we don't meet a traffic jam,' Jack said. 'It'd be like sitting in a slow cooker.'

A little over an hour later, Jack reached the outskirts of the city and threaded his way through nearly empty streets towards the prison. He parked close to the main gates and opened his door. Dry, dusty heat rushed in and made him gasp.

They left the car, walked to the gate and began the laborious booking-in process. Inside the building the heat was oppressive and stifling.

Prisoners obviously didn't have the luxury of air conditioning. The prison officers were short-tempered and grouchy, sweating in their uniforms behind the check-in desk. One of them reluctantly escorted Ben and Jack to the visiting hall, where they had to wait nearly half an hour before Leo Phillips was brought in. When he did appear, he looked worn out. He scowled when he recognised the detectives sitting at a round table on one side of the hall. An officer guided the prisoner to a seat, then backed off to take his place behind a desk at the end of the large room.

'Shit,' Phillips said, 'thought I'd seen the last of you.' He flopped onto an orange, plastic chair. 'Why are you here? Can't you just leave me alone?'

'You can refuse to speak to us,' Ben said, 'but we are still investigating the death of your wife and her friend Jonathon Haddon. We have some more questions to ask you.'

Phillips frowned. 'Go on then, ask your questions, but do it slowly. We're on twenty-three-hour bang-up due to lack of staff, so it's good to get out of the cell.' He sighed. 'You know I shouldn't really be here. I wouldn't be if you weren't so vindictive. There was no need to lock me up. I apologised after all.' He glanced briefly at Ben's healing nose.

'The court handed down the sentence, not us,' Jack said, 'and you broke a senior officer's nose. Bearing in mind your previous conviction, what did you think would happen?'

Phillips folded his arms. 'Whatever,' he said. 'Just get on with it.'

Jack opened his notebook and took a pen from his inside pocket.

'OK,' Ben said. 'You told us previously you had never met Haddon. You said you didn't recognise the man from the photo we showed you.'

Jack continued, 'But you knew Rowan, Kitty's brother. Stands to reason you also knew Haddon, that you had met him on several occasions, one of which was at your wedding to Kitty.' He grinned. 'We looked at your wedding album.'

Phillips shook his head. 'Who remembers random guests at a wedding, especially your own?'

'Maybe you were pissed that day too,' Jack muttered.

Phillips snorted. 'You're a piece of work aren't you? Are you married? Was your wife killed while out with another man? No? Thought not. How on earth can you know how that feels?'

'The night your wife died,' Ben said, 'and Haddon was shot, you told us you were working late. You said you had made phone calls and sent emails which would prove you were at home.'

'That's right I did.' Phillips wiped his sweaty face on a sleeve and leaned back in his chair.

'We have checked with your phone and internet providers and the latest call you made was at eleven thirty.'

'So? What of it?'

'Haddon was killed sometime after one in the morning. You had plenty of time to drive to Builth, shoot him and return home. In other words, your alibi doesn't hold up.'

'Can't help that, can I?' Phillips growled.

'What did you do after making that last call?' Jack asked.

'Went to bed. It was late and I was tired. Had a lie-in the next day and hadn't been up long before you two banged on my door to tell me my wife was dead.' He dropped his eyes to the tabletop. 'I want to know who killed my wife, probably more than you do, but I've told you all I can. I didn't leave the house the night she died and I didn't shoot Haddon.'

'You weren't straight with us though,' Jack said. 'You didn't admit to knowing him, or how you learned to shoot at university. We had to find that out ourselves and that doesn't look good.'

'For Christ's sake, I didn't know him. I'll admit I'd heard his name, but to my knowledge I have never met him. If he did attend my wedding, then I wasn't aware of it. Over two hundred guests came to watch me marry Kitty. Apart from our families, I can't say I remember anyone else.'

'Probably cos you were pissed,' Jack said.

'Give it up, will you?' Phillips grumbled. 'It's way too hot for this and I have nothing more to say to you.' He glanced at the screw behind the desk. 'Officer, I want to go back to my cell. These two are leaving.'

Phillips was removed from the hall and after a short wait, the detectives were walked back to the main gate. They left the prison and returned to the car.

'Didn't shake anything loose from Phillips, did we?' he said.

'Nothing,' Jack said. 'Be different if we actually had some hard evidence against the man, but we don't.'

'Looks as though Natalie Turrell is our best bet so far. We've proved she was in Wales the night in question and she's obviously not willing to tell us why.' He groaned. 'We must work harder to uncover some hard evidence against her.'

'Well,' Jack said, 'it's definitely too hot to be out today so we'll work with Elsa in the office. Maybe she can discover a blackmail note from Haddon to Turrell.'

'You think, like I do, that Turrell was responsible for Haddon's death?' Ben asked.

'Certainly starting to look that way, guv. The fraud charge will keep her remanded for a week or so, she could be considered a flight risk, but her solicitor will have her out soon.'

Jack put the car in gear, pulled out of the car park and headed in the direction of the A470.

Chapter twenty-nine

The return journey to Wales from Reading was probably the worst Stacey had ever experienced. Erica drove steadily, eyes fixed, staring through the windscreen, but Stacey doubted her friend was actually seeing anything. She had tried to talk to Erica about the visit to the industrial estate and how they might begin the search for Heidi, but Erica hadn't answered. Thankfully, due to the weathermen's warnings, the motorway was much quieter than usual and the traffic kept flowing, although a few vehicles had overheated and were stuck on the hard shoulder, with not an inch of shade anywhere.

Miles passed and as Erica drove over the first Severn Crossing and took the road to Usk, Stacey tried again.

'We will find her,' she said. 'I know we will.'

'How do you know that?' Erica snapped. 'Finding people is part of my job and I know how many times we aren't successful.'

'At least you have resources to make a search, and who knows what resources Freddie has. He'll move heaven and earth to find his daughter, you know he will.'

'Doesn't mean he'll pull it off though.' Erica thumped the steering wheel. 'Heidi never learns does she? Rampages through life thinking nothing can touch her.' Erica groaned loudly. 'After her brief spell in jail you'd think she'd be more cautious. Besides, the resources you talk about are only really useful if you know where to point them and I haven't a clue where to begin.'

'Where you'd begin any other case – trace her vehicle, and check her bank card and mobile usage.'

Erica didn't look impressed and passed no comment.

'I know,' Stacey said. 'We'll ask Molly to help.'

'The young autistic woman who lives down the road from you?'

'Yes, that's Molly. She has access to Heidi's facial recognition program. If Heidi's been picked up on a camera anywhere, Molly will find her. It's bound to help that Heidi looks so distinctive.'

'Maybe.' Erica didn't sound convinced.

'I'll give her a ring,' Stacey said. 'Molly will do anything for Heidi, her first proper friend.'

Without waiting for Erica to reply, Stacey pulled out her mobile and prayed for a signal. Eventually, two bars appeared on the screen and Stacey dialled Molly's number. The call was answered quickly.

'Hi, Molly. It's Stacey.'

'I know it is,' Molly said in her inflectionless voice. 'I recognised your number. Do you want something?'

'You make it sound like I only ring when I do.'

'I know that isn't true, you ring often, but your voice is tight.'

'OK, you've got me. I could do with a hand. Erica and I would be grateful if you could look for Heidi.'

'Has she gone away again?' Molly asked. 'Like she did before?'

'We don't think so, but we're not sure.' Stacey took a deep breath. 'A couple of days ago, Heidi and I went to talk to some bad people.'

'What sort of bad?'

'People smuggler bad.'

'Really bad then. Perhaps they have taken her, they might hurt her.'

'We don't know any of that has happened. Heidi's dad is helping to search for her but I'm sure you'll want to help and you might be quicker. Do you still have access to Heidi's facial recognition program?'

'Yes, I have and I'll look. Where should I start?'

'Her apartment in Brecon and an industrial estate in Reading. I'll send you the postcodes.'

'What about her truck? Should I look for that too?'

'Good idea. Erica and I are on our way to my place so we'll pop in. You might need to ask us more questions.'

'OK.'

Molly disconnected the call and Stacey knew the young woman would drop everything to begin the search.

'Do you think she'll be able to find anything?' Erica asked.

'Wouldn't be surprised. Molly is bloody amazing and she'll keep at it until she does. She's another ace in your pack. We'll find Heidi, I know we will.'

Erica shook her head. 'You don't get it, do you? She's been missing for the best part of two days. If she hasn't gone walkabout again and *has* been snatched, we haven't heard anything and that's not good.'

'What do you mean?'

'Surely, if she's been taken whoever has her would have been in touch. No one has so maybe…' Erica ran out of words.

'No! You can't be thinking she's dead. Even if people smugglers did take her, what reason would they have to kill her?'

'What reason would they have to keep her, especially if they thought she had told anyone about them, broke the promises the two of you made?' Erica glanced at Stacey. 'Have *you* told anyone about the meet in Reading? Written anything about it?'

'What? No! We established earlier I haven't even told Ben.'

Erica nodded and fell silent once again as Stacey replayed the meeting with the boss, and remembered how he had warned them not to betray his trust. Had she done something which had upset him?

Soon after four, Erica pulled up outside Molly's fieldstone cottage, a little way down the lane from Noddfa. Even though the sun was past its zenith, the temperature hadn't dropped at all. They walked up the path and Erica hammered on the door using a brass knocker in the shape of a horseshoe. A few moments passed before a small woman in her early twenties appeared. She had long straight hair dyed a neon orange.

'Hi, Molly,' Stacey said.

'Hello. Come inside, it's cooler,' Molly said, looking at a point somewhere to the left of Stacey's actual face.

Stacey and Erica stepped inside the old building and Molly was right, the thick stone walls had managed to keep the temperature down by at least ten degrees and the cooler air was welcome.

'I made iced coffee,' Molly said. 'It's in the fridge.'

Stacey smiled and followed her friend to the kitchen. 'Perfect, thank you.'

'Have you had any luck?' Erica asked.

'The programs are running – nothing so far. I can't make them run faster. There are over five million CCTV cameras in the UK, plus another thirteen thousand ANPR devices, which submit an average of fifty-five million "read" records to the national systems every day.'

Erica perched on a stool next to the counter and put her face in her hands. 'I didn't realise how enormous the network is. You'll never be able to check all that on your own.'

'Don't worry, Erica,' Molly said, 'I don't have to. I have a computer and know where to look. If Heidi's image has been captured by a camera, I'll find it. I only have to search two days. I'll set alarms on my system, run the programs overnight and will phone you when I've found her.'

Molly went to the fridge, removed a jug of iced cafe latte and after lining up three glasses on the counter with minute precision, poured the drinks. Erica grabbed one, gulped gratefully and wiped her lips with the back of her hand.

'All I can say is, I hope you're right,' she said, 'because I'll be honest, I'm not convinced.' She took another mouthful of coffee and looked at Stacey. 'Now you have to tell Ben what's going on.'

* * *

The ancient air conditioning in the incident room, tried – and failed – to make much of a dent in the oppressive heat. Ben looked around the room and recognised that the team were struggling, but he couldn't do anything about it. Now Natalie Turrell had been charged and remanded, the paperwork had to take priority. Elsa Duffin worked the fraud and passed evidence to Ollie and Tegan who began preparing documents for court, while he and Jack hunted for more evidence relating to the murder. Ben groaned and rubbed his face.

Jack glanced up from his screen. 'Problem, guv?' he asked.

'Only this bloody case. It's so messy. What started out as a murder investigation has become so much more and we don't know nearly enough about any of it.'

'I agree and that's why I think all of it is linked somehow.'

'Me too, but try as I might, I can't see how, except…'

'What?'

'Jonathon Haddon. All the players we are aware of so far knew him.'

'Everyone apart from Natalie knew Rowan too,' Jack said.

'They did, yet despite our best efforts, he's still in the wind. We have all this amazing technology but it's still bloody difficult to find someone who doesn't want to be found.'

'Do you think he's purposely avoiding us?'

'I don't know, but maybe he's just keeping his head down. I'd probably do the same in the circumstances. Heidi said something about Rowan and Haddon passing on information relating to people-smuggling gangs, and that Freddie was planning a visit to discuss it with her.'

'Has he been over?'

'If he has she didn't let me know. I haven't heard from her for a couple of days.'

'Could be worth chasing that up.'

'Hmm.' Ben sighed heavily. 'What I'm having difficulty with is where Natalie fits in. The fraud she's committed is significant, a definite jail term if she's found guilty. If Haddon was blackmailing her that is a strong motive for murder, yet we have no proof of that, or proof she is involved in any way with refugees. That's the bit that doesn't fit.'

'I really want to nick those responsible for the deaths of those in that truck,' Jack growled. 'I can't stand the idea we have individuals in Mid Wales making money on the backs of those poor, desperate people. I know we've got the delivery boy, but I want them all, right to the top.'

'I'm with you.' Ben checked his watch, saw it was after five, got to his feet and addressed the room. 'Let's call it a day, troops. Gonna be another scorcher tomorrow, so be in as early as possible. Go and cool off, the lot of you.' The team nodded their thanks and the room emptied. 'Us too, Jack. God, I hope it's cooler on the mountain. I'm sure my brain is melting.'

* * *

'You did what?!' Ben yelled after Stacey told him about her recent trip to Reading. 'I warned you how dangerous this business could be. I begged you and Heidi to keep away from it and you obviously took no notice.'

Erica, not able to cope with listening to an argument, and having her own worries, retreated to the living room, shut the door and turned the radio on.

'I didn't ignore your warnings,' Stacey said. 'I passed them on to Heidi and we were careful.'

'Goes without saying, not bloody careful enough!' He lowered his voice and glanced at the kitchen door. 'This could be really bad shit, Stacey. We don't know anything about these gangsters, where to look for them, nothing. Heidi could be in real trouble.'

Stacey dropped on the carver and put her head in her hands. She knew everything Ben said was true. This mess was her fault. She had got Heidi involved, then she was swept along by her friend's confidence. Now Heidi was missing, and it was down to her.

'We've got to get her back.'

Ben nodded. 'Did you say Freddie and Molly are running independent searches?' he asked.

'Yeah. Phone and internet records. Molly is also using one of Heidi's own programs, same one she used to pick out that Parry bloke in London who ran county lines.'

'We couldn't provide anything like that,' Ben muttered. 'No budget, no staff. What does Freddie bring to the table?'

'I guess his contacts and considerable clout, but I don't really know.'

'OK.' Ben rubbed his chin. 'I'll talk to Molly first thing about making her an independent adviser. That will give her some latitude and if she does find good stuff, we have more chance of being able to use it in court if we get that far. Then I'll ring Freddie.'

Ben sat at the table and scrubbed the top of his head.

'I'm sorry I yelled,' he said. 'It's worry, that's all. What you appear to have got tangled up with seems to be a satellite of a large and dangerous criminal network, stretching all the way to Iraq. This really isn't the place for you or Heidi.' He got to his feet. 'I'll go and apologise to Erica for our behaviour, we'll eat supper, then you can spend a couple of hours online.'

'Doing what?' Stacey asked.

'Talking to an excellent police artist I know. You will describe the guys you saw to him, every single detail, and he'll make sketches.'

Ben leant over Stacey, brushed a tear from her cheek and kissed her forehead.

'I'll ask Erica to stay here tonight. She shouldn't be on her own,' he said and headed for the living room to eat humble pie.

Chapter thirty

Ben and Erica left the cottage just before the sun had fully risen above the mountains. Another ridiculously hot day had been forecast and they wanted to accomplish as much as possible before the temperature ramped up. Stacey remained in bed until she heard the thump of car doors in the lane, then she shambled to the bathroom, splashed cold water on her face and stared at the dark shadows beneath her eyes. She found painkillers in the cabinet behind the mirror, swallowed two, then headed down to the kitchen without getting dressed.

She had talked to the police artist for well over two hours the previous evening, describing the men she was sure had taken Heidi. When the artist had heard enough, Stacey had dragged herself to bed but any sleep she did manage, was plagued by unsettling dreams. Now, she was running on empty – or not running, to be precise. There wasn't a single useful thought in her pounding head, so she sat outside and stared into the middle distance.

The sun burst above the tops of the parched mountains and hot, golden light shafted across the back garden, but Stacey remained where she was, the tops of her feet pinking in the UV glare. An hour or so later, the phone broke her trance. Thinking it could be Heidi, she leapt up, steadied herself on the door jamb as a wave of dizziness threatened to overwhelm her, and fumbled with the landline's handset from the top of the counter.

'Hello?'

'Good morning, Ms Logan. I am ringing from Insulate Now, part of a government scheme. Can I–'

'Sod off!' Stacey yelled, lobbing the device across the kitchen.

She shook her head. She knew she needed to get a grip and worked at taking a deep breath, filling her lungs until they hurt, then another and another. Slowly her head stopped spinning, her pulse slowed and her mind tentatively flickered back online.

Stacey put the kettle on and went upstairs to dress. A few minutes later, wearing loose-fitting cotton clothes, she was drinking a fresh cup of coffee and beginning to feel more like herself. Halfway down the mug, she opened her laptop and discovered an email with four attachments sent by the police artist. She took another deep breath and clicked on the first. The little man who had searched her stared out from the screen. The likeness was uncanny, and Stacey's breath quickened again as she looked into his mean, weasely eyes. Opening the next attachment, the giant with the thick gold earring suddenly glared out at her. Stacey eventually located the telephone handset, poking from beneath the fridge, dug it out and dialled Molly's number.

'Hello, Stacey,' Molly said. 'Have you heard from Heidi?'

'No, I haven't, sorry. Are you OK?'

'Maybe. Why are you ringing?'

'I have an email I'm going to forward, four sketches of some of the men I met with Heidi in Reading. They might be useful. Have you found anything yet?'

'Heidi's truck on the outskirts of Brecon and again approaching Abergavenny. Nothing else yet.'

'That's great! Felicity Savage lives out that way, maybe Heidi has gone there. I'll send the email then I'll give Fliss a ring.'

'Tell me what she says?'

'I will. We'll talk again soon.'

Stacey dialled Miss Savage's number and after a couple of rings, she came on the line.

'Llwyn-glas, good morning.'

'Morning, Fliss. Stacey here. How are you?'

'All is well thank you, Stacey, apart from being old and decrepit that is.'

Stacey chuckled. 'You are old, but hardly decrepit.'

'You don't live in my body, dear. How are you and Heidi?'

'That's why I'm ringing. Is Heidi with you, or has she been to visit in the last couple of days?'

'No, she isn't here and I haven't seen her. Is everything OK? You don't sound like your usual self.'

Stacey groaned. 'That's because I'm not. No one has seen Heidi for a couple of days, and she hasn't contacted her partner, Erica.'

'Does Heidi make a habit of this sort of behaviour?' Fliss asked.

'Uh, not really, although she did go away for a while a couple of years back, some sort of sabbatical, but not recently.'

'You sound concerned.'

'That's because I am. I've made an awful mistake and think I've put Heidi in danger.'

'How do you think you've done that, dear?'

Stacey took a deep breath and confessed all, while Fliss listened patiently.

'The first thing,' Fliss said, when Stacey had finished speaking, 'is for you to accept this is not your fault. You didn't conscript Heidi, she volunteered.'

'But–'

'No,' Fliss said, 'you both made the decision. If there is any blame, you share it equally. I'm glad you rang though. I might be able to help the search.'

'Really? How?'

'I might not go out much these days, but I know lots of people, good people. I'll send a message.' Fliss chuckled softly. 'It's helpful that Heidi is so memorable, and not just because of how she looks.'

'Thank you,' Stacey said. 'Let me know if you hear anything.'

'Of course I will. Would you like to stay here for a couple of days? You'd be most welcome.'

'That's kind and it's tempting, but I can't run away. Have you seen or heard from Rowan?'

'Yes, he called last night. He's in Dunkirk. I told him he should come back, but I'm not sure I convinced him. I'm concerned he'll overdo things again, let everything overwhelm him, like the last time when he was so ill.'

'Do you know anyone in France who might help him, or check on him?'

'There will be someone. I've put my feelers out. Don't worry about Rowan, I'll see to that. You worry about Heidi, so I don't have to do that too.'

Stacey disconnected the call and was about to dial Freddie's number, when she heard a knock at the front door. Hoping it would be Heidi, she dashed down the hall, yanked open the door and her brain took several seconds to recognise Bilbo Blaggins.

'Oh,' was all Stacey could manage.

Bilbo's face almost split in two as he smiled and said, 'Not the best welcome I've ever had. Are you OK? Heat getting to you?'

'No, I was expecting… what are you doing here?'

'I guess your technique is improving, slowly.'

'Sorry.' Stacey opened the door wider. 'Please, come in. Go to the kitchen, coolest room in the house. Would you like an elderflower cordial with ice?'

Bilbo nodded. 'That would be good, thanks.'

He headed down the hall to the back of the cottage and into the kitchen. His eyes swept around the room before he sat on the carver.

'Lovely place you have,' he said and smiled again. 'I almost forget that most people don't fill their houses with shitloads of boxes and bags.' Stacey put a glass in front of him and he drank deeply. 'So then, my lovely, tell Uncle Bilbo what's bothering you.'

For the second time in an hour, Stacey related her sorry tale. When she reached the end, she said, 'Now you know my story, tell me why you're here. How did you even know where to find me?'

'I gave Sorrell a ring and got directions.' He opened an old-fashioned, brown leather satchel. 'This is all very embarrassing,' he said as he rummaged inside.

After some searching, he pulled out a large brown envelope and slid it across the table to Stacey.

'What's this?' she asked.

'The envelope Jonathon Haddon dropped in at Builth golf club just before he was murdered.'

* * *

The team had all arrived early. Ben had been rereading statements taken during the investigation when the phone on his desk rang.

He picked up the handset. 'DCI James.'

'Morning, Chief Inspector,' said a female voice. 'Governor McCourt from the remand centre.'

'Good morning, Ms McCourt. What can I do for you?'

'I'm calling about one of your cases involving Natalie Turrell. She has put in an application to talk to the police.'

'Did she say why?'

'I had a word and she says she wants to provide a new statement. She isn't doing particularly well in here, so I'm not sure if she does actually have anything new to tell you. She has refused to discuss the matter with myself.'

'OK, I'll pop over with my sergeant.'

'That's not going to work I'm afraid. Turrell has said she will only talk to a female officer.'

Ben sighed heavily. 'I'll arrange something. Should be there this side of lunch if that's OK with you.'

'I'll let the gate staff know to expect you. I'm in the office all day, if you should like a word.'

'Good to know. Thank you, ma'am.'

Ben hung up. 'Elsa?' he called. 'Newport remand centre has been on. Turrell wants to make a new statement and wants to talk to a female officer. Best if you come, you understand the fraud better than anyone.'

'Me, sir? I haven't done much interviewing and never in a jail.'

'You'll be fine, I'll coach you on the way. Grab what you need and I'll meet you downstairs. Jack?'

'Yes, guv.'

'Keep this lot on track and try to speak with Freddie Holtz, find out exactly what is going on. I haven't been able to get hold of him.'

'Will do and I'll call if there's anything you need to know.'

Ben nodded, draped his jacket over one arm and followed Elsa to the car park.

Chapter thirty-one

As Natalie Turrell shuffled into the small interview room, Ben thought the governor's opinion that Turrell wasn't "doing well" was a vast underestimate. The woman was hunched, her eyes red-rimmed and dull, hair lank and greasy-looking, and she was sweating profusely.

One of the prison officers set up a fan before he left the room, but the device did little more than move hot air around. Natalie grasped the edge of the table and lowered herself onto a chair. She glanced at Ben then looked away and focussed her gaze on Elsa.

'Hello, Natalie,' Elsa said. 'I'm Constable Duffin. How are you?'

'How the fuck do you think I am?' Natalie muttered. 'I'm locked up in a lunatic asylum.'

'Governor McCourt rang us this morning,' Elsa said. 'She told us you requested a meeting because you want to make a change to your statement. Is that right?'

'Yeah, that's about the size of it.'

'We've also been told you're happy to talk to us without legal representation. Is that also correct?'

'Yeah, it is. It's not like Jacobs was doing me any good.'

Natalie wiped her damp face with the bottom of her grey T-shirt.

'So tell me what's on your mind.'

Natalie stared at the palm of one hand, picked at something with her thumbnail and kept her eyes low. Ben wanted her to confess. He wanted to reach across the table and shake the prisoner but knew the interview couldn't be rushed, so he remained silent while Elsa asked questions.

'We've come a long way to see you, Natalie,' Elsa said. 'It won't look good in your position if you are wasting our time. Tell me what this is about. Something about the fraud? Something else?'

'The night Jonathon died,' Natalie said, voice cracking.

Elsa risked a quick glance at Ben who nodded almost imperceptibly.

'What about it?'

Natalie looked up. 'It's difficult, OK? Nothing about this is easy.'

'Take your time, we're in no rush.'

'I *was* in Wales that night,' Natalie said and gulped a huge breath. 'I came to meet up with Jon but I didn't kill him, I swear I didn't.' She looked up at Ben. 'You've got to get me out of here. I can't deal with it and I haven't killed anyone, so promise me bail and I'll go into chapter and verse.'

'It doesn't work that way,' Elsa said. 'You need to tell me everything.'

'If I do, will you get me out?'

'I can't promise anything, but depending on what you say, it could make a difference at your plea hearing in a couple of weeks.'

Natalie's lip began to tremble. 'Couple of weeks? In here?'

'Just tell me.'

Natalie wiped her face for a second time. 'Jon knew about the fraud,' she said, 'and how much money had gone… missing.'

'Was he going to report you?' Elsa asked.

'He said he wouldn't, as long as I stood down as CEO of the charity and paid back every penny, but I didn't have it.'

'What happened to the money?'

'I lost it,' Natalie muttered.

'How did you lose it?'

'Online poker. I'm an addict, a victim, not a fraudster or a murderer. You should let me go. I need help for my mental health issues, not incarceration.'

'So why did you come to Wales to meet Jonathon?'

'To talk the thing through. I saw on his website he'd be at the Caer Beris in Builth Wells, closer to Bristol than Carmarthen where his office is, and I wanted to meet on neutral ground.'

'What did you intend to say to him?'

'Oh, shit, I don't know. Try to reason with him or something.'

'Did you choose the venue?'

'No, that was Jon. I rang him that evening, said I'd come to the hotel, but he said no, we should meet at a car showroom in Llanelwedd. He said he'd be there at 1am, that he couldn't get away before then, but it would give me enough time to drive there.'

'So, did you go to the showroom?' Elsa asked, while Ben held his breath.

Natalie nodded. 'Yes, but I was late. The weather was awful and there was a hold-up on the motorway just after the bridge. I arrived about twenty past. The rain was lashing down and it looked as though the river would burst its banks. I was about to drive into the car park, when I saw someone by the main doors, a man I think. I panicked, turned the car around and headed back to Bristol.'

'Why did you go home when you were expecting to meet Jonathon? Was that who you saw?'

'No, it wasn't Jon. The man was shorter, heavier. Jon was tall and slim. Even in the rain I could tell I wasn't looking at Jon, and there's something else.'

'What's that?' Elsa asked.

'Before the lights in the showroom went out, I'm fairly sure I caught the glint of a gun in his hand.'

* * *

Stacey stared at the manila envelope on the table and saw Rowan's name written on the front in a large, looping hand.

'How did you get this, Bilbo?' she asked. 'The police went to the golf club looking for it and no one admitted they'd even seen it.'

Bilbo sighed. 'I collected a vanload of donations from there, over two weeks ago. I only got around to looking through the stuff last night and found the envelope in one of the boxes. Maybe a cleaner put it there. I rang Sorrell and she suggested I bring it to you. She said your fella is a cop and he'd know what to do with it.'

'Did you open it? Look inside?'

Bilbo nodded. 'I took a quick shuftie. There's a letter for Rowan and some photographs.'

'OK if I take a look?'

'Knock yourself out, my lovely.'

Stacey gingerly picked up the envelope and tipped the contents onto the surface of the table. She saw about twenty photos of different individuals, all candid shots. With the pictures was a sheet of cream paper, headed with the country hotel's monogram, beneath which was what looked to be a hastily scribbled note. Stacey placed it in front of her and began to read.

> *Hi, Rowan,*
> *Without being too dramatic, this is my "just in case" letter. I was hoping we could meet up, while I was in*

Builth, but things got a little complicated, so... just in case...
The photos are hard copies of UK members of the smuggling gang my darling Yezda managed to get herself involved with. Kitty and I have been able to track a few down, and put names and address to some of the faces, but not all. I kept this off the internet for safety reasons. Knowing you often park up overnight at the golf club to spend time with your mate who works there, I knew this would find its way to you. Really sorry I couldn't pass it on in person, but as we know, plans often don't work out.
Funny thing, one of my clients has been cyber-stalking me, ever since I confronted her and told her I knew she was fleecing thousands of pounds from a charity she ran. She saw my name on the guest list of the annual FIA bash, rang me there and asked for a meeting. She requested neutral ground, Kitty suggested the showroom as she had the key, and I agreed. Two birds with one stone and all that. Anyway, I'm sure we'll meet up soon, it's been too long. Hope all is good with you
Take care and stay safe
Jon

'Bloody hell,' Stacey said and began sifting through the photos. The third she looked at was of the giant she'd met in Reading, the gold hoop in his ear plainly visible. She separated the snap from the rest and handed it to Bilbo.

'I met this guy,' she said. 'He was one of the heavies at the meeting I told you about.'

Stacey examined the other shots carefully but couldn't recognise anyone else. She turned back to the note and read it through again.

'Do you understand anything Jon's talking about?' Bilbo asked.

'Some. I think the cyber-stalker could be a woman called Natalie Turrell. She was in court yesterday charged with fraud and murder.'

'Fuck. So she lured Jon somewhere quiet and shot him. Is that what you're suggesting?'

'It's possible, but I don't understand his comment about two birds and one stone. He and Kitty must have had another reason to be at the showroom, otherwise it doesn't make sense. Do you have any idea what he meant?'

'Not a clue, sorry.'

'OK, I'll give Ben a ring. Put the kettle on, I could do with a cuppa.'

Stacey picked up the phone, noticing a small crack in the plastic sustained when she'd launched it across the kitchen earlier, and dialled the number of the incident room at the station. She fiddled with the photos impatiently until her call was answered.

'DS Trent,' Jack growled.

'Hi, Jack, it's Stacey. Is Ben there?'

'No, he's out of the office. Can I help?'

'Hope so. Something interesting has just come into my possession. The envelope Jonathon Haddon dropped off at the golf club just before he was killed.'

'How the hell have you got hold of that?'

'It's complicated. Would you like me to bring it over?'

'No, stay there, don't drive out in the heat. I'll come to you. See you in thirty minutes or so.'

Stacey hung up and filled a teapot.

'I ought to get off,' Bilbo said. 'Got loads to do and I'm not keen on getting involved with the cops.'

'You can't leave,' Stacey said. 'Jack Trent's a good guy and he's bound to want to talk to you.'

'But I feel so useless, not finding the envelope before now. It could have made a difference.'

'It probably still can but it isn't going to change the fact Jonathon was shot. Nothing can change that, but this information will help the investigation into his murder.

You really should stay and talk to Jack, please?' She grinned. 'He looks like a handful but he's more of a pussycat – between ourselves that is.'

'Go on then, but if it gets spikey, I'm off.'

* * *

Ben and Elsa were glad to leave the remand centre. The interview had taken it out of Elsa, so Ben got behind the wheel for the drive back to the station.

'You did really well in there,' he said, pulling onto the main road. 'You're a natural interviewer.'

'Thanks, sir, but I don't think it's helped. I reckon pretty much everything she said was rubbish.'

'Why do you say that?' Ben asked.

'It's obvious Turrell wants out. I think she invented the guy with the gun to shift suspicion away from herself.'

'That is a possibility, but I'm not convinced. She didn't need to tell us about the proposed meeting at the showroom. It's not like we've been able to prove where she went after she drove into Wales.'

'I guess not, but it just seems too convenient to me. She doesn't say anything before, then she gets banged up and all of a sudden she tells us she saw a guy with a gun? *Way* too convenient.'

'Then we need to disprove her new statement, look at the case from another direction. For example, recheck the mobile phone records of Haddon and Turrell. If we can confirm the small details, then maybe this time Natalie is being truthful.'

'Maybe,' Elsa said and wiped her face with a tissue. 'God, I'm knackered.'

Ben grinned. 'But you did well, Constable.' He overtook a slow-moving caravan. 'Have you ever thought of applying to be a detective?'

'Not really, sir.'

'Well, you should. I know CS Warren has been impressed with the work you've put in on this case – me too.'

'I'll think about it,' Elsa said, 'when I'm not so tired and it's not so hot.'

'Fair enough.'

They travelled in silence for a few miles before Elsa asked, 'What do you think has happened to Heidi?'

Ben groaned. 'I can't honestly say. It doesn't look great, bearing in mind she and Stacey went for a chat with people smugglers a couple of days before she disappeared.'

'I don't understand how Heidi managed to find those people and we haven't. Do you think it's the same lot who put those poor refugees in that truck?'

'Worth bearing in mind.'

'Do you know how Heidi found them, sir?'

'Not a clue. I'm hoping her father will be able to shed some light on it.'

'I'm hoping she's OK. I like Heidi and hate the idea something awful might have happened to her.'

'You and me both, Constable.'

Chapter thirty-two

Jack was as good as his word and pulled up outside Noddfa just under half an hour later. Stacey met him on the doorstep, and he scurried out of the heat.

'Bloody hell,' he said. 'I love sunshine, but this is mental. Too hot to think straight.'

'We're in the kitchen,' Stacey said as she closed the door.

'We?' Jack asked.

'I have a guest, a charity worker from Cardiff called Bilbo. He found the envelope.'

Jack nodded, stomped along the hall and into the kitchen.

'Afternoon,' he said. 'I'm DS Jack Trent. Stacey says you're Bilbo.'

'Yes that's me.' Bilbo hauled himself upright with the help of his stick and the men shook hands.

'You found an envelope we've been looking for, is that right?'

'Yes. I'm sorry I didn't find it before. I collected a vanload of donations from Builth golf club a couple of weeks back, dumped the stuff in my place and didn't open any of the boxes until last night. I found it then.'

'Let's see what you've got,' Jack said and took a seat.

Bilbo handed over the thick envelope, while Stacey made another jug of elderflower cordial and added handfuls of ice to tall glasses. Jack cast his eyes over the photographs, then bent to read the note, a deep frown creasing his forehead.

'Bloody hell,' he said. 'Jonathon's talking about Natalie Turrell. Looks to me like this proves her guilt. Bloody hell,' he said again and wiped his face. 'Ben and Elsa went to the remand centre this morning. Natalie said she wanted to change her original statement. Maybe she's confessing.'

Stacey handed out glasses and tapped the photo of the Reading giant.

'This is one of the guys Heidi and I met.'

'Recognise any of the others?' Jack asked.

'No, just him.'

Jack glanced up at Bilbo. 'Do you know what Jonathon meant by "two birds and one stone"?'

'Sorry, not a clue.'

'Jack, is there any news about Heidi?' Stacey asked.

'Not so far. You?'

'Molly found an ANPR record of her truck heading to Abergavenny soon after she left me. I called Fliss Savage, but she hasn't seen her.'

'OK, I'll let the others know. I've been trying to speak to Freddie, but he seems to have vanished as well. Did he say anything significant when you and Erica met him?'

'Not much, only that he'd look for Heidi and would ring when he has anything to say.'

Jack nodded and drained his glass. 'Right then,' he said, 'better get back to the nick with this.' He got to his feet. 'Good to meet you, Bilbo. Have you met the Ahmadis? A couple discovered recently in the back of a truck?'

'Yes, I have,' Bilbo said. 'They are about as good as they can be in the circumstances. I'm keeping an eye on them and one of our volunteers is guiding them through the Home Office paperwork.' He hesitated. 'I wonder…'

'What?' Jack asked.

'They're Muslim, and like to bury their dead soon after death.' He sighed deeply. 'Any chance you can speed up the process? I'm sure being able to put their son to rest would help them.'

'I get it,' Jack said. 'I'll have a word and find out what can be done.'

'Many thanks.' Bilbo scribbled on a scrap of paper and offered it to Jack. 'My mobile number. Easiest way to get hold of me.'

'Thanks.' Jack tucked the scrap in his pocket. 'I'll see myself out, Stace. Ring me if Molly has any more discoveries.'

* * *

Ben and Elsa walked into the incident room just a few minutes after Jack. While Elsa worked out how to use the new coffee machine, the detectives swapped notes. Ben read and reread the letter Haddon had written to Rowan. No matter which direction he came at it from, the letter, plus Natalie's startling admission, made a conviction much more likely.

'Why didn't we have this earlier?' Ben grumbled.

'The guy wasn't aware he had it and took it to Stacey first thing.'

'Why Stacey?'

'This Bilbo character met her recently and Sorrell had told him she was the partner of a cop. I got the feeling Bilbo didn't want to get involved with us.'

'Did he say why?'

'Usual stuff, guv. Confidence in the police at an all-time low, even lower trust, especially if you live on the edges of society.'

Ben nodded. 'We need to be able to prove or disprove what Natalie told us she saw, just before Haddon was murdered and Kitty Phillips dry drowned.' He looked around the room. 'Ollie and Tegan, get back to the showroom. I know the flood took out most of the internal cameras, but check any historical footage and look for cameras further afield, on the nearby service stations maybe.'

'I've worked out where Natalie must have parked that night overlooking the car park,' Tegan said. 'While we're there, I'll check exactly what she could have seen of the showroom from her vantage point.'

'Good idea,' Ben said. 'If the answer is not much, we'll know she's spinning us a line. If you can see the main door, go back after dark and check the lighting. Natalie said she saw the gun because it glinted in the lights.'

Ollie snorted. 'Sounds to me that she got that straight out of a crime novel. Glinted? Yeah right.'

'Check it out though and if either of you can think of something clever while you're in town, follow up on it.'

'Yes, sir.'

'Elsa, you keep on with the accounts. Now Natalie has confirmed she did ring Haddon, it would be good to know about any other contact she had with him up to the day he died. She told us he had asked her to pay the money back to the charity and stand down as CEO. Surely there would be some emails or messages discussing this, so keep looking.'

'Yes, sir,' Elsa said.

'Bilbo gave me an update on the Ahmadis,' Jack said. 'He told me they were very distressed about not being able to bury their boy. Any chance we can speed up proceedings?'

'Maybe,' Ben said. 'Kevin, that's your job. Talk to the CPS, find out what you can then liaise with the couple. Now they have a place to live, they might be easier to talk to and any information would be useful. Take copies of the artist's sketches and the photographs from the envelope. We might get lucky – we're certainly overdue.'

* * *

When evening arrived and the sun began to sink, the heat finally started to lift. Stacey sat in a chair beneath the apple tree and enjoyed the gentle coolness on her skin. She was worried about Heidi but tried to remain focussed and work out how to find her friend without throwing things across the kitchen.

She looked at her watch, Ben should be home soon. She hoped things would be better than the previous evening. The row had unsettled her and she didn't want to repeat the experience. After Bilbo had left, she'd worked in the office, researching what was available online regarding smuggling gangs. There had been a few raids, a few arrests of truck drivers, some confiscated cash and weapons, but if as many refugees were on the move as the boss had claimed, there would be many more takedowns, she was sure of it.

She'd studied mug shots of those who had been convicted of the trade in UK courts. Not one matched the photos from the envelope and that made sense when she thought about it. The pictures had come from Haddon, information he and Kitty had somehow discovered about the gang which had sold Yezda and her family places on a blow-up boat.

When she found that she could no longer focus properly, Stacey got to her feet, checked on supper and returned to the garden. She leaned back and gazed up at the clear night sky, picking out stars she knew the names of, and wondering at the millions she didn't, as a large, yellow-tinted moon rose gracefully above the forest. The metallic click of the side gate made her look earthwards and Ben walked around the end of the cottage.

'Sorry I'm late, *cariad*,' he said, 'something came up.' He bent and kissed the top of her head. 'Heidi's truck has been found.'

'Has it? Oh, thank God. Is she OK?'

'The truck was found on a council estate in Bath. It had been torched. Heidi wasn't inside.'

'Bloody hell.' Stacey rubbed her face. 'This situation is just getting worse, isn't it?'

'Unfortunately, things like this often do. We'll have the vehicle brought here and get SOCO to go over it. A burnt-out vehicle doesn't often contain much evidence. We get lucky sometimes though.'

'But what if you don't? Heidi wouldn't have torched her own truck. To my mind that proves someone has her. It removes the element of doubt.'

'Yes, it does. CS Warren has promised more staff and ensured full cooperation from Avon and Somerset force.'

'Can I ask you something?'

Ben smiled. 'Yes, of course.'

Stacey swallowed hard. 'Do you think Heidi's been hurt, killed maybe, her truck burnt to destroy evidence? Do you think we should be looking for a body?' Stacey noticed her voice trembled.

Ben took hold of her hand. 'No point in jumping to conclusions. We should work on the premise that someone has her, but until the vehicle had been examined, together with any available CCTV, I can't tell you any more than that.'

Chapter thirty-three

The next morning the heat was manageable, less fierce, and Ben left for work at a more sensible time. As soon as his car had pulled away, Stacey picked up the phone and made a call.

'Hi, Stace,' Erica said. 'I'm guessing you've heard about Heidi's truck.'

'Ben told me yesterday evening. Are you OK?'

'What do you think?' Erica grumbled. 'I'm gonna drive over to Bath and take a look at the scene.'

'Why? Ben said the vehicle is being brought here.'

Erica sighed. 'I have to do something so I can feel I'm being useful. I've been in touch with Freddie and am also planning to drop into Milebrook Manor. Are you busy? Fancy keeping me company?'

'Of course. I'll drive to Brecon and meet you at your place.'

The drive across the ranges was uneventful and Stacey pulled up outside the apartment under an hour later. Erica heard her arrive and ran up the stone steps.

'We'll take your car,' she said. 'I've been granted a few days' compassionate leave, but not the use of the car.'

'Not a problem. My old banger might look a bit tatty but it runs OK. Do you know where we're heading for in Bath?'

'Council estate called Twerton. Heidi's truck was burnt out behind a community centre. We won't have to go into the city. It's a couple of hours' drive if we're lucky. Should be there before lunch.'

'OK, you navigate then. Sorry I haven't got air con.'

'No worries. Must be ten degrees below yesterday's high and we can open the windows.'

The journey wasn't trouble-free, even though Stacey stuck to B roads when she could. There had been a bump on the Severn Bridge and the accident added another hour to the trip. Eventually they arrived at a sprawling housing estate. Erica concentrated on the satnav and a few minutes later directed Stacey into the car park of a run-down, and seemingly unloved, community centre. A group of teenagers kicked a football around the tarmac and scattered when the women left the car.

'Over here,' Erica called and pointed at a fire-stained section. 'This is where the truck was torched.'

Stacey walked closer and stared at the blackened ground. 'What now?' she asked. 'There isn't really anything to see.'

Erica didn't answer and wandered around the car park, eyes cast down, searching. Stacey did the same in the opposite direction but neither found anything. Erica leaned on the bonnet of the car and began to cry. Stacey wrapped an arm around her friend's shoulders.

'Hey now,' Stacey said. 'Come on, don't cry. It was always unlikely we'd find anything here.'

Erica sniffed. 'I know, just wanted to take a look.'

'Let's get over to Milebrook, maybe Freddie will have something good to tell us.' Stacey dug a packet of tissues out of the car. 'Wipe your eyes, love. Won't take us long to get there.'

Erica nodded, blew her nose and settled in the passenger seat. Stacey started the car, found her way back to the main road and headed for the Cotswolds.

* * *

The patch of gravel outside the main entrance of Freddie's manor house popped musically beneath the tyres as Stacey pulled up. The women left the car and by the time they reached the door, Freddie Holtz was standing on the step.

'Afternoon, ladies. You're a little later than I expected. Problem?'

'Nothing more serious than traffic,' Stacey said. 'How are you?'

'Busy as usual.' Freddie stepped closer to Erica and brushed a kiss on her cheek. 'How about you?' he asked. 'Holding up?'

Erica shrugged. 'I guess.'

'Let's go to the study,' Freddie said. 'I've kept your visit to myself to keep the residents at bay.'

'How is everyone?' Stacey asked.

'Muddling along nicely but worrying about Heidi like the rest of us. Go on through, I'll rustle up some coffee. Won't be long.'

Stacey and Erica went to the study and sat in a pair of antique upholstered chairs in the bay window.

'Doesn't feel right,' Erica said, 'being here without Heidi.'

'Maybe Freddie has some news.'

'Yeah, maybe. Did you bring copies of the stuff in that envelope?'

Stacey nodded and patted her bag. 'After what Haddon wrote about keeping the photos off the internet, I didn't want to email them.'

The study door opened and Freddie entered carrying a large tray which he placed on a round table next to the chairs.

'I made a couple of plates of sandwiches earlier,' he said as he filled mugs with coffee. 'Don't expect either of you have eaten anything today. Tuck in while I look at what you've brought.'

'Thanks, Freddie,' Erica said, 'but I'm not hungry.'

'Probably not, but you must eat. At least try the ham and cheese, both from a farm just down the road.'

Stacey passed over the bundle of photocopies, Freddie took them to his desk and switched on a green-shaded banker's lamp. He didn't say anything as he read Haddon's note and examined the pictures carefully, using an ornate magnifying glass. After several minutes he got to his feet and dragged a third chair closer to the table.

He took a deep breath. 'What I am about to tell you must not – under any circumstances – be repeated outside this room,' he said. 'I've known you both long enough to trust you, but nevertheless I need your assurance you will not mention anything to another living soul.'

'Goes without saying, Freddie,' Erica said. 'You're my father-in-law after all and I will never let you down.'

'And I won't say anything,' Stacey said. 'You know I won't.'

Freddie nodded and took a sip of coffee. 'OK then, here goes.' He put his mug back on the table. 'I have been speaking with a friend of mine in the Home Office, someone I trust. It seems that Haddon and Rowan, and to a lesser extent Kitty Phillips, had for some time been passing on information they gathered by working in the refugee camps in France.' He waved the bundle of photocopies. 'This would have found its way to Whitehall long before now if a couple of links in the network hadn't fractured.'

'When Haddon and Kitty died,' Erica said, 'and Rowan didn't pick up the envelope?'

'Correct,' Freddie said. 'The late delivery blew some plans out of the water and delayed others.'

'Can you tell us about those plans?' Stacey asked.

Freddie offered the hint of a smile. 'Calm your inner journalist. I'll tell you what I can.'

'Sorry. I'm very wound up about Heidi disappearance. I feel as though it was my fault.'

Freddie sighed. 'You attended a meeting Heidi arranged. She convinced you to go along by telling you I had given her a tip. Isn't that what happened?'

'Yes, but I got her involved with the murder case.'

'And that led to the people smugglers, who Heidi had presumably tracked, then contacted to arrange the meet. We haven't got time to beat ourselves up.' He selected a sandwich and took a bite. 'To answer your question, a large – and I do mean large – operation is in the final stages of preparation. These photos will complete the picture and the plans will be tweaked accordingly.'

'So you know about these scumbags,' Erica said, 'and you – or whoever – is picking the time for the bust carefully.'

'That's a pretty fair assessment. The scale of the op means simultaneous raids in the UK, France, Belgium, Germany and the Netherlands. Intel has already provided locations of warehouses full of RHIBs and thousands of life vests, and a list of over eighty individuals we want to detain. Thanks to the three musketeers, we now have photos of nearly all of them.'

'When will it happen?' Erica asked. 'A few days, a week, a month? Do you think Heidi is with them?'

Freddie took a deep breath. 'I know she is. Our undercover guy saw her. She wasn't badly injured – a few cuts and bruises, nothing more.'

'Bloody hell, Freddie. If you know where she is why hasn't she been rescued?' Erica asked.

'I know this is difficult for you to accept, but we must wait until everyone is in place. Don't worry. If Heidi is in immediate danger I'll authorise the raid myself, but if we're to catch those responsible for the people-smuggling racket, a little patience is called for.'

'I don't agree!' Erica snapped. 'We should bring her home, right now! Tell me where she is and I'll go and get her.'

Freddie shook his head. 'That's not possible. There's a lot at stake.'

'Yes, there is. The safety of my wife – your daughter.'

'Erica,' Freddie said, 'you've been in the force long enough to know how these things go. If we don't apprehend as many of the gang as possible – including those at the top – more innocent people will drown in the English Channel. More bodies will wash up on our beaches.' He reached out and took both of her hands. 'You must trust me. I won't let you down.'

Erica pulled her hands away. 'I want to be there,' she said, 'when the raids happen. I want to be there to make sure Heidi is safe.'

'I understand, my dear. Really I do. The National Crime Agency will handle the operation in the UK, but I'm intending to involve Ben James as the cases he's currently working are linked to this.' He smiled at her. 'I will do my very best to ensure you're included.'

Erica nodded reluctantly. 'When do you think the raids will happen?'

'If I had to put money on it, by the end of the week. You just need to hold your nerve for a few days.'

'Can't say I'm overjoyed,' Erica grumbled, 'but it doesn't seem as though I have a choice.'

Freddie patted her shoulder. 'Just trust me.'

'A minor matter I know,' Stacey said, 'but when you spoke to your friend at the Home Office, I don't suppose you asked about Bilal, Sorrell's husband?'

'I did as it happens. On first inspection it does appear something has gone awry. My friend has begun an investigation into what has happened.'

'Does that mean Bilal might be able to return to live with his family?'

'Too early to tell, but let's not abandon all hope.'

Chapter thirty-four

Ollie and Tegan returned to the incident room just after lunch. Ben glanced up from the stack of paperwork he was working through.

'You look pleased with yourselves,' he said.

Ollie held up a memory stick. 'Guess what this is.'

'A memory stick,' Elsa muttered from behind her screen.

'Yeah, whatever. Only CCTV footage, captured by cameras on the main entrance of the Royal Welsh Showground, covering the last month.'

'Is the showroom on it?' Ben asked.

Ollie grinned. 'Yep. Cameras cover all three exits on the roundabout, and pick up the showroom, front and side. All we've gotta do is look through it.'

'Brilliant. Who thought to ask at the showground?'

'I did, sir,' Tegan said.

Ben nodded. 'Well done. Anything new from the showroom?'

'Nothing. We spoke to Caleb and the new guy on reception, but Tomos Jones was on a day off.'

'Right, then you'd better start looking. Check twelve hours before the flood and twelve after.' Ben handed the memory stick to Elsa. 'Copy the files and send them to each of us. Is Jack still with SOCO at the garage looking at Heidi's truck?'

'Yes, sir.'

'OK.' Ben got to his feet. 'CS Warren is expecting me in her office. If Jack's back before me, get him on this too. Maximum effort, everyone.'

* * *

An hour passed before Ben walked back upstairs. CS Warren had listened to his update carefully, then passed on astounding details regarding an upcoming raid, headed by the NCA, and how it was connected to his investigation. He took off his jacket, made coffee and dropped onto his chair. The incident room was quiet as the team examined the new CCTV footage.

'Oh my God!' Elsa exclaimed. 'Sir, come and take a look at this.'

Ben got to his feet, mind still clogged with the information his boss had imparted, and walked down the room to Elsa's workstation.

'Look.' Elsa pointed at the screen. 'Natalie Turrell wasn't lying.' She tapped the image. 'There's her man, caught on the middle camera from above the RWS entrance.'

Ben leaned closer as the rest of the team gathered to peer over his shoulder.

'Bloody hell,' he said. 'I was sure she was making it up. What time was this captured?'

'01.23,' Elsa said, pointing at a time signature at the top of the image.

Elsa ran the section forward slowly until the lights in the showroom went out as the river burst its banks.

'Run it again will you?' Ben asked. 'Wind it back to 01.00, then scroll through slowly. See if we can work out where the guy came from.'

'I already know,' Elsa said and reset the recording. 'He drove.'

She pointed at the screen again as a car drove in through the exit and parked. Ben watched as a man got out and walked towards the main doors. Elsa paused the footage, minimized the image and replaced it with a view from a different camera.

'Watch carefully, bottom left.' She ran the footage then hit pause. 'There! Natalie's car. Parked for three minutes before she turned around, drove towards town and vanished.'

'Go back to the shot of the car our mystery man arrived in,' Ben said.

Elsa tapped the keyboard and Ben peered at the picture for several moments, then straightened and smiled.

'Ollie, find Sergeant Trent, we need to make an urgent house call. You and Tegan need to attend too. I want to be away in ten, so get a move on and round up a couple of uniforms. Chop chop!'

As his officers scrabbled out of the room, Ben sent Stacey a text to say he wouldn't be home that night.

Fifteen minutes passed before the team had assembled. Jack was the last to arrive. He slipped behind the steering wheel and pulled onto the main road. Two vehicles followed, Ollie and Tegan in the first, a white patrol car containing two uniformed officers brought up the rear.

'Where are we heading, guv?' Jack asked.

'Take the Erwood road. We need a word with Tomos Jones.'

'The manager of the showroom?'

'The same. Doesn't appear he's been straight with us since the beginning. He is the man Natalie saw. We have discovered CCTV footage which clearly shows he went to the place shortly after one in the morning, just before the river broke its banks.'

'Have you warned the team? If he is our man, he could be armed.'

Ben nodded. 'I'll pass the word.' He removed his mobile from a pocket and made calls to officers in the following cars. He tucked the phone away and said, 'As soon as Tomos opens the door, nick him and get him in handcuffs. No mistakes on this. I don't want anyone hurt.'

'Got it, guv.'

A little while later, all three cars pulled up outside a small cottage just off the main road and the officers spilled out. Jack strode up to the main door, rang the bell and as soon as the door opened, took a step forward. He dropped a firm hand on Tomos' shoulder, spun him around, grabbed his wrists and snapped on cuffs as Ben recited the caution.

'What the hell?' Tomos yelled. 'Get your fucking hands off me. What do you think you're doing? Let me go!'

'No chance,' Jack growled and pushed his prisoner up against the wall. 'Are there any firearms in your house?'

'Of course not. I don't own a gun,' Tomos said, shaking his head. 'Why are you treating me like this? I don't understand.' He glanced at Ben. 'You're making a huge mistake, Chief Inspector. Tell your man to release me.'

'Can't do that,' Ben said. 'You've been arrested on suspicion of the murder of Jonathon Haddon and causing the unlawful death of Kitty Phillips.' Ben turned and addressed his team. 'Make a start on the property search and ensure you do it properly.'

'You can't search my home,' Tomos protested. 'You haven't shown me a warrant.'

'Don't need one,' Jack said, 'given you're under arrest. Why not save us some work and tell us where the gun is?'

Tomos shook his head and looked away.

'Fair enough,' Ben said. 'Ollie, Tegan, you take upstairs. The rest of us will work down here. Let's crack on then.'

Ben walked along the hall and into a living room which took up most of the ground floor. A desk sat beneath the window on which four screens were set up, a keyboard beneath. The screens were on and it didn't take Ben long to realise he was looking at four separate live feeds from security cameras covering the showroom, inside and out.

'Bring Tomos in here, Jack,' he called. 'He has some explaining to do.'

Jack nudged the prisoner into the room and closer to the desk.

Ben glanced up. 'What's all this, Tomos?' he asked.

The man shrugged. 'Security for the showroom.'

'Do you retain footage from these cameras?'

Tomos didn't answer and looked at the carpet.

'I'll ask again,' Ben said. 'Have you got any recordings?'

'You wouldn't believe me whatever I said,' Tomos muttered. 'Anyway, you aren't supposed to ask me questions unless I'm in an interview room with a solicitor. I know my rights.'

Ben nodded then moved away from the desk as uniformed officers began pulling out drawers and riffling through the contents. Any CDs, flash drives and other storage devices were placed inside plastic evidence bags. While they worked, Ben watched the screens. He saw a few customers inside the cavern-like building, walking between the cars, some opening doors and sitting inside. Others stood at reception and talked to a young man in a dark suit. Ben shifted his gaze to the screens which displayed the outside of the showroom. He saw the car park and at the back of the plot a large service bay, where other cars were parked in spaces next to the garage area. He went to the hall, took out his phone and called the incident room.

'Elsa,' he said. 'We need a couple more officers and a small van to bring the evidence back.' He gave her the postcode of the cottage.

'OK, sir. I'm on it.'

'Jack and I are gonna come back to the station. Could you let CS Warren know we've made an arrest? She may want to observe the interview. Tell her we'll start the questioning as soon as the prisoner is booked in.'

'Yes, sir.'

Ben disconnected the call and returned to the living room.

'Jack,' he said, 'we'll leave the team to it. There's more manpower on the way. Put Tomos in the car.'

Jack nodded then he took hold of the cuffs and led Tomos from the house.

Ben addressed the searching officers. 'You two, I want all the computers, mobile phones, diaries, cameras – you know the drill.'

They nodded and began unplugging the electrical equipment. Ben walked to the bottom of the stairs.

'Ollie?' he called.

Ollie appeared on the landing. 'Yes, sir?'

'Take the place apart. Collect all laundry, footwear, outdoor coats and if possible – a handgun.'

Ollie grinned. 'I'll do my very best, sir.'

Ben left the house, got in the car and Jack sped back to the station. When they arrived, anxious to get Tomos in an interview room as soon as possible, Ben allowed the man to ring his solicitor before the booking-in process began. A little over an hour later, Ben faced Tomos and his solicitor across the desk. Jack switched on the recording device, and after he had verbally logged on, the interview began.

Chapter thirty-five

Jack slid an enlarged copy of a single frame captured by a camera on the RWS entrance across the table. He tapped the centre of the photo which depicted a dark-clad figure outside the main doors of the showroom, looking as though it was about to enter.

'That's you isn't it, Tomos?' Jack asked.

Tomos leaned forward in his seat and peered at the image.

'When was this taken?' he asked.

'Approximately six and a half hours before you discovered your deceased receptionist and her companion.'

'I told you,' Tomos said, 'the earliest I was at the showroom was ten past seven. I'd heard on the local news the river had flooded so I rang Caleb and asked him to meet me there, help move the cars.' He sighed. 'I've told you this before.'

'In that case, tell me where you were between one and two that Sunday morning?'

'As I've already said, at home in bed.'

'That's the problem,' Ben said. 'It's not what the crime shows call a cast-iron alibi. Take another look just in case you've made a mistake.'

Tomos pushed the picture away from him. 'This is stupid. I've told you that's not me and before you ask, I don't know who it is.'

'How many people have keys?' Jack asked.

Tomos sighed. 'Me, Kitty, Caleb – for emergencies – and one of the mechanics in the service garage.'

'Looks to me,' Jack continued, 'that whoever that is, is about to use a key. That makes sense because we found no signs of forced entry.'

Tomos leaned back in his chair. 'Must have been Kitty,' he said. 'I found her inside.'

Jack tipped back his head and laughed. 'Kitty, yeah of course.' He laughed some more.

'I object to your attitude, Sergeant,' the solicitor said. 'This is not a laughing matter.'

Jack reined in his mirth and held up the photo in front of Tomos' face. 'Is that person dressed in a shimmery, aqua-blue ball gown? This isn't Kitty. This is you.' Jack grinned. 'We also have an eyewitness who saw you by the doors. Their statement together with this footage means I'm intending to charge you on one count of murder and one of aggravated manslaughter.'

'No, that's not right. I didn't kill anyone. I found them dead after seven. Caleb was with me.'

'An elaborate charade,' Jack said. 'You knew they were there – you spotted them entering the showroom hours earlier, on your array of screens. The flood gave you a perfect excuse to call Caleb in early on Sunday. A pre-arranged witness. Nice touch.'

'*Our* witness,' Ben said, 'who saw you by the door, reported seeing a gun in your hand.'

Tomos laughed. 'Not a chance. This is just an enormous wind-up. She was too far away to see anything.'

Jack pounced. 'You saw the witness then? Knew she was female?'

'Just a turn of phrase.'

There was a knock at the door. Jack opened it and Elsa handed him a cardboard file. He shut the door, flipped through the documents and removed another photo which showed a low-slung saloon car, parked a little way from the entrance.

'That's your car, Tomos,' Jack said and slid the photo across the table.

Jack leaned back in his chair and watched the prisoner carefully. He saw the man's face change, spotted a twitching beneath one eye and his skin break out in a damp sheen. Picking his moment, Jack decided now was the time to hit Tomos with the extra, astounding discovery, the link that would more than likely hang him. Jack opened the file again, removed two photographs of a white, refrigerated truck parked close to the service bay. The shot of the back doors clearly recorded the registration number of the vehicle.

'Recognise this?' Jack asked.

Tomos shrugged. 'Just a truck. Heaps on the road like that.'

'Not just a truck,' Ben said, 'but the *actual* truck used to transport refugees from Dover. The truck in which seven individuals, including a child, suffocated to death.'

'Chief Inspector,' the solicitor said, 'if you wish to continue this line of questioning, you should prove my client is linked to this vehicle. I can't allow you to run a fishing expedition.'

'He's not,' Jack said and placed another document on the table. 'We discovered many sets of fingerprints inside the cab of the truck.' He grinned. 'Just so happens some belonged to your client.' He pointed at the document. 'See where it says "perfect match"?'

'Can you explain how your prints came to be in the truck, Tomos?' Ben asked.

The prisoner shook his head. 'I can't,' he said. 'You must have got it wrong.'

Yet another document was removed from the file and placed on the table.

'This records the result of a GSR test on a waxed cotton jacket, recovered from a coat stand in your hall,' Jack said.

'What does GSR mean?' Tomos asked.

'Stands for gunshot residue. The test came up positive. Proves whoever wore it fired a gun.'

Tomos stared at the document but said nothing.

'I think we could do with a break,' Ben said. He glanced at the solicitor. 'You should talk to your client, sir. I think even you will now agree this is not a fishing exercise.' Ben got to his feet. 'Interview terminated at 20.05.'

Jack switched off the machine and the detectives left the room.

* * *

The next morning, Ben and Jack sat together in the incident room planning the resumption of Tomos Jones' interrogation. The man's solicitor had spent over an hour with his client the evening before and the decision had been made to continue the interviewing process after the prisoner had been given the opportunity to get some sleep.

The detectives gazed up at the incident board, satisfied smiles on their faces.

'Do we really need to question him again?' Jack asked. He waved a hand at the board. 'Everything is there and the CPS will agree. Put Tomos in front of a jury and they'll convict him in a heartbeat.'

'Great to have such a strong case,' Ben agreed, 'but I want him to tell me why he killed Jonathon Haddon. Why and how he is involved with the smugglers.'

'Not sure we'd get an answer,' Jack said. 'All he did yesterday was lie to us, but thankfully we have enough hard evidence and a witness. Re-interviewing him will be a massive waste of time I'm sure. We should just charge him. He'll be remanded and in due course he'll be found guilty and locked up. I'm praying for a whole life sentence.'

Ben nodded. 'I wonder if Tomos was the guy Afran Ahmadi said he saw on the beach in Dover. How did he describe the man who took his money?'

Jack grinned. 'Something along the lines of short, overweight and balding. Why not send Kevin over to Cardiff with a pack of photos? If Afran picks Tomos out it'll be the last nail in his coffin.'

The desk phone rang. Ben answered the call, listened briefly then hung up.

'CS Warren wants us in her office,' he said.

'Both of us?' Jack asked.

'Seems so.'

The detectives put on their jackets, walked down to the second floor and found the chief superintendent's door was standing open. She glanced up from her work.

'Come in, gentlemen. Shut the door and take a seat.' Once they were settled she said, 'I've just taken a call from the NCA. They have informed me their planned operation will take place tomorrow morning at 4am.'

'They still want us involved then?' Ben asked.

'Yes, particularly in the light of yesterday's arrest.' She smiled. 'Well done by the way.'

'Thank you, ma'am.'

Warren nodded. 'You're to assemble in the truck stop at Cardiff West services, junction 30 on the M4. You'll receive more details then. NCA are concerned about leaks after all the work they've put in over the last ten months, so not a word to anyone. We don't want anyone escaping.'

'No, we don't,' Jack growled.

'I suggest you go home and rest up. I've been informed that DS Bevan will be attending together with a local print journalist.' She paused and looked at Ben. 'I have a feeling you might know her.'

Ben raised his eyebrows in surprise. 'How on earth did Stacey manage to get included in this?' he asked.

Warren shrugged. 'Friends in high places?'

'Yeah, maybe. Any suggestions as to what we do with Tomos Jones?'

'Unsurprisingly we've been granted an extension which helps. I think Elsa Duffin and Ollie Langdon could continue the questioning today. The case is strong enough that another interview isn't really necessary, but Elsa did such a good job with Natalie Turrell I'd like to broaden her experience.'

'She did do very well,' Ben said. 'Yes, I'm happy with that.'

'Good,' Warren said. 'Make sure you prepare properly for tomorrow, bulletproof vests are essential, and remember… this is not your operation. NCA is in charge, not you. Don't let me down and stay safe.'

'Yes, ma'am,' the detectives muttered in unison.

'Off you go then. Updates directly to me when you can, and absolutely no chatter about this until *after* it's happened.'

Chapter thirty-six

Ben and Jack spent the rest of the day at Noddfa. Ben cooked a meal, spoke briefly to Stacey and said he'd see her later without going into details, then the detectives tried to get a few hours' sleep.

Just after midnight, they got up, drank strong coffee, then left the cottage and Jack drove across the army ranges lit by a bright, full moon. Neither said much, brains swamped with concerns regarding the upcoming raid. They hoped everything would go to plan, that the smugglers would be arrested, no one would be injured, and that Heidi would be found safe and well and released.

A little over ninety minutes later, Jack pulled into the truck stop at Cardiff West. The assembly point. A group of vans were parked at the far end of the area in the shadow of a few scrubby conifer trees. As Jack drove closer, one of the vans flashed its headlights briefly and he parked next to the vehicle. The side door slid open and Ben and Jack slipped inside.

'Morning, chaps,' a voice said and they saw Freddie Holtz sitting in the front seat, Erica and Stacey squashed next to him. They smiled at the officers but remained quiet.

‘I want you to meet the team leader,’ Freddie said, nodding towards a large, heavyset man dressed in black and wearing protective gear. ‘You can call him Dave. He will be in charge of the operation tonight and you must do exactly as he says, understand?’

‘Yes, sir,’ Ben said and stretched out a hand towards Dave who grasped it tightly and shook. ‘I’m DCI James, Ben, and my companion is DS Trent, Jack, from Dyfed-Powys Police.’

‘Good to meet you both,’ Dave said. ‘Now listen carefully and I’ll outline how we’re going to play this.’

Dave spoke for nearly thirty minutes. Calmly and quietly he explained what would happen in the next few hours and tried to cover all eventualities. It was decided that Erica and Stacey would remain in the van with Freddie until NCA officers had entered a large property to the north of Newport and judged the situation to be under control. Ben and Jack would be positioned closer to the action but under a watching brief. They were not expected to take part in the actual raid.

Dave summed up by saying, ‘Be prepared folks. I’m going for shock and awe, catch the bad guys unawares. Leave no time for them to grab guns and start firing but you need to be aware of the possibility.’ He fixed the group in his gaze.

‘You probably know,’ Jack said, ‘I’m a firearms officer. I worked close protection for a while and trained during my time with the Met. I’m armed.’

Dave frowned. ‘Fair enough, but there is no room for heroics of any sort. The NCA have been working on this for months, any of you steps out of line there will be consequences. Do you all understand me?’

The four nodded their agreement even though Stacey looked nervous.

Dave spotted her disquiet. ‘I’m not gonna force anyone into this. If you’re not up for it, now is the time to say so. No one will think any the less of you.’

No one spoke, so Dave nodded, then he opened the side door and stepped out into the shadows. He turned back to look at Freddie.

'Follow us then, sir. You have the radio I've given you. Any shit comes your way just holler. Good luck, everyone.' He closed the door and walked away.

'Bloody hell,' Jack said, 'he means business.'

Ben looked at Stacey. 'You heard what he said, *cariad*, you don't need to be involved, you could wait here.'

Stacey shook her head. 'I'll be fine. Anyway if I chicken out now, Sam would have my hide.'

'You'll be quite safe,' Freddie said. 'I shall make sure of it.' He peered through the windscreen and watched as the small convoy of vehicles began to move off. He tucked on at the end of the line, followed them out to the motorway and headed towards Newport.

No one spoke, nerves getting the better of them all. Erica fidgeted in her seat, clasping and unclasping her hands, while Stacey fiddled with the camera which hung around her neck. Ben and Jack perched on the wheel arches in the back of the van, checked their personal safety equipment and worked hard at staying put as the vehicle rocked and swayed. Thirty minutes later Freddie slowed, turned off the motorway and drove towards a patch of open countryside north of Newport.

'Nearly there,' he said. 'When we park up, Ben and Jack will transfer to an NCA vehicle, the ladies will stay with me.'

'Will we be able to see anything of the actual raid?' Stacey asked.

Freddie chuckled. 'You heard what Dave said, it'll be hard to miss. Remember, no getting out of the van until we've received the all-clear. I'm too old to chase after either of you and drag you back.'

'Have you heard if Heidi is with the gang?' Erica asked.

'Available info suggests she is.'

Freddie pulled up next to the NCA vehicles. Ben and Jack opened the side door, stepped out and climbed into one of the Land Rovers which sped away. Freddie turned off the engine and looked at his passengers.

'Now we wait,' he said.

Stacey stared through the windscreen into the darkness, moonshine the only light. A large house stood just off the narrow lane, not a glimmer from inside, and a large group of black-clad officers, weapons clasped in gloved hands, began creeping towards the building. She realised she had stopped breathing and took a deep lungful of cool air through the open window. Erica was completely still, concentrating on the scene in front of her while Freddie peered through binoculars. A few minutes passed and the stalking men melted into the darkness. Everything was quiet, all Stacey could hear was the sleepy grumble of a nearby flock of sheep which looked like ghostly apparitions under the full moon.

Suddenly, she heard the tinkle of breaking glass, followed by several violet explosions as stun grenades were hurled through windows. NCA officers leapt to their feet and charged forward, screaming a challenge, guns held in front of them. Stacey quickly lost sight of the men as thick smoke from the grenades drifted across the scene. She heard a gunshot, wondered who had fired, then another. Erica looked as though she was planning to jump out of the van and Stacey grasped her arm, willing her to stay put.

Ben and Jack, tucked away behind a thick hedge, also heard the shots. They kept low to the ground, trying to follow what was going on while thick smoke swirled around them. Jack suddenly nudged his boss in the ribs.

'Look!' he said. 'There's a car.'

A dark vehicle shot through the yellow fog, around the end of the building, and sped towards the hidden detectives. They lowered their faces as the car passed, then leapt to their feet and ran towards an empty Land Rover.

Jack fired up the engine and was on the move before Ben had slammed his door.

'Heidi's in that car,' Jack said. 'I'm sure I saw her on the back seat.'

'Then don't lose them.'

'Do my best not to,' Jack growled through gritted teeth as his quarry swerved around a tight turn and joined a wider section of road.

'Don't get too close,' Ben warned, 'can't risk him crashing.' He stabbed at the screen of his phone. 'Shit! No bloody signal.'

'Keep trying, we need back-up.'

'Can you see how many are in the car?'

'Looks like just a driver with Heidi in the back.'

The fleeing gangster kept his foot down but couldn't shake Jack. Luckily the roads were still quiet. Too early for people to be leaving for work, too early for the night shift to be returning home. After approximately five miles the leading vehicle made another sharp turn. Jack followed and found himself in a sprawling mass of ex-miners' houses, back-to-back terraces, bisected by a maze of narrow streets, cars parked on each side of the road leaving a tight corridor in the middle.

'Slow down, Jack,' Ben said as he fiddled with his mobile. 'If anyone steps out–'

'We'll lose him.'

'Where's he gonna go? I've managed to get a text to Freddie and he'll send back-up, maybe the copper chopper too. Don't worry, we'll get him.'

Jack slowed a little. Ben checked out the side streets as they passed and scanned parked vehicles.

'We've lost him,' Jack snarled and thumped the steering wheel. 'Shit!'

'Take a breath, Jack. Turn left at the end of the road and drive around the block. He can't have got far.'

Jack snorted but made the turn, then another past an old primary school, next to a modern Methodist chapel.

'Wait,' Ben said. 'I think I saw something. No, don't reverse, pull in and we'll walk back.'

Fifty yards or so further on, Jack squeezed into a tight space and turned off the engine.

'Where's the back-up, guv?' he asked.

'Freddie says they're on their way and to wait.'

'Not me,' Jack said and opened his door. 'I'm gonna take a look. What do you think you saw?'

'Large guy, dark clothes, standing close to a car parked in front of the chapel.'

'Then let's spilt up. You go around the back. I'll get as close as I can and try to work out what we're dealing with. You up for this, guv?'

Ben nodded. 'Recon only, OK? If Heidi is with the guy, we can't do anything to put her at risk.'

'Yeah, I get it.'

The detectives began walking quietly back towards the chapel using parked cars as cover. Ben crossed the road and slipped down a narrow alley, while Jack moved slowly towards the target. About thirty feet away, he crouched behind a dark blue people carrier and, keeping his head low, peered over the short bonnet. He squinted into the dark.

A dim bulb glowed above the entrance of the place of worship and movement in the small car park caught his eye. He shifted his gaze and saw Ben had been right as a large man opened the back door of a parked car. He reached inside and dragged out a small figure. Heidi! She was hunched over and shuffled forward awkwardly. Jack saw she was cuffed and her ankles were shackled. He became aware of an anger building inside him, tension at his temples, teeth clenched, pulse quickening. He forced himself to stay calm and remain hidden.

The man pulled Heidi towards the entrance closer to the dim, overhead lamp. Is he going inside? Jack wondered, just before he spotted a gun in the hostage taker's hand. Jack swallowed. He'd made the decision to arm himself as soon as he'd heard about the raid, so he reached inside his jacket and removed his own weapon from a shoulder holster.

Halfway across the car park, the man paused, looked up, and with horror Jack saw Ben standing at the corner of the building. The man with the gun had seen him too.

'Stay there!' the man yelled. 'If you move I will shoot you, then I'll shoot her.'

'Put the gun down,' Ben yelled back. 'You're surrounded. Shoot me or your hostage and you'll go away for the rest of your life. Do the right thing.'

'You're talking rubbish. You're on your own. There's no one here that I can see.'

He waved the gun wildly and let go of Heidi's arm. She took two small shuffling steps away from him.

'Freeze!' the man ordered. 'One more step and I *will* shoot you.' He held the gun at arm's length, the barrel about two feet from the back of Heidi's head.

'Don't do it,' Heidi warned. 'You'll regret it forever.'

The man laughed. 'I doubt that. I regret nothing of my life.'

'On your own now though, aren't you? Where are the heavies you had in Reading? Bit of luck they're all dead, and what did you do, *boss-man*?' she sneered. 'Oh yes, you ran away.'

'Put the gun down,' Ben shouted again. 'There's no way out of this for you.'

'You could run away again,' Heidi suggested. 'Just make a better job of it this time, cos I promise, they will hunt you down.'

Jack wished Heidi would stay quiet, he couldn't see the benefit of winding up her captor. He watched as the man refocused his aim.

'Shut the fuck up!' he screamed. 'I'd shoot you now if I didn't need some insurance. Now walk slowly back to the car and get in.'

Heidi held her head high. 'Make me, cretin.'

Jack's brain went into overdrive and made its decision. The gunman was three feet away from Heidi, he wasn't pressing the barrel into her head. Something else in Jack's favour was the thug wouldn't hear the bang if Jack pulled the trigger, bullets travelled faster than the speed of sound. The bastard wouldn't know he'd been hit until he began to drop and it would be highly unlikely he would be able to fire his own gun. The final advantage was Jack had the perfect shot, the man's head in a direct line with the barrel of his standard-issue police firearm. Visibility was good, wind minimal and best of all, he hadn't been spotted.

He took a quick glance at Heidi. From twenty yards away, she looked like a child, her short white hair catching the light. Her tormentor stood a couple of paces to her right, his head lit perfectly by the low-wattage bulb above the door of the chapel. Jack took a deep breath. He checked his aim, breathed in for a second time, held it, and gently squeezed the trigger. Above the barrel he glimpsed a red mist as the man's head exploded. Heidi dropped to her knees. Jack began to run towards the building.

'Heidi!' he screamed. 'Speak to me. Let me know you're OK.'

'I'm OK. Scumbag's dead. Nice shooting, matey.'

Chapter thirty-seven

Immediately after the raid Freddie had taken Heidi, Erica and Stacey to Milebrook Manor and two days later they were still there. With Freddie's permission, Stacey had laid claim to his study and written a long, and detailed article. Not only did the piece appear on the front page of *The Mid Wales Times*, but many of the nationals picked up the story and printed her work on the front of their own papers – much to Sam Jenkins' delight.

While she worked, Freddie and Erica fussed over Heidi, to her disgust, but she bit her tongue, understanding how much distress her abduction had caused. Following her dramatic rescue, she had refused point blank to attend hospital so as soon as they arrived at the manor house, Freddie had called in the local family doctor. After a thorough check-over, and treatment of a few scrapes and bruises, he passed her fit and everyone relaxed a little.

On the third day, Ben and Jack joined the Milebrook residents for lunch in the large downstairs kitchen. When Jack walked in, Heidi – in a rare display of emotion – hugged him as tightly as she could. When she released him, Freddie grabbed the detective by the hand and shook it vigorously.

'Good to see you, man,' Freddie said. 'I shall forever be in your debt.'

'Rubbish,' Jack muttered embarrassedly, 'only doing my job.'

'Well, you won't have any trouble with the internal investigation, you have my word.'

'I'm grateful, sir, thank you. Can't say I was looking forward to that much.'

'Now, sit all of you,' Freddie said. 'Help yourselves to food and fizz, don't be shy, we have plenty to celebrate.'

He plonked a silver cooler filled with ice and a large bottle of champagne on the long table.

Wooden chair legs scraped and squealed on the flagstone floor. Freddie removed the lid of a dish containing an enormous beef casserole, then ferried platters of roast potatoes and steaming vegetables from the old cast-iron range. As the meal began, Freddie took his place at the head of the table, a broad smile on his face.

'So tell me, Ben,' he said, 'how have things worked out at your end?'

'Pretty bloody well, to be honest,' Ben said. 'While we were busy with the raid, two of my officers interrogated Tomos Jones, manager of the car showroom in Llanelwedd.' He took a sip of champagne. 'In view of the evidence we have accumulated, his solicitor was able to convince him to co-operate.'

Jack chuckled. 'More than that, guv. Elsa Duffin managed to persuade Jones to turn King's evidence. He's been singing like a choirboy ever since. Still at it I believe. We've got names, together with phone numbers, addresses, full details of vehicles used to transport refugees, his contacts in Europe… and his sorry part in the affair.'

'Did you find the gun?' Stacey asked.

'Said he'd chucked it in the river. Little chance of recovery but the underwater unit is having a go.'

'And the screens in his house? What was that about?'

Ben took up the narrative. 'Tomos told Elsa the screens and live feed from the showroom were purely for his benefit, not security for the building. Seems he had hidden records relating to the vehicles he'd obtained for the smugglers. Logbooks, insurance documents, that sort of thing – together with a lot of cash. He knew who Haddon was – a photo had been circulated amongst the network – and thought he was there to remove the stash, which it seemed he was.'

'That's what Jonathon meant when he wrote that phrase about two birds and one stone,' Stacey said. 'To meet with Natalie Turrell and then collect the evidence he knew Tomos must have had.'

'That's the conclusion we came to. After Tomos told us where his hidey-hole was, we recovered the lot and added it to the substantial evidence bundle.'

'What about Rowan?' Heidi asked. 'Any news regarding him?'

'Yes there is,' Jack said. 'He rang the station after speaking with Sorrell. He *is* working in the camps but he's been told about the raids and plans to return to the UK in the near future.'

'How successful were the raids?' Erica asked. 'Did they get everyone?'

Ben nodded. 'Seems like it. I spoke with Dave at the NCA. The prisoners are being questioned but he's sure he'll be able to charge all of them. The information Kitty, Jonathon and Rowan had been funnelling their way has been invaluable.' He sighed. 'A crying shame two of them weren't able to see the extraordinary results of their efforts.'

'Were those arrested the gang responsible for the deaths of Yezda and her family, as well as the refugees in the truck?' Stacey asked.

'Certainly looks that way, and many more have been arrested in Europe. The whole network has been blown out of the water.'

'Bad turn of phrase,' Heidi muttered, 'but I hope they get what they deserve. They caused so much misery and heartache.'

'You caused some of that too,' Erica said. 'Why didn't you tell us you'd tracked down the people smugglers yourself?'

Heidi shrugged. 'Cos you don't like me messing about on the dark web and would have given me grief.'

'If you'd shared, you might not have been snatched.'

'Maybe, but I'll be honest, I didn't see that coming. Thought I'd covered my tracks and had no idea I was being followed.'

'Where did they grab you?' Ben asked.

'In a service station toilet on the M4. I was on my way here to pass on what I'd learned to Freddie.'

'You were lucky,' Ben said. 'It could all have ended very differently.'

Heidi nodded and topped up her glass.

'Anything new regarding Natalie Turrell?' Stacey asked.

'She's intending to plead guilty to the fraud,' Jack said. 'She stole so much money that she will do some time but not as much as she should. Judges are obliged to knock a third off any sentence if the accused admits their guilt. Her goods and chattels will be seized though. Life will be very different for Ms Turrell when she is released.'

'All sounds excellent,' Freddie said. 'The courts are going to be busy for months to come.' He glanced at Stacey. 'I guess your editor is a happy man? The feature you wrote was just brilliant.'

'Sam's beside himself,' Stacey said and chuckled, 'although he manages to hide it well. Thank you so much for giving me the chance to be part of this.'

'My pleasure. The story needed reporting – correctly.'

'Glad the top dog was nicked,' Heidi said around a mouthful of food. 'Will he be extradited or tried in France?'

'Too soon to tell,' Freddie said, 'but he won't escape justice. No other poor souls will risk their lives in his nasty little boats. The teams operating the other side of the Channel raided warehouses full of boats, outboard motors and life vests.' He grinned. 'Fair few bad guys too.'

Heidi's mobile chirped and Erica frowned, she hated calls at the table. Without checking the screen, Heidi answered the call.

'Speak first, you're paying.'

'Excuse me?' a male voice said. 'I am trying to contact Ms Heidi Holtz.'

'That's me. Who are you?'

'Friend of a friend,' the man said.

'Make more sense, will you? I'm eating and my food is getting cold.'

'I apologise. Our mutual friend is Felicity Savage. She would like to see you. Can you come now?'

'Fliss? Is everything OK?'

'Can I tell her you are coming?'

'Just tell me who you are and how Fliss is.'

The line disconnected and Heidi stared at the phone angrily.

'What's up, love?' Erica asked.

Heidi got to her feet. 'I have to go out.'

'What, now? You haven't finished your lunch. Where are you going?'

'Just out. Got something to do.'

'I'll come with you.'

'No. Stay here. Don't worry, I'll be back. I just need to go alone.'

'But why?'

Heidi didn't answer. She got to her feet, kissed Erica soundly, and strode from the room. Erica heard Heidi's new truck fire up outside the front door and tyres spin on loose gravel. She put her head in her hands and groaned. Stacey rubbed her back.

'Don't worry,' she said. 'She'll be back.'

'I've only just got used to having her with me again.'

'I'm absolutely sure it will be fine. Now finish your meal. We're celebrating, remember? We solved the case and the bad guys will get what's coming.'

Erica didn't look convinced, but she nodded, clinked her glass with Stacey's and drank deeply, spluttering as champagne bubbles found their way up her nose.

Epilogue

Heidi shot down the long drive to the lane then onto the main road and headed for Wales. Nearly ninety minutes later, she slid to a halt outside the dolly mixture house, turned off the engine, marched up to the front door and repeatedly swung on the metal bell pull. The door was opened by a tall, brown-skinned, slim man, with very dark hair and a full beard.

'I'm Heidi,' she said. 'Who the hell are you and where's Fliss?'

'I'm Bilal,' the man said, 'Sorrell's husband. Auntie is in the library, but…'

Heidi pushed past him. She dashed through the large hall and shoved open the heavy library door. She saw Fliss lying on a *chaise longue* in the large window next to the French doors, an open book lying on her chest, a red tartan blanket draped over her legs.

'Fliss,' she called. 'I'm here. Is everything OK?'

The elderly lady didn't respond or move. Heidi walked closer and lifted the book. Bilal moved to stand by her side.

'Ms Holtz,' he said, 'I am very sorry to say, but Auntie has passed.'

'Passed?' Heidi dropped to her knees and gently took hold of Fliss' hand. It was cool to the touch. 'Oh no,' Heidi moaned and held the hand to her cheek. 'How long has she been gone?'

'Not long. Soon after I called you.'

'I should have got here faster.'

'Don't say that. She went quickly and very gently. There is a letter.'

Heidi ignored him, eyes fixed on her friend's face. 'Why are you here?' she asked without looking away.

'I live here. I have been here since I was refused right to remain in UK. Auntie needed help as I did. She hid me and I cared for her.' He held out the letter for the second time.

'Has the doctor been?'

'He has not. Auntie wanted you to be here before any doctor. Please, read the letter.'

Heidi took the envelope and saw her name on the front written in an elegant copperplate script. She slipped a finger beneath the flap and removed a sheet of good-quality paper. She unfolded the letter and ran a gentle thumb across the ink.

> *My dear Heidi,*
> *Please do not mourn my death, I do not wish to cause you any unhappiness. Death comes to us all in the end and I was very old and needed a rest. I have lived a long, full and useful life, so there is nothing to regret about my passing. The world will not miss me, not really, and not for long.*
> *No doubt my friend Bilal is with you as you read this. He has been a great supporter and I love him like a son. I want you and your father to do whatever it takes to return him to his family, to Sorrell and little Rebin who misses his daddy every day. There is plenty of money in my estate to pay for lawyers, so use it. As I said – whatever it takes.*

Heidi glanced up at Bilal, noticed his cheeks were wet and patted his arm. She continued to read.

> *The remainder of the cash should go to Rowan. As I've named you executor, it will be your duty to see that he receives this money. The rest of my worldly goods I leave to you, house, contents, the lot, but there is a condition. Please set aside some rooms in the house for those who need somewhere safe to be. If you don't want to live here, my solicitor has been instructed to set up a trust which you would manage. I won't bore you with the legal details, there is a will in my desk.*
>
> *Lastly, I want you to know I am very happy and consider myself lucky to have met you, a kindred spirit! Such a short time we knew each other, but the instant you walked into my house, I felt as though I'd known you forever. Make sure you live a good life, my child.*
>
> *All my love and many blessings*
>
> *Fliss.*

Heidi returned the letter to the envelope, perched next to her friend and bent close. She kissed her powdered cheek and whispered, 'I miss you already. I will carry out your wishes, and thank you, my dear Fliss. I promise I won't let you down.'

THE END

If you enjoyed this book, please let others know by leaving a quick review on Amazon. Also, if you spot anything untoward in the paperback, get in touch. We strive for the best quality and appreciate reader feedback.

editor@thebookfolks.com

www.thebookfolks.com

More fiction by Nicola Clifford

NO REFUGE (book 1)

Reporter Stacey Logan has little to worry about other than the town flower festival when a man is shot dead. When she believes the police have got the wrong man, she does some snooping of her own. But will her desire for a scoop lead her to a place where there is no refuge?

THE CONSORTIUM (book 2)

Whilst reporter Stacey Logan is investigating illegal raves in the Welsh countryside, her boyfriend DI Ben James is dealing with a suspicious death. When drugs enter the picture, their two separate inquiries will collide. Can they find a way to collaborate and catch a dangerous killer?

NOT FORGOTTEN (book 3)

When journalist Stacey Logan's policeman boyfriend disappears with little more than a note, she suspects he has been abducted. But his colleagues refuse to pursue her leads. She'll have to go it alone, but must brace herself for the worst.

RIGHT OF SANCTUARY (book 4)

When DC Heidi Holtz's sister Greta joins a cult, she has trouble convincing her superiors of foul play. And there is nothing the detective can do if Greta went by her own free will. Holtz will have to find evidence to discredit the sect, or risk losing her sister for good.

CODDLING MOLLY (book 5)

A teenager is found dead after a fall from a bridge on a winter night in Brecon. Identifying her proves a challenge. DI Ben James and DS Erica Bevan discover links to a drugs gang. But when these crooks bother someone dear to ex-detective Heidi Holtz, she too will jump on their trail.

GONE TO THE DOGS (book 6)

Reporter Stacey Logan is looking into the case of a missing teenager, but she can't help but put her nose into Detective Ben James' murder investigation. Tensions within the community reach fever pitch as events come to a head.

MURDER SPIKE (book 7)

Reporter Stacey Logan lands a scoop when she discovers the body of a man placed on top of a statue in the town square. But that's just the first in a series of bizarre crime cases that hit her small rural town. What is causing the crime spike and will she get to the bottom of the matter before the police do?

GREEN SHOOTS (book 9)

Police are called out to an commune on a country estate. The owners of the land want the environmentalists off their turf. Someone is going to get killed. Let's hope it isn't journalist Stacey Logan, who is heading there for a scoop.

Other titles of interest

WINTER'S CRY by Cheryl Rees-Price

When a farmer clears some trees from a field, he unearths a corpse. Suspicion immediately falls upon the neighbouring commune, a collection of makeshift huts and tents which house a reclusive group of people. Having grown up there, DI Winter Meadows goes to talk to its members, who are wary of the police. But what he finds will have him questioning everything he knows about his past.

STILL WATERS RUN by Mark West

A short holiday at the end of summer should be a chance for sixteen-year-old Dan and his recently divorced mother to unwind. Yet despite quickly striking up new friendships, their break takes a nasty turn when a holiday worker is murdered. Dan becomes embroiled in events. Can he get out or is he in too deep?

Printed in Dunstable, United Kingdom

81407417R00163